JAKE HOWARD:
Multiverse 101

By

Will Castillo

Dedicated To:

Gina, Harlee and Victoria

Thanks for dealing with all of my stuff.

PROLOGUE

The concept of a Multiverse has always been something that has fascinated scholars and ordinary people alike. *Back to the Future* showed us the promise of time travel with possible consequences, both good and bad, and the concept of diverging timelines creating an "alternate" timeline. Stretching back further than that, bending time to man's will has been a topic in a countless number of books and movies.

But what if the focus has been on the wrong thing? What if it's less about time and more about space? What if alternate timelines exist alongside the current perception of reality and both timelines just continue on, blissfully oblivious of the others existence?

For example, imagine a world that is much like the current world with slight differences:

What if Kurt Cobain never killed himself and continued to make great music?

What if instead of airplanes people flew on the backs of dragons?

What if America and Russia did launch attacks on each other in the eighties?

Imagine just those tweaks impacting the current world of 1997 and beyond. Here's the thing though, I always thought that they were just fantasy. Just stories that were made up for movies and television shows. As it turns out, I was wrong.

There actually is a multiverse. It's been there all along, undetectable to nearly everybody. The only trace of it is those cases where something seems familiar, almost like a bout of *deja vu* but different. The reality is that the feeling that you feel is a type of link to The Multiverse. In a different world, maybe you did

2

something that triggered a different reaction than what you experienced. Maybe it was good that you didn't go to a party, or maybe not kissing that girl was a mistake that had dire results.

All of those things that happen, on a global or personal level, create an alternate world with a different reality; each decision in those worlds spawn a new world with different realities and on and on. It's all held together with a thin thread that, if disturbed, could unravel it all and send the entire Multiverse colliding in on itself...

And I think I might have just accidentally done that.

CHAPTER ONE

In late summer of 1997, I was beginning my junior year at the State University of New York at New Paltz. I grew up around there, about thirty minutes away in a little town called Wallkill, but I spent a lot of time in New Paltz. Actually, technically, it's the Hamlet of Wallkill but no one ever calls it that. The town of Wallkill is actually around twenty minutes away from my Wallkill, which is actually named Shawangunk, but that is a nightmare name to say so locals just say Wallkill and leave it at that. Upstate New York geography can be a little messy and a lot of towns up here end with the suffix 'kill'. Wallkill, Fishkill, Plattekill, when I was little I thought I lived in a very violent part of the world.

Wallkill didn't have much to do unless you just wanted to go hang out at someone else's house just so you weren't bored alone. The town had a pizza place, where I was the reigning Street Fighter II champion, a small car dealership and a couple of convenience stores. New Paltz, however, had some major stores, a movie theater, a great comic book store, and one of the coolest record stores around, Rhino Records. All of that was just what's available uptown.

Downtown New Paltz is the quintessential college down. Little privately owned shops and cafes run up and down the streets, there's always a buzz of activity at nearly all times. New York City may be the city that never sleeps, but New Paltz on a Saturday night is a pretty lively place, usually followed by sleeping in on Sunday.

Even though I lived close enough to drive here every day, near the end of my sophomore year I chose to stay on campus. I told my parents it was to get the "full college experience" but, really, I just wanted to get out of the house and kind of live on my

4

own. It's not like my relationship with my family is bad, it is strained at times, but not bad. My family is very working class. Dad works all the time and when he gets home; he just crashes and doesn't really want to be bothered and leaves the day-to-day operations of the house to my Mom. The problem with that is Mom is a nurse, and works a lot, too, which usually left me, good ol' Jake Howard, to take care of my little brother and sister. Because of that, my entire freshman and most of my sophomore year was spent either in class or at the house watching my siblings. On the rare cases that I did get to go out, my parents needed the phone number to where I was "in case there was an emergency". Most of the time there wasn't an emergency, but more than a few times I had to leave wherever I was to go attend to the kids.

Near the end of my sophomore year my sister turned fourteen. Through a debate that is still legendary in the Howard household, I convinced my parents that my sister was old enough to stay home alone with my eight-year-old brother and that they would be fine. My parents could be called slightly over-protective and hated the idea of leaving my sister home alone with my brother because my Mom said it was illegal because they are both minors. I'm pretty sure she just made that up because my sister could be a bit moody and my brother was a holy terror. I never bothered to research or ask about it, I just took her word for it.

The debate started with some pretty obvious points about our general location. My family lives on a secluded street where a two hundred foot driveway leads up a hill to the house. If anyone was going to break in to the place they would be winded and nearly passed out by the time they go to the front door. On top of that my Dad installed lights everywhere because he's a little eccentric so it's very well lit. There have been many times where people (myself included) have come to visit my parents at night only to be blinded by the power of a thousand suns. I'm pretty sure that man just adds new lights when he gets bored. He also added a security system to the house and detached garage because he was scared that someone was trying to steal his tools and construction equipment. I swear it's easier to sneak in and out of Fort Knox that it is to get in or out of the family property.

Eventually the unthinkable happened and my parents agreed that it was time for me to get out there and experience life, even the limited capacity of just living twenty minutes away. I would still stop in about once a week to make sure everyone was ok and to grab some of Mom's cooking. Campus life is fun, but the food kind of sucks.

The other reason this was the perfect time to move out was my best friend Scott's roommate decided college was too much for him and just left one night. No words or anything, just *POOF*, gone. Scott and I were headed back to his room to play some Battle Arena Toshinden on my brand new Playstation, and when we got back, all of his stuff was gone. It looked like no one was even there, ever. All that was left on his side of the room was the bare gray walls and a neatly made bed, it was actually kind of creepy. Scott almost instantly suggested that I take the space, and since I really needed to get out of the house, it was a win-win.

Scott Connelly has been in my life since sixth grade. We crossed paths then because we both liked the same girl in our class, Jennifer Andrews, and we were constantly trying to one-up each other in order to impress her. Jen was really cute with blond hair, blue eyes and a smile that could light up a room. With our wild, sixth grade level resources we each showered Jennifer with assorted candies, cheap bracelets, sparkly (but ever so fake) gold-ish jewelry and whatever else our young, dumb asses could get our hands on. Scott had the charming good looks and I was a chubby kid with a great sense of humor. We used every meager asset we had to try and win Jen over. In the end we both realized neither of us were going to wind up with her and decided that it all just wasn't worth it.

Honestly, looking back (as bad as this sounds), I think we just both liked her because she was the first girl in sixth grade to have boobs.

After putting Jennifer behind us, we became pretty much inseparable through our junior high and high school years. If there was an event going on people knew Jake and Scott were a package deal. Scott was the jock and I was the art kid that skateboarded so, even though we essentially had a different friend circle, he always had my back and I always had his.

He actually saved my life once, even if he doesn't know the full story of how it happened.

We were on a class trip to the Mohonk Mountains in New Paltz for our Earth Science class in the fall of ninth grade. The area where we live is really nice in the fall. When you live there, you kind of take it for granted, but the colors are breathtaking. Autumn turns our whole area into a tourist attraction with people from the city areas coming to upstate New York to see the colors of the leaves change and to enjoy pumpkin and apple picking. There are a ton of farms up here so this whole area becomes gridlocked for about two weeks in October, usually around Columbus Day weekend.

Our class was taking a hike to the top of the Mohonk Mountains the week before Columbus Day to observe all of the orange and red autumn leaves that from far away made the woods look like they were on fire starting from the Mohonk Mountain House, which is an upscale resort and spa, to the Albert K. Smiley Memorial Tower (known to the locals as the Skytop Tower) at the top of the mountain range.

As a kid, before I knew what that tower was, I always thought it was a really tall man pointing at the sky. That's just what it looked like to me and it was visible for miles so I thought it was a giant or something. Eventually I learned it was a tower but I've always loved the look of it for some reason. It looks both ominous and inviting no matter the time of day. I'd like to think that one day if I ever move away from here, I will see that tower and just feel a bit of comfort.

Our hike started and our group, consisting of myself, Scott, Jen (who became one of our best friends) and a couple of other people that I can't remember, started our climb. I might be a little dramatic in calling it a "climb". It was more of a nature trail walk but, as a slightly chunky kid (I've thankfully slimmed out a bit since then), this was more exercise than I was planning to do today. I packed some snacks in my backpack, because I was a little fatty, so I was happily eating a chocolate covered granola bar and following behind the group. Scott and Jen were hanging back with me for a while but after a while it seemed like I was quite a bit away from the group.

I wasn't sure how I got so far away from the group. It was almost as if one minute I was chatting with them and looking at the colors of leaves and making jokes, and the next minute I was alone. The bright colors of the woods were still there and everything looked normal, but suddenly the trail got creepily quiet.

I kept on the trail to catch up to the group. I'm not sure how long I was walking, it seemed like it was a couple of minutes, when I heard something. It wasn't a normal sound, not like an animal or anything because the woods along the trail were still dead silent, but some weird, unusual sound.

I started to branch off the path a bit to follow it. A smart move? No, probably not. Many a horror movie has started with a sound in the woods that turns out to be something terrible. Entire plots could have been avoided if somebody just said "What's that? A weird sound? Oh, no thank you!" and went on their way.

So me, being a curious (and kind of a dumb kid) followed this weird noise not quite sure what was causing it. It sounded, for lack of a better explanation, like the sound of a lightsaber humming with the roar of a tiger over it. It seemed to fade in and out at set intervals, like a pulse or a heartbeat, and after a few more minutes of walking I moved through a heavily wooded area and saw something.

I only saw it for a blink of an eye because in an instant it was gone. It looked like a glowing blue doorway. The portal, or doorway really, stood about seven feet tall. It was pulsating and it had something like a swirling vortex inside of it. There were sparks coming off the edges of it like something was short circuiting. It was the coolest and most terrifying thing I had ever seen.

I moved closer to it and it vanished in a flash of light and a force wave knocked me on my ass. Disoriented, I started sliding on my behind, being pulled somehow toward the edge of the precipice where the portal was perched. I couldn't hold a grip on the ground. I don't know if it was me panicking in fear of if there was just nothing to grab on to, but I was convinced that I was about to fall to my death.

Suddenly I stopped sliding as someone grabbed the shoulder of my jacket. I looked up to see Scott and Jen, with panic in their eyes, holding on to me as my feet were dangling off of the cliff. Scott was yelling my name, I think, because I could read his lips but couldn't really make out his voice. Everything seemed garbled and muffled. I twisted my body up to grab his hand and he pulled me up. He asked what happened but, honestly, I wasn't sure. I wasn't sure what I saw at all. A portal? A floating door from out of nowhere? There was nothing around showing that anything was there. No marks on the ground or anything that would indicate that something weird happened here at all. Maybe I was just delirious from all of this unplanned exercise.

I said that I dropped my granola bar and fell trying to get it. I don't think they bought my story, but I stuck to it and eventually it passed. It was the only thing I could think of and the only time I've ever lied to Scott and Jen.

CHAPTER TWO

I awoke to the sound of my scratchy clock radio playing "Touch, Peel and Stand" by Days of the New on the morning of my first day of junior year. As I tried to clear the sleep from my eyes and let the room come into focus, I noticed Scott left a note on my nightstand that he had already left to grab us some coffee. He might be getting us coffee or he might be getting a better view at some of the new girls on campus (probably the latter). In any case, I wasn't in a rush to get out of bed. My clock read 8:00 A.M. on the glaring red digits and my first class wasn't till ten. That was the earliest I wanted a class in my junior year. Even at that time, my brain is barely functioning.

I swung my feet out of bed and hit the grey linoleum tile with a shock. We kept the air conditioner at a frigid temperature when we slept. Some people in DuBois Hall may have thought it was morgue-like, we thought it was just right. Besides, what better way to start your day than stepping into the arctic as soon as you wake up?

DuBois Hall was one of the better dorms on campus due to the fact that the rooms came in two-, three-, or four bedroom suites. They were spacious and afforded the people staying in them a little more privacy instead of putting the ol' "sock on the door" if you were entertaining guests. The suites also had a common bathroom shared between roommates instead of a community bathroom shared by an entire floor, which avoided any potential foot fungus outbreaks (I've seen some of these peoples feet...) and a common living room area. All of the residence halls were coed, but not all of them had private bathrooms which had the potential to lead to some awkward situations.

Movie and comic posters littered most of my walls along with a couple of posters of barely dressed women that I bought when I still lived at my parents house but wasn't allowed to put up because my Mom forbade it. My argument was that Jenny McCarthy was on a bike and working out, but Mom didn't buy it. I was allowed to have my *Batman Forever* poster of Nicole Kidman as Chase Meridian there because she was fully clothed, even though she had cleavage for miles. My mom is weird like that.

On the whole, my room was pretty clean, other than some laundry that had to get taken care of next time I visited my parents, or made my way to the laundry room downstairs.

I stretched, said good morning to the poster of my future wife (Jenny McCarthy) and headed out to the living room on my way to the bathroom. Between Scott and me our room was pretty well set up. Scott's an only child and, as such, is spoiled. Whatever Scott didn't have, I had. The big television was his, the stereo system with five disc changer was mine. We had a bunch of game systems, movies and all other kinds of entertainment. We wanted to be the "go-to" dorm and based on the turnout from our "back-to-class" Mortal Kombat tournament it looked like we were on our way. I lost because Mortal Kombat has a stupid block button instead of just holding back to block, but it was a fun time. The living room was a little trashed from the party, but nothing too bad. Pizza boxes and chinese food containers were stacked on our tiny center table that Scott must have conveniently forgotten to throw out this morning and beer cans that were piled in the trash can. I'm not a big beer drinker but a lot of the other guys, Scott included, could hammer them down. Drinking was never really my thing. I might have a drink or two at a party, but I prefer to watch other people make asses out of themselves or be there to bail people out of trouble if necessary.

Scott must have left fairly recently because the bathroom was still kind of steamy from his shower. I stepped in, wiped off the mirror and got a look at myself for the first time today.

My mess of shaggy brown hair was out of control, but nothing a shower and a blowdryer couldn't fix to get me to achieve my Jordan Catalano *My So Called Life*-esque level of hair control. I had slimmed out quite a bit since high school, might I even be detecting some muscle tone? I lost a lot of weight going into my senior year at Wallkill Senior High School but once I hit college, and I had access to a free gym that didn't have rusty, outdated equipment I started exercising with a bit of frequency. I would try to go about three times a week, and just getting around campus gave me a lot of exercise. I wasn't trying to get jacked, just comfortable enough in my own skin. My six foot frame was in decent shape now, at least nice enough that I felt more confident when Scott brought a girl over to talk to me. Looking decent wasn't enough to get me over crippling shyness from time to time though.

My wardrobe consists of various t-shirts, jeans or shorts and a couple of flannels. I settled on my favorite Nirvana shirt with a yellow smiling face on it, jeans and my black and white flannel. In September it's warm in the morning but might get kinda brisk at night. I put on my checkered Airwalks, grabbed my bag, my Walkman, blew a kiss to Jenny McCarthy and left to start a brand new world of junior year at SUNY New Paltz.

"Aneurysm" by Nirvana came through my headphones as I passed through the doors of DuBois Hall and headed out. The temperature was warm enough to still be summer but a slight cool breeze that let everyone know that fall isn't too far away. Campus was buzzing with activity, everything from new students finding their way around, looking like tourists holding a map in a new city, to various frats and sororities looking for new pledges. I considered joining a frat in my sophomore year but decided it wasn't really for me since I lived off campus and I didn't want to commit to something that I might have to be pulled away from if there was a "family emergency". Even though I was now living on campus I still didn't have an interest in joining. I'd rather just go to the parties they host and even then I'm not that big of a partier.

My first class of the day was Astronomy. I've always liked space since the first time I ever saw Star Wars when I was six years old, but maybe if I ever need to make the jump to lightspeed in the middle of an asteroid field, this will help me navigate it. Probably not, but we do get to have classes in the planetarium so I can hopefully imagine how that would look or, at the very least, take a nap.

I've kinda floated through my last two years not really sure what I was here for. I came to college with no plan, just the idea that after high school you either go right to work or go to college. Neither of my parents went to college, they went to trade schools. My father joined the Ironworkers union, which is not really a trade school per se, but has an apprentice program where they teach you everything about the trade with basically hands on training. Mom went into nursing. They are both successful in their fields, but I knew neither of those fields were for me, so I headed to college with basically no clue and no plan of what to make of my life.

I did have to take some pre-reqs for Astronomy and, boy let me tell you, there is a lot of math involved in looking at the stars! Of course I knew there was going to be various sciences involved which itself has a bit of math, but holy shit, calculus. Calculus can go straight to hell, do not pass go, do not collect two hundred dollars. I did enjoy physics though, it's been one of my favorite classes regardless of the math involved. There are so many fields of study, it's mind boggling. Scott and I started taking physics together and he decided to change course and study atmospheric science and meteorology.

The planetarium and science hall was pretty much on the other end of campus from the dorm but I had plenty of time. The path there was along a large pond that provided nice views of campus with trees close enough to provide shade but not so dense as to block out the sun entirely. I was taking my time getting lost in my music, "Supernova" by Liz Phair, when I felt my left knee buckle but not enough for me to wind up on the ground, just stumble a bit. I turned to see what dastardly person could have caused this and was not surprised by who I saw.

"Watch your step dude, you're always so clumsy!" Scott said, chuckling to himself like he was the funniest man alive. This was how we greeted each other if we were lucky enough to catch the other off guard. Take out the person's knee by kicking it from behind and say something terribly unfunny. He held a cup out for me to grab.

I caught my balance. "Yeah, not quite sure why. I'll have to get that looked at." I grabbed the coffee, took a sip and gave Scott a slight punch on the arm.

Scott made a disgusted face as I took a sip. "I don't know how you drink that, man," as we started walking. "That shit is way too sweet. I like my coffee black with sugar, the way God intended."

"Black coffee is the number one drink of psychopaths. There's been studies." I took another sip. As far as I know there had been no studies, we would just add 'there've been studies' after statements since we took a class freshman year and our professor would start nearly every sentence with some variation of those three words. Besides that, my coffee was delicious. Regular coffee with a hot chocolate packet added in, so good. "There have also been studies that having hair that looks like Brian Austin Green makes you a douchebag psychopath."

Scott feigned hurt. "How dare you! My hair is way better than his. He may have me beat in getting some ass department though by a narrow margin though." It almost isn't fair that Scott was smart, athletic and really popular with the women on campus. He could be lying about his various escapades, but he usually has a gaggle of girls around him and has no problem talking to them. "Hey, did you check your email yet?"

"No, why?" I asked.

"Nothing major," Scott started. "Jen emailed us from B.U. It seems that Shelly transferred up there."

My body involuntarily shuddered, almost visually pausing for a brief moment.

"Yeah," Scott continued, "she kept it a secret and showed up at her 'best friends' dorm and announced she's moving in, on the same floor I think too".

"Best frenemy more like it." Talking about Shelly still hurt, even after splitting over half a year ago. We met through Jen right before my freshman year here. Jen met her while she was lifeguarding the summer, before she left for Boston University, and thought we would hit it off. We did almost immediately, even though she was kind of annoying. She loved *Clueless* and seemed to be doing her best Alicia Silverstone impersonation all the time. It was cute, for a while anyway. Shelly was really hot and we had a great time together, but something had been weird almost from the start.

Right before Valentine's Day this past year Scott showed up at my parents house where I was still living. Apparently Shelly showed up at Scott's dorm a bit drunk at midnight-ish looking to hook up. Scott refused, because he is a good guy that only looks like a douchebag, and came by my house the next morning to pick me up.

Scott and I went out for breakfast and he told me what happened. I wasn't mad at him at all and I let him know that I had thought something was up with Shelly for a while. That night I took her out to the diner and confronted her. She confessed that she did try to hook up with Scott, and also has been BANGING THREE OTHER GUYS while we were together for over a year and a half. Her reasoning was that I didn't live on campus and she would get bored at night and just liked sex.

I left her at that diner and never looked back.

"Yeah, I don't know why Jen stays friends with her." Scott's head turned to admire a group of women jogging on the path. "I don't know what you saw in her." he remarked, leaning around me, still watching the joggers.

I shrugged and let out a deep breath. "I thought I loved her."

"Turns out she just loves dick." Scott turned back to me with a wry smirk.

I nearly spit my coffee out. "Well, it's hard to argue with that logic, honestly."

Scott put his hand on my shoulder and swallowed some coffee. "You're better off man," he said, "That girl is batshit crazy. I feel bad for whoever she jumps on next! Man, she probably has one of those deli take-a-number ticket machines at the base of her bed."

I laughed and we kept walking, in silence for a little bit. As we rounded the corner we arrived at the Student Center which was a hive of activity. Students both new and old were everywhere and even more clubs and organizations were here looking for new recruits.

"Is it always like this on day one?" I asked Scott. I always came in from the opposite side of campus and usually just barely on time for class.

Scott nodded. "Everyone out here is looking for fresh meat for their gang." He struck a dumb pose like he was flashing some gang sign. "SUNY NP Crew, Yo!"

I chuckled and shook my head. "You're an idiot."

He replied, "Yes, yes I am."

We turned to go around the crowd, but then I suddenly bumped into someone and nearly knocked them to the ground. The girl I bumped into dropped her book and a few other things. I rushed to help her pick them up.

"I'm so sorry!" I said, trying to grab a piece of paper before it flew away.

Her voice seemed disinterested and annoyed at the same time. She snatched her book from the ground.

"Yeah, whatever, just watch where you're going." she said.

I looked up at her and for a moment I couldn't speak.

She stood a few inches shorter than me and was dressed mostly in black with black Doc Martens and some multi-colored bangle bracelets. Her scoop neck black dress clung to her in all the right places and she had a necklace on with a red jewel hanging from it. Dark, heavy eyeliner gave her an intensity in her stare that was both sexy and terrifying and her lipstick was so dark red it was almost like the color was trying to escape an infinite black void. The way the sun hit her dark red hair made her look unreal, almost like a painting.

I managed to find my voice. "Yeah, um, yeah I really should pay more attention." I handed her the papers I picked up. "I think I got everything."

"Yeah." She opened her book, turned and walked away.

"Hey, I didn't get your name!" I called to her as she scurried away.

She disappeared into the crowd in front of the student center. For a moment I stared in the direction that she walked until Scott snapped his fingers in front of my face.

"Hey man, you there?"

I shook the cobwebs out of my head. "Huh? Yeah."

"So, she was interesting! I don't remember seeing her around here ever."

"Do you keep a log of all the girls on campus?"

"Well, no," Scott explained, "But I think I would remember," he made a circular motion with his hand "that whole look. She looks like one of those witches from The Craft."

Scott went to take a sip of his coffee and when he put it up to his mouth the lid popped off and spilled some of it on him. "Shit!"

I couldn't help but laugh. "That coffee stain completes your look, buddy!"

"Whatever, man, I got time before class. I'm running back to the dorm and changing. Meet up at My Hero for lunch?"

"Yeah, later dude."

Scott went off and I continued on my way to the planetarium, my head still a little muddled. Hopefully I would see her around again, maybe even get her name.

CHAPTER THREE

The rest of the way to the planetarium was uneventful. The class was pretty full already, probably full of students that were looking for a quick nap before starting their day. I saw some of the guys from last night's Mortal Kombat tournament near the middle of the classroom and made some small talk with them. I hate making small talk normally, but I didn't mind talking about video games and my coffee got me pretty wired up.

The door opened and our professor walked in. He was a slightly younger than middle age man, almost like an older Denzel Washington from *Virtuosity*. He dressed like you would expect a college professor to dress almost to a stereotypical level, brown suit jacket and pants, white button up.

He dropped his briefcase on his desk and turned to write his name on the whiteboard, Professor Cline

"I am Professor Cline," he began, "and this is Exploring the Solar System. Those of you expecting nap time can leave now."

It seemed that everyone sat up a little straighter in their seats.

"Can anyone here tell me what the basic forces that underpin the Universe are and what they do?"

The room was silent. This guy was intense. Near the front of the class a hand raised in the air. Those bracelets seemed a little familiar.

"Yes, Miss Davenport."

"The four basic forces that underpin the Universe are strong nuclear force, weak nuclear force, electromagnetic force and gravitational force."

My ears perked up a bit. I've heard that disinterested voice before. Was that the girl from earlier? Also, did Professor Cline memorize the entire class roster?

"Both nuclear forces work at the atomic level, the other two govern the assemblages of atoms." The mystery voice continued.

"Resulting in all matter. Correct Miss Davenport."

Professor Cline continued spewing out facts about the universe and the class rushed to take notes. He was talking about the vastness of the universe and how our solar system is just a speck of dust in the grand scheme of everything. I swear our collective pens were about to catch fire from the speed we were writing. I decided that when I head back to the dorm later, I might have to see if we have a tape recorder somewhere, I think I saw one. If we don't I can always head to my parents house, channel my inner Kevin McAllister and grab my old Talkboy that did not work nearly as well as advertised in *Home Alone 2*.

As I took notes I was trying to get a better look at Miss Davenport. Now that I had a last name in my head I was trying to match up what could possibly be her first.

Katie? No, she definitely did not give off a Katie vibe.

Jennifer? No, too common. The number of Jennifers I've run into in my life is staggering. Seriously.

Rebecca? Maybe, she looks like she could be a Rebecca.

I was deep into my Mystery Name Game when I was snapped out of it by a hand clapping down on my desk. I nearly fell out of my chair and heard a chorus of chuckles as I composed myself. Professor Cline was standing right in front of me.

"Mister…?"

"Uh, Howard." I struggled to find my voice. "Jake Howard."

Professor Cline started to walk to the front of the class. "Well, Mister Howard, would you like to answer the question?"

Oh shit, the professor asked me a question. I had to think of a bullshit excuse that didn't include me trying to figure out Mystery Davenport's first name.

"Uh, I'm sorry, Professor," I started, "I was busy taking notes and didn't even realize you were asking me something. Can you repeat the question?" I heard a bit of muffled laughter from the guys next to me.

"Mister Howard," Professor Cline sat on the edge of his desk and stared at me, into my very soul it seemed, "I am not accustomed to repeating myself but consider this your one repeat for this year. What can you tell the class about meteorites? Formation, frequency of striking Earth, anything?"

I shuffled uncomfortably in my seat. "Well, aren't they basically broken off pieces of an asteroid?" I'm pretty sure I gathered that from playing Asteroids on my Atari 2600.

"Yes, Mister Howard," Professor Cline seemed to be enjoying torturing me. "What else can you tell us?"

"Um, I know a lot of them burn up in the atmosphere and I don't think that many of them wind up on Earth, at least you never hear about them."

A familiar, almost monotone, voice came from the front of the room.

"Actually, a few hundred tons of meteorites fall to Earth each day but most are lost by frictional heating and disintegration or vaporization."

Professor Cline rose from the edge of the desk.

"Very good Mister Howard, Miss Davenport." the professor locked eyes with me. "Mister Howard, I suggest you work on listening and writing at the same time. You won't be able to count on Miss Davenport every time I call on you."

The class chuckled a bit and I shrank down into my seat a little more.

For the rest of the class the professor went on about the infiniteness of the universe, the possibilities of other Earth-like planets out there that have yet to be discovered due to them being light years away, and theories about what other Earth-like planets could be like. It was really interesting even though I was still a little distracted, now even more so because of my run in with Professor Cline.

Professor Cline dismissed the class and everyone started to shuffle out. Like a hawk, my head turned towards where Mystery Davenport was talking and I saw her grab her books and walk out of class. I quickly shoved all of my stuff into my backpack and rushed out of class to talk to her.

At first I didn't see what direction she was going but then I caught a glimpse of her heading outside. I hurriedly made my way through the crowd of students and headed to the door.

What was I going to say to her? I had no freaking clue, maybe thank her for backing me up? At the very least I just wanted to find out her first name.

I felt the warm nearing-the-end-of-summer air on my face and saw her almost at the bottom of the stairs. Damn, she moved really quick. I yelled out the only thing I could think of.

"Miss Davenport!" I called out to her, louder than I meant to. Even I was embarrassed.

I saw her stiffen up and turn to see me. I swear I could *hear* her eyes rolling when she saw that I was the one that called her name. I ran down the stairs, nearly stumbling and falling on my face. I'm sure that would have been a great third impression considering my first two were bumping into her and looking like a moron in class.

"I just wanted to say," I stammered out as I caught my breath "thanks for helping me out back there. And I wanted to apologize again for knocking into you earlier."

"Yeah." she said as she stared at me. Her gaze was a little unsettling. I could feel myself getting hot from being flustered and a little out of breath.

"Anyway," I continued, "Thanks. I'm Jake. I figured since we are in class together maybe we should know each other's names."

She adjusted her books in her hand. I'm pretty sure she wanted to be anywhere but here.

"Beth." She said flatly.

The lighting made her hazel eyes pop. The way the sun reflected in them was mesmerizing, the way the color picked up the sunlight made her eyes look almost like a smoldering fire. I felt I should shake my head a bit to break the spell that her look had me under.

"Beth," I repeated, "That's a pretty name." Holy shit that was lame, did those words actually just come out of my mouth? I wanted to crawl in a hole and die.

"Uh, thanks."

I needed to go die of embarrassment and get out of this conversation, like now.

"Well, anyway, I guess I'll see you around campus. I'll try not to knock into you next time!" I think I made finger guns. What the hell is wrong with me? I must be having a stroke.

I think Beth was sensing a need to get away from this weird goon that really seemed like a whole ball of awkward.

"Uh, yeah, bye." She turned and walked away. I watched her go until she vanished into the crowd.

I stood there for a moment, reliving the terribly awkward interaction I was just a part of. It was almost like my mouth just didn't want to say anything that would even try to make me look good, like at all. It's not like I was trying to flirt with her. Well, I totally was, but you sure as hell couldn't tell.

It was almost noon so I hoofed it over to My Hero to meet up with Scott and tell him how terrible I am.

My Hero was a pizza and sub place pretty close to campus in the heart of the village of New Paltz. Next to Rob's Pizza in Wallkill, this place was definitely in the top five when it came to pizza in the area. The place was too small for its popularity, and usually filled up quickly. Since the middle of freshman year either Scott or I would try to get there right around noon to get a decent spot.

As I approached I saw the place was already packed. Scott was sitting at a table in the front, not looking pleased.

"What's up man?" I brought over an unused chair from a different table and dropped my bag under the table. Scott looked really annoyed.

"Man, you know I hate eating outside." he started. "I came here early like usual and this place was fucking swarmed."

"You want to go somewhere else?"

"Nah," Scott took a sip from his Jolt Cola. "I already ordered us some fries and a pie, half meatball and onions, half ham and pineapple." He grimaced when he said my half.

"Dude, you know it's good. You tried it, you even liked it!" I cackled

"Not dying from eating that abomination, and liking it are two different things," he quipped.

I scoffed. "You just don't appreciate good things."

"You are wrong and probably part ninja turtle." He pushed the basket of fries toward me. "How was Astrology?"

Our pizza arrived and we each grabbed a slice. I made sure a piece of pineapple fell on his slice and he flung it into the street.

"Astronomy," I said, correcting him. "Good, interesting. The professor is a little intense." I took a bite of my slice and probably gave myself third degree burns on the roof of my mouth from the molten pineapple. After my mouth regained function I continued, "That girl is in my class."

"What girl?" he was still chewing through forced exhalations because of the volcanic fresh pizza. We both need to learn how to blow on our food first.

"The girl from earlier, the one I bumped into." I gestured with my pizza in hand.

Scott laughed, "That weird one?"

"Yeah man, her name is Beth." I told him the story of our after class conversation and every awkward interaction it contained. Scott nearly choked from laughter.

"You're a mess and she's something else." Scott wasn't wrong on either count.

"Yeah, she's something else." I trailed off my train of thought. "There's something about her that I dig."

Scott grabbed another slice. "What, the fact that she doesn't even want to talk to you? Cut and run dude, she'll probably curse you if you don't leave her alone." He made a wiggling motion with his fingers.

"Whatever man. It's not like I'm looking for anything anyway." Since everything that happened with Shelly I really have been a little cautious, maybe even a little scared, about getting into another relationship. It sure as hell wasn't for lack of Scott trying to hook me up with girls, I just wasn't feeling anything toward anybody.

"Sure you're not." He winked exaggeratedly, using his whole face.

"Really!" I insisted. "I just wanted to know her name."

CHAPTER FOUR

Over the next month I settled into my new life of living on campus and balancing classes. My grades were pretty good, The dorm I shared with Scott was popular, people hanging out in there at most times, and summer was almost over. I love the temperature at the beginning of fall, that high-sixties to low-seventies weather. If I could find somewhere that was this temperature all year long, I would move there in a heartbeat.

I've gotten to talk to Beth a few more times and actually received more than one word answers a couple of times; whole sentences even! I think, possibly, I got her to slightly crack a smile once. I think it was more due to the fact that I tripped and almost ate pavement when I was talking to her, while heading to my next class, which was one hundred percent in the opposite direction. However her next class was the way I was walking, and I nearly fell over on a branch in the path. I played it off in classic Pee-Wee Herman "I meant to do that" mode, but she didn't buy it and I know I saw one side of her face maybe possibly raise in a smirk. It's a start.

I was relaxing after class in our living room playing some Final Fantasy VII when Scott came home with a weird grin on his face. He tossed his bag down and sat next to me on the futon.

I had to ask, "What's with the dumber than usual look?"

"I just ran into Jen and a couple of her friends downtown." He breathed these words with no effort.

"Oh, really?" I pulled up the game menu to pause it. "She's back in town?" I was intrigued.

"Yeah for the weekend. I was coming out of Jack's Rhythms when I heard a car honking. I looked over and Jen with a couple other girls were waving all crazy." He waved his hands in my face like someone trying to flag down a taxi.

I batted his hands away. "And?"

"And," he continued, "Her and her two *very hot* friends want to meet *us* at The Griffon tonight around like ten-ish to catch up."

The Griffon was the bar in town that the students on campus loved. It had cheap drinks, cool atmosphere and usually had some great live music. After Woodstock II, Green Day supposedly stopped in there to play a quick set. Every now and then a pretty big act would roll through for a surprise set on their way from Albany or Poughkeepsie, so the place was always packed, especially on Friday nights. I went there mostly for the music and have my obligatory one drink.

"Man, that place is always packed on Fridays." I reminded him.

Scott looked at me, "And?"

"And," I said, "You know I'll be there even though I hate the crowds on Fridays."

"Goddamn right you'll be there!" Scott jumped up and went into his room to get ready even though we had a few hours until we had to be there.

Part of me has always thought Scott and Jen hooked up the night of graduation. Neither of them will confirm it, but I'm pretty sure they did at one of the graduation parties we went to that night. I don't care if they did, I've been over Jen for years and consider her one of my best friends, but Scott always has a little extra spring in his step when she's around. He will, of course, deny this too.

"Hey!" I yelled to Scott, "Shelly's not with her, right?"

"I said her two hot friends, not a dick sucking demon," he called out from the other room.

I laughed. "Alrighty then."

I looked at the clock and went back to my game. It was four thirty and we were meeting Jen at ten. That is just under six hours and I could be ready in about ten minutes. Scott would need all this time to get ready. I swear he's worse than my sister when it comes to getting ready. I think he probably spends a good two of those hours on his hair alone, his hair will be spiky and crisp. It might as well be a weapon.

After no less than six outfit changes, and whatever other mystic rituals Scott had in getting ready we were ready to head out. All I needed to do was change my shirt. I would throw on a poncho that covered it anyway. It was about nine thirty and The Griffon was kind of within walking distance, another feature that made it popular to the student body here, so we were on our way.

As predicted, The Griffon was packed. There was a short line outside and the music sounded decent tonight, probably a local cover band. I could clearly hear Toad the Wet Sprokets "All I Want" when I got grabbed from behind in a hug.

"Jake!" Jen yelled, "I missed you hun!"

I turned and gave Jen a big hug, lifting her off of her feet. Her normally long blond hair was cut into a short bob with a bunch of little hair clips in it. It looked cute, like that's how her hair should have always been. "Hey! Missed you too. You look great! How's B.U.?" I beamed.

"Thanks, great!" she said excitedly. "Let me introduce you to my friends, Courtney and Erin!"

I saw Scott mouth the word "hot" behind them. They were cute, almost like they could be related. Both of them had light brown hair, brown eyes and stood about the same height, pretty short, maybe about five feet or so.

"Nice to meet you. Are you two sisters?" I inquired, attempting to break the ice.

They giggled, almost in unison. "No, not related. We both cheer though so we're like cheer-sisters!"

Oh boy, Scott would have a ball with this. Jen cheered in high school and was the only non bitchy one in the bunch. My experience with cheerleaders, at least from high school, was either they were super giggly bubbleheads, bitchy, snotty or batshit crazy.

When I got to college I met Shelly who was a cheerleader. She started off giggly but then fell into the batshit crazy category. These two, from their first impression, hopefully just fell into the giggly one.

The five of us chatted for a moment outside and I could tell Scott was showing off a bit. I wasn't sure who he was trying to impress, either Jen or the cheerleaders. I did see Jen give him a couple of glances and a smile. I swear there's something there.

After about a half hour, we made our way inside and grabbed a table. We ordered some drinks and some nachos (they make the best nachos at The Griffon). Courtney and Erin had to go to the restroom so Scott, Jen and I started babbling like it was old times.

"So," I started, "Scott told me that Shelly showed up on your doorstep." I took a sip of my Guinness.

Jen rolled her eyes. "Oh my God, yeah. Just kinda showed up at the beginning of the year." She took a swig of her Corona. "Listen I've always kind of liked her but, I don't have to tell you, she can be a bit much. And after everything that went down-"

"And everything she went down on." Scott added.

Jen tossed a napkin at him and continued, "I tried to distance myself from her because I love you and you are, like, one of my best friends and she's just, Shelly, you know?"

"Yeah, I get it." Believe me, I get it.

"Anyway," Jen continued, "She shows up at the beginning of the semester like 'Hi roomie!' and just moved in. I was looking forward to having my dorm to myself this year because my old roommate moved out. She took extra classes to graduate early. I never reported it to housing and she said she wasn't going to either, but they must have found out anyway, because they stuck me with Shelly." Jen took another sip. "So are you all recovered from what she did to you?"

I shrugged. "Pretty much, I guess. Leaving her at the diner was pretty therapeutic for me."

Jen laughed. "I'm sure it was."

"Man, fuck that girl." Scott muttered, downing his first Budweiser and motioning for another one. "So what's the deal with the cheerleaders? Think we can get old Jake here some action based on his heartbreak?"

"I'm not looking for any-" I was cut off.

"Silence, young padawan." Scott said, mimicking the Jedi mind trick hand motions.

"Listen," Jen started, "These two are interesting. I knew them from my first couple of years from cheering up at school and we stayed friends after I stopped cheering. They are nice but…" Jen trailed off.

"But, what?" I asked

"But," Jen continued, "they are not exactly picky with who they hook up with. After everything you went through with Shelly I don't know if you want to get involved with that."

"Who cares?" Scott said loudly. "Jake hasn't had any action since that bitch. Have I mentioned how much I hate her?"

"Yes Scott." Jen and I both said in unison. We clinked our bottles together.

"Well I'll say it again, I hate her. Anyway," he said, "My man needs to get back on the horse, or *horses* as it were."

Honestly, I wasn't looking to hook up with anyone at the moment. Plus, given what Jen just said, I really didn't want to hook up with some loose cheerleaders. I'm sure it would be a fun time, but I wasn't looking for that kind of fun. I had to go to the bathroom so I stood up. "I'm going to let the two of you figure out my love life, I gotta pee."

"I got you dude!" Scott saluted me. Jen rolled her eyes and laughed.

I made my way through the sea of people bopping to a cover of Sublime's "What I Got" on the way to the bathroom and noticed Courtney and Erin being chatted up by a group of guys at the bar. It looked like they were downing shots and laughing. Yeah, that looked like a bunch of crazy I didn't want to get involved with, I think Jen was right.

After taking care of business I headed back to the table when I noticed Beth. She was sitting at a table by the window alone, her nose still stuck in a book. Who brings a book to the bar?

I was going to walk right over and say hi when I saw Professor Cline approach her. I've never seen a professor in here before, and to see a professor like Cline in here was a little strange. I stayed by the bar and checked out what was happening.

Professor Cline sat down across from Beth and started talking to her. She put her book in her bag and Cline appeared like he was laying into her about something. He wasn't yelling at her, but from his posture and body language he was definitely being stern. Beth had her arms crossed and was listening but it really seemed by her body language that she wasn't happy with what Cline was saying. He got up and left The Griffon. Beth stayed in her seat but looked a little upset and peered out of the window. At least, I think she looked upset. It's really hard to read her.

I decided to head over to her and ask her if she was alright. I swam through the ocean of bodies while the band played "She" by Green Day and sat across from her. She turned towards me with a look of possible annoyance but maybe also relief.

"Hey are you okay? You look a little upset?"

Beth sat up a little, startled, "Yeah, I'm fine. Why?"

"Well," I started, "I saw Professor Cline in here talking to you and it looked like he was laying into you about something."

"What are you, like, stalking me or something?"

"No, not at all!" I insisted. "I was just making sure you're all good. You looked upset, that's all."

She got up and grabbed her bag, a medium black backpack-purse thing. "Nope, I'm fine." She didn't sound fine. "I gotta go. See you around."

Beth stormed off and I sat there for a second. Scott noticed where I was and came over.

"Hey the girls came back to the table, get your ass over there." he started, "What's wrong?"

"Nothing man. Beth was just here and Professor Cline was too. He was talking to her about something and she looked upset."

Scott laughed. "She always looks like that! Maybe Cline was banging her and just broke it off."

"I don't think it's that at all." I got up and started to leave.

"Dude, where are you going? Those girls are waiting for you to come back."

"I'll be back in a few minutes, I just want to make sure she's ok."

Scott got a little annoyed. "Man what is it with her? She obviously wants to be alone and she is going to like, turn you into a frog or something if you keep bothering her." He went to take a sip of his beer and it fell out of his hand, and spilled on him and the floor. "Goddamnit!"

"I'll be back dude." I said and ran out the door.

The air was crisp and cold and it struck my face hard. It took a moment for me to recover from the shock and started walking the way I saw Beth go. I crept up the alley next to The Griffon and noticed that the outside basement doors to the bar were open. I started to sneak down there when I heard a sound. A sound I haven't heard since I was in ninth grade.

I immediately froze halfway down the stairs and was filled with an immediate sense of dread. Why the hell was I hearing this sound? I also saw a strange, but familiar, blue-ish light coming from deeper in the basement.

I continued down the steps and saw what looked like a swirling, glowing doorway in the bricks. The brick wall looked like it was trying to close around the portal but couldn't for some reason. It was almost like they were trying to shuffle in some crazy puzzle but just couldn't configure itself properly.

"No. Fucking. Way." I whispered to myself. A thousand questions started forming in my head. Why is this here? Am I dreaming? Am I drunk?

I found myself drawn closer to the glowing doorway and the bricks slowly stopped shuffling themselves and stayed open.

This was one of the coolest and most terrifying things I've ever seen. The last time I saw this it was gone in a flash, this time it just stayed here.

I realized I was inches away from the portal when a hand reached out, grabbed me by my collar and pulled me in.

CHAPTER FIVE

I could feel my body twisting and contorting as I was pulled through the portal. The feeling is difficult to describe. It was almost as if over the span of one second, my body was trying to stretch, shrink, twist and fold onto itself at the same time. I also immediately felt like I was going to vomit and shit my pants simultaneously.

In a flash I felt myself land on my stomach on a cold floor in a pitch black room. The air seemed cool and damp and, from what I could tell, the floor felt like stone. One thing was certain though, there was not a speck of light in here. I slowly stood up and patted myself down to make sure *every part of me* made it through the portal, I tried to convince my eyes to focus on something, anything in what seemed like an infinite amount of darkness. That weird queasy feeling left over from the portal journey had lifted, but I was filled with another sense, terrifying dread.

"H-hello?" I called out somewhat quietly but my voice still resonated. It seemed like I was in a cave but I was too scared to move. I could be on some type of ledge or pillar or something and I couldn't even see my hand in front of my face. No way was I going to move anywhere, at least at the moment. "Is anyone there?"

The echo of my words seemed to go on forever. After it faded there was nothing, no type of sound at all. There didn't seem to be anything at all in this cave. I guess at the very least that was a good thing, at least there were no scratching or clawing sounds. If I was going to die here, I figured it would be best to be taken by surprise; I really didn't want to hear if anything was coming for me.

34

"WHAT DID YOU DO?" A woman's voice boomed in the infinite silence almost coming from everywhere at once. The voice sounded almost otherworldly but not quite and was almost deafening after hearing nothing but myself. I wasn't nearly that loud. "WHAT DID YOU DO TO MAKE THE GATEWAY NOT BE ABLE CLOSE?"

Gateway? I guess that's what I was pulled through. I tried to find the courage to address whatever being was addressing me.

"Uh, I didn't do anything," I said meekly.

"LIAR!" The voice boomed at me. It seemed louder and super pissed off.

"No, I'm not!" I protested. I was pretty sure I was about to be killed by something, some type of alien-demon type thing. I started rambling. "I just followed a sound that I heard a long time ago and went down a set of stairs and saw a blue portal thing and got pulled through, I swear!"

I heard a shuffle in the cave and almost immediately felt a hand grab me by my shirt. *This is it*, I thought to myself, *this is how I die.* I closed my eyes and waited for the inevitable end. I felt an intense heat near the left side of me and figured I was about to be roasted.

"I know," the voice said. It was not as loud as before but still sounded foreboding. "I pulled you through and I want answers. Now!"

I opened my eyes slowly, not knowing what to expect. What I saw was something I will never forget. It's also the last thing I would have expected to see in a situation like this.

Beth stood in front of me, but this wasn't the same Beth I saw everyday. No, this Beth was confident and looked like some type of goddess. She was still wearing what she wore in The Griffon, very much the same type of outfit she wore every time I saw her, but her dark red hair seemed to be radiating light framing her face like an eclipse, and with a look of rage that her normally hazel-with-a-hint-of-sunrise eyes were practically glowing orange. Her right hand gripped me tightly by my collar and her left hand held a ball of flame. *Holy shit*, I thought, *Scott was right.* I was speechless.

"I'm going to ask again," Beth said with a commanding tone pulling me closer to her till my face was inches away from hers, "What did you do to make the gateway stay open?"

I got lost in her eyes for a moment before speaking.

"Beth," I stammered. "I swear to God I didn't do anything. I thought you were upset at The Griffon and followed you. That's when I heard that sound that I haven't heard in a long time and saw the wall in the basement; I was freaking out. It calmed down as I got closer to it and then, apparently, you yanked me through. That's it, I swear!"

She stared at me for a moment. "What do you mean 'a sound you haven't heard in a long time?'" Her grip on my shirt loosened a bit.

"Elizabeth, please let go of Mister Howard's shirt." I knew that voice.

Professor Cline stepped out from the shadows and started to approach me. He looked normal, although he didn't have a blazer on and his sleeves were rolled up a bit. Beth released her grip and the fire in her left hand subsided. The glow that she seemingly had before faded and she looked like ordinary Beth again, but still with a commanding posture. Professor Cline stopped just behind Beth and put his hand on her shoulder.

"Very good, Elizabeth," he said to her in a genuine compassionate tone. "You are getting much better at controlling your abilities." Beth looked at Professor Cline and gave him a little smile then the professor turned his attention toward me. "So, Mister Howard, I'm sure you have some questions," he started.

Questions? That didn't even begin to plumb the depths of what I was experiencing.

I opened my mouth to speak before Professor Cline cut me off.

"Before you start, why don't we brighten the room a little. Elizabeth, if you would?"

Beth closed her eyes and snapped her fingers and a little flame appeared in her hand. Professor Cline and I stood still while Beth stepped over to an old looking switch and pulled it. The lights started to come up and I could see where I was. Upon seeing my surroundings I was even more confused.

The scene looked like a cross between the old Batman show and Doctor Frankenstein's laboratory. There were various monitors humming to life and ancient looking equipment being revealed to my eyes. The room we were in was a bit dangerous looking with some pitfalls, none near us thankfully, and the air was cool and kind of moist. We were in a cave, I just had no idea where.

"That's better, thank you Elizabeth." Professor Cline started to walk away from me towards the various monitors and had a seat. "Now, Mister Howard, you were about to say?"

I was about to say? What I wanted to say was to ask what the actual fuck was going on here, but I held my tongue. Why was Beth on fire? Why did a gateway or whatever appear at The Griffon? Is this all some fucked up dream? I started with what I hoped would be the easiest question.

"Where are we?"

"We are in the heart of Mohonk Mountain," he started. "Only a few miles from The Griffon. The area where that establishment was built has been the entrance for The Conclave for centuries."

I felt myself furrow my brow, "The what now?"

"The Conclave." Beth calmly stated as she walked past me and leaned on the desk near Professor Cline with her arms crossed. She looked like she was back to normal and her tone changed to her normal voice.

Professor Cline continued, "We belong to an ancient order called The Conclave that has been tasked with protecting The Multiverse." He paused for a moment, allowing me to soak in what he just said. My brain was still a little scrambled, but I thought I knew what a Multiverse was at least.

"The Multiverse," I repeated, "Like in the comics?" Comic books were the only example I could think of. Different realities fighting each other for control or whatever was needed to sell issues that month. I saw Beth roll her eyes and shake her head gently.

"To a point, yes." Professor Cline replied. "Although The Multiverses we keep guard of are slightly different. They are referred to as Daughter Universes."

I think the professor could see the blank look on my face and continued. He marched confidently over to a whiteboard and drew a horizontal line.

"In simple terms, Daughter universes are decision based. For example," Professor Cline drew a dash on the line, "Three years ago you decided to continue your education at SUNY New Paltz. What if, instead, you decided to start a band?" The professor drew a line skewing off of the main line he drew. "There would be a whole other set of experiences, circumstances and consequences that would erupt from that. A Daughter universe is just that, every decision spawns another world with those decisions and then more worlds spawn from decisions made in those worlds and so on." He kept drawing lines until there was essentially a spider web pattern on the board. "There are, essentially, infinite worlds that exist and we are tasked with protecting them and make sure that they do not interfere with one another."

I looked at the board, trying to process all of the information I was just given. "Okay." I said, not totally processing all of this information yet and continued, "I kind of get that, kind of, but why was Beth's hand on fire?" I was hoping this was a more simple explanation.

"I'm a Caster." Beth said, turning towards me. "Basically I'm part of a line of people that has," she paused for a moment, "gifts, passed down to them from generation to generation."

"So you're a wit-" I was cut off.

"I don't like that word." Beth said with a touch of anger in her voice. "I don't have a cauldron full of stew and live in a woodland cottage luring kids in to eat them. Also, your friend Scott is a douchebag and if he keeps calling me that I'm going to keep making things drop on him."

Ah, I thought, *so that explains that.*

"Elizabeth's heritage has been part of this organization for a centuries," Professor Cline walked over to Beth and put his hand on her shoulder in a reassuring way, "And I have been trained by The Conclave to assist a Caster in my charge. I have done so for a long time. I have no gifts myself, but I help train her to use them responsibly. Elizabeth still gets a little overcome with her abilities, she has only had them for a short time." Beth put her hand on Professor Cline's hand. "I'm helping her to overcome the rage that fills her when her power shows itself to help her stay more in control." He stared at me and continued, "If this situation had happened a year or two ago, she may have evaporated you on the spot, given that she was bestowed the gift of Pyromancy."

I didn't know what to say to that.

"Okay, I have a question for you," Beth said staring what seemed to be into my soul, "What did you do to make the gateway not close behind me? And," she said in a slightly softer tone, "you said you heard that sound the gateway made before. When, and where did you hear it?"

"I didn't do anything to the gateway," I insisted, "When I saw it the bricks in the wall were kinda just shuffling, like a slide puzzle. I walked closer to them and the sliding stopped and then, you pulled me through. I really didn't do anything to it!"

The Professor and Beth looked at me before Beth spoke up again. "And the sound? When did you hear it before?"

"Ninth grade. We were on a field trip to Skytop Tower on the mountain and I wandered off from the group. I heard that sound and followed it. I saw what I guess was a gateway, it flashed closed and knocked me over and I almost fell off the mountain."

Beth looked at me intensely for a moment and then looked away. Under his breath I heard Professor Cline say something that sounded like "Fascinating."

The Professor stood up and approached me with a bit of excitement and interest on his face. "Well," he started, "This has been quite a night and I think we are all a bit tired. I'm sure Mister Howard has a lot to process, as do we. Elizabeth, would bring Mister Howard back to his dorm please?"

"Sure." Beth said, sounding a little choked up.

I got a little worried. "Uh, how are we getting there?"

"By gateway, of course!" Professor Cline said. "It's the only way in or out of here."

Before I could protest Beth grabbed my arm, opened the gateway, and pulled me through. I felt my body twist and contort again and in an instant we were in the basement of The Griffon. I gave my body a moment to acclimate itself before turning to Beth.

"I hate that." I said, still getting a hold of my surroundings.

"You get used to it." Beth said, not really looking at me. "I gotta go."

I started to tell her to wait but she was gone in a flash. As I plodded back to the dorm, I tried to wrap my head around what I just experienced. At the moment I just felt the need to sleep. Maybe I was already sleeping and this was one of those dream-in-a-dream scenarios. Either way, I was done for today.

CHAPTER SIX

By the time I made it back up to my dorm it was nearly three o'clock in the morning and I just wanted to either wake up from this crazy dream or go to sleep and forget this night happened. I woke up the next day around noon and just lay there, in the silence of my room, my brain still spinning from the events of the night before. As it turns out it wasn't a dream, and everything was burned into my mind. I wasn't going to forget it.

I tried to unpack everything in my head from all of the information I was given last night. There's a multiverse, which itself is a terrifying concept. The way that Professor Cline explained, it seems that nearly every choice that every person makes spawns a new universe and then new universes spawn from decisions made there and everything keeps repeating itself infinitely. I wondered what the consequences of me never leaving my bed again would be now that I was too scared to ever do anything again that might cause some bullshit to happen. Still, I woke up freaked out and was debating the pros and cons of building a pillow and blanket fort in my room and never leaving.

Then there was the whole thing with The Professor and Beth. They are part of some secret organization to guard The Multiverse? What the hell? And the fact that Beth was on fucking fire? Why did she seem really weirded out with me hearing that sound a long time ago? This all was a lot to process and their reactions to me didn't seem to clear anything up.

While all these thoughts were spinning around in my head, I heard a knock at my door. Without thinking I clutched my blanket tight and pulled it up halfway over my face. I used to do this as a kid. I think it started after I watched The Lost Boys. My tiny kid-mind believed that by pulling the blanket up over my face

41

I would be protected from neck bites, like a vampire wouldn't ever be able to pull the covers down from my child grip. I also haven't eaten rice since I watched that movie, but that is a whole other set of issues.

"Dude, you awake?" It was Scott on the other side, not a blood sucking monster. Maybe? Who even knew at this point anymore.

"Yeah." I released my grip from the covers but stayed laying in bed, my head was still swimming a bit.

Scott opened the door, walked in and plopped down on the oversized bean bag chair that sat in the corner of my room opposite of the bed. He looked tired and a little annoyed.

"How was last night?" I asked, hoping to hold off any questioning of what I was doing last night, at least for a little while. It's not that I planned on bailing, not at all. How was I supposed to know that following Beth would lead to crushing my expectations of what reality actually is?

"Last night was fun," Scott started, "Courtney and Erin were something else. Jen and I didn't see much of them until last call so it was just us hanging out." He stared at me for a bit before adding. "She was kind of annoyed that you just disappeared last night. At first she thought she made you mad about the whole Shelly thing but then I told her you are just crushing on a girl that pretty much hates you and decided to stalk her."

"I didn't decide to stalk her, I just wanted to check and make sure she was okay." I decided not to add the fact that she opened a portal and has magical powers.

"Well you were gone all night. So what happened? Did you get some from witchie-poo?" He really didn't seem interested in my answer.

"Don't call her that." I said, groggily. Honestly, I didn't know if Beth could hear Scott all the way over here. Better safe than sorry. "We actually talked all night. It was," I paused for a moment to find the right word, "Fascinating." Yeah, that pretty much summed up the night. It's not like I was going to tell Scott it was terrifying, that would lead to a whole lot of questions I really didn't know the answers to.

"Whatever, dude." Scott got up off the beanbag chair and started to leave the room. "I have soccer later and Jen said that she might want to hang out again tonight since she's leaving tomorrow. Let me know if you want to come."

"Alright, man." I felt bad for not telling him everything. "Hey, sorry for snapping at you. I'm just really tired, it was a late night."

"Yeah, it's alright. I'll talk to you later." It felt like he had more to say.

Scott left the room and a moment later I heard the door to our dorm close too. I lay in the safety of my bed alone once more. I really wanted to tell him everything that happened, but I wasn't even really sure how to verbalize it.

After a little while I got up, brushed my teeth and went to our kitchenette and poured a bowl of cereal in the biggest bowl I could find. In times of stress, I could always turn to Tony the Tiger to make things feel alright. I plopped down on the futon and put on *Star Wars*. I've seen the original Star Wars so many times I could recite it by heart and, if I'm tired enough, it's almost like a lullaby that can put me to sleep. I wasn't that tired, but I just wanted something that was comforting while I ate and processed.

When Luke and Obi-Wan got to Mos Eisley I decided to grab another bowl of cereal. On my way back to my seat I stopped for a moment to look out of the window overlooking the campus. I've always loved the view, our dorm faced Mohonk and I could see the tower from here too. The leaves were changing nice orange and red colors and the whole scene almost looked like a painting. I could see a few other students just walking around, probably on their way to grab something to eat. I was standing there for a while when my sight fell on the bench in front of the building. There was a girl sitting there alone, seemingly waiting for someone.

It was Beth.

I felt a little wave of panic come over me and nearly dropped my Frosted Flakes. I ducked to the side to avoid her seeing me while I figured out what to do. What the hell was she even doing here? I've never seen her on this side of campus since school started. Hell, I didn't even know if she lived on campus, she probably just lived inside the mountain.

I peeked back around the corner and she was still sitting there but now she was looking up at my window. We locked eyes and I saw her take a big breath, probably a sigh, and motioned for me to come down. I did a motion like 'who, me?' and she stared at me and nodded her head. Well, shit. There goes thinking there was another person she was about to drag to The Twilight Zone.

I figured I should probably not go downstairs in my boxers so I threw on a pair of jeans and headed down. I walked down the four flights of stairs like a man heading to his death, got to the front doors and shambled out. The crisp autumn air hit me with a refreshing coolness, probably because I was overheated from wondering what fresh hell I was getting myself into and dragged my feet over to the bench where Beth was sitting. As I got closer she stood up, but didn't walk closer to me. She looked like normal Beth, not the fire goddess looking Beth from the night before.

"Hey, what's up?" I tried to sound cool and calm, but I know my voice was shaking a little and I'm pretty sure I was about to piss myself.

Beth looked at me and took a deep breath.

"Cline wanted me to come here and tell you that he would like to see you." she said begrudgingly. Beth continued, "Now that you know about us he wants to make sure you don't tell anyone and that you aren't in danger."

"I didn't tell anyone, not even Scott. But why would I be in danger?" I was audibly nervous.

Beth sighed. "Listen, I have no idea," she started, "sometimes Cline gets these thoughts in his head and it's just better to go along with them. He just wanted me to come here and get you."

"Beth, listen, last night messed with my head pretty good." I could feel my anxiety levels rising. "If I knew what was going to happen after I followed you I probably would have thought twice."

"Yeah, well, it's too late for that now."

"Too late for what?" I questioned.

"You know about us," Beth stated as she came closer. "Well, you know a little about us." She stopped in front of me and took a deep breath again. "Cline wants to make sure you are protected and I…" she trailed off a bit.

"You, what?" I had to make sure I heard what she had to say.

"I want to see why the gateway didn't close." She was insistent.

Oh, I thought to myself. For a fleeting moment I thought maybe she was going to say something else.

"Follow me," Beth said before gently adding, "please."

Against my better judgement I followed her. Why? This was just going to lead to another mindfuck, I could feel it. Yeah, I had a little crush on her. That was before I knew what was going on. Now, I still had a small crush on her, but it was wrapped in a large layer of fear. She was heading around the back of DuBois Hall when she turned to me.

"You ready?" she asked me, deadpanned.

"Ready for what?" I looked around, confused.

Beth was matter-of-fact. "We gotta go."

Before I knew what was happening Beth grabbed my arm, touched the gem on her choker, opened a gateway, and pulled us through,

CHAPTER SEVEN

We landed back in the main room from the night before, except this time, the lights were already on. The same wave of physical feelings happened again after coming through the gateway with Beth.

Nausea? Check.

Feel like I'm about to crap myself? Double check.

Does my whole body feel wobbly? Well, I'm on my ass again so I'm saying triple check.

"How did we get here again?" I asked after getting some feeling of normalcy back. "I thought the only way in or out of here was through The Griffon?"

Beth touched the gem on her choker.

"This allows me to make, basically, a one way gateway." She explained. "It only works once a day so I usually use it to get here and then usually use The Griffon to get back."

I started to get to my feet and tried to find my balance.

"Seems like the kind of thing that would be good for emergencies." I responded.

"Cline says the same thing," Beth said before adding, "Besides, this was kind of an emergency."

"Oh, really?" Why did I ask that?

"Yeah," she smirked, "I wanted to see you come through a gateway again."

I tried my best to sound nonchalant, "I'm glad my torment is amusing you." I gave her a little smile.

"It's pretty funny." Beth said with a hint of a grin.

A door opened on the far side of the room and Professor Cline strode in. He was wearing what I saw him in the night before but had some type of apron on over it. It reminded me of a welding apron.

"Still looking a little green, Mister Howard," Professor Cline said as he made his way over to his desk and sat down, "Your body will get used to travel by gateway in time."

I started to ask why he wanted to see me and why he thought I was in danger and he cut me off.

"After our conversation last night, it occurred to me that now that you know about us. The fact that you had an interesting reaction to the gateway, and that you might require a bit of protection." Professor Cline leveled his gaze at me. "Also, a bit of study as to why the gateway didn't close until you passed through.

I felt my mouth go dry. "Study?"

"Mister Howard, no need to worry. Other than a blood test everything is non invasive."

"I, uh, really don't like needles." I was desperate to get out of there.

Beth sighed, grabbed my wrist and pulled a little device out of her purse.

"Don't be a baby," she said as she pulled my arm out straight in front of her. "It takes like a second."

Before I could protest any further she clamped the device down on my finger and I felt a little prick. The light on it turned from blue to red and she removed the device.

"There, all done." Beth reached in her little black backpack purse and pulled out a Band-Aid. "I'm glad you survived the horrific ordeal and torture that you were just put through." Her snarky tone was followed by a smirk.

"Okay," I said as I grabbed the Band-Aid from her, "That wasn't as bad as I thought it was going to be."

Beth brought the little device over to Professor Cline who inserted it into something attached to his massive computer. Looking at his setup now it looked like the Batcave computer in the cartoon.

"Mister Howard, would you come here please?" I didn't want to, but I found myself walking towards him.

I approached the pair not knowing what to expect. Beth was leaning on the edge of the desk with a look that I really couldn't discern and looking at something in front of Professor Cline. As I got closer he spun in his chair towards me.

Cline started, "While we wait for the results of the blood test-"

"Wait a second." I interrupted the Professor, which really was against my nature. This last twenty-four hours has been a whirlwind and I wanted some answers that were straightforward and not cryptic.

"Before I hear anything else," I continued. I felt my blood pressure rising and became a little agitated. "What are you looking for in my blood? Why am I back here? I feel like I am at the edge of my sanity right now and I haven't even fully processed what happened last night! Why do you think I am in danger?" I was ranting a little bit but I felt like I was about to go nuts.

Professor Cline did not seem at all surprised by my reaction, neither did Beth.

"Mister Howard," he calmly started, "I was just about to explain that to you. Please, come here."

I composed myself and sat in the chair the professor motioned for me to sit in.

"As I was saying, it's going to be a little while before we get the results of your blood test. I have reason to believe that you have some type of, what's a good term," He paused to find the correct word, "Enzyme? Yes, that works, enzyme in your blood that makes you able to interact with gateways and, possibly, rifts."

"Rifts?" I tried to piece it all together in my brain.

"Yeah," Beth chimed in, "Rifts are how people can travel between multiverses."

As I was about to unpack that bombshell the professor continued. "Because of that, pending the results of the test, I feel that we should take precautions in case this were to become a bit complicated." Professor Cline reached into the pocket of his apron and pulled out a leather strap. "In order to keep you safe and to protect yourself in case something were to arise, I have this for you." He extended his hand towards me.

"A bracelet?" I asked, puzzled.

"It's what Elizabeth calls a Rig," Cline explained, "we couldn't come up with a better name for it, so that's what we're calling it, for now anyway. Please, put it on"

I grabbed the ordinary looking strap and inspected it. It didn't look like anything special, just a thick black leather wristband with some metal studs on it. The one thing that did stand out on it was it had a green gem in the middle that almost looked like Beth's red gem on her choker. "Ok, so what is it?" I put it around my right wrist and buckled it.

"It allows you to create weapons." Beth said, standing up and raising her wrist in front of her, showing me her assortment of bangle bracelets. One of them had a gem similar to mine except it was a dark red like her choker. "If you think of something basic, not like a gun or anything, it will appear in your hand."

Beth closed her right fist and with a flick of her wrist and a sword with a reddish blade appeared. She flicked her wrist again with a flourish and the sword disappeared. I was dumbfounded, that was one of the coolest things I've ever seen. All I could get out of my mouth was "Wow."

The professor continued, "You're here now because I want Elizabeth to give you at least a basic training on how to use it in battle."

"Wait, what?" Beth seemed surprised.

Professor Cline turned to her and explained. "I want you to train Mister Howard on the use of the Rig. He needs to know how to protect himself if the need arises, and you still need practice in controlling your abilities. A little sparring is good for that."

That last bit concerned me a little bit. I had never really been in an actual fight at all. The only time I ever was in any kind of physical confrontation was on my school bus one time when I was in seventh grade. There was a kid that was in high school, tenth grade I think, that was messing with me on the way home constantly since the beginning of the year, and started to get physical with me. I stood up to him finally and he took a swing at me. I ducked and took a wild swing, I'm pretty sure with my eyes closed, and the next thing I knew he was on the ground. Apparently I hit him on the side of the head and knocked him out cold. He didn't mess with me again after that.

"Um, I'm not going to fight anyone, especially Beth." I protested.

Beth turned and glared at me. "What do you mean 'especially Beth'? Is it because I'm a girl?"

Honestly, that didn't even occur to me as my first thought.

"No," I explained, "You can set me on fire and I'm not trying to be roasted today."

Professor Cline let out a laugh.

"A legitimate concern, Mister Howard," he said amusingly, "but I don't think it will be a factor today. Elizabeth has enough control of herself to not accidentally make you a flambe'."

"Fine." Beth took a deep breath and started to walk away from me toward another section of the cave. After a moment she stopped and turned her head a little over her shoulder. "You coming?"

Professor Cline turned back to the task of analyzing my blood and fiddling around with other objects on the desk, so I followed Beth towards whatever mind bending experience I was about to go through. After a couple of minutes we came to a set of doors that Beth opened with a wave of her hand. She led me into what looked like a type of gym mixed with an armory. There were various weapons and armor hanging along the walls, some that looked pretty common like staves and swords to others that looked exotic and almost other-worldly. She walked towards the middle of the room, turned and faced me.

"Are you ready?" she stared at me with an impatient look.

I walked towards the middle of the room, "Uh, not really. I don't even know how to use this." I motioned with my right wrist.

"It's actually not as hard as you think." She flicked her wrist and the sword she held earlier appeared in her hand and she flicked it again and it was gone. "I've been using it for years so my Rig is attuned to me."

I tried mimicking Beth's actions but nothing was happening. "Nothing's happening." I said.

"Yeah. Yours isn't going to work like that, at least for a while," she said with a slight smirk, "You're going to have to think a little more about what you want."

I tried to think of a weapon that possibly wouldn't get me totally destroyed and that was good for training. Swords were out of the question immediately, it was Beth's weapon of choice it seemed and plus I didn't feel like possibly getting impaled. I was going through weapons I'd seen in movies, games and cartoons when it hit me. I felt something forming in my hand and my hand instinctively closed around it. I looked down and saw that I was holding a Bo staff. I let out a little shout of joy and looked at Beth.

"A staff? Really?" Beth did not seem impressed.

"What's wrong with a staff?" I asked, "It's a good weapon, considerably less lethal for training purposes and has a decent reach. Besides, Donatello is my favorite Ninja Turtle." I tried to give her a little smile even though this whole situation had me a bit rattled. Hopefully all of my years of training with sticks or wrapping paper tubes would help me out now, I also guessed it probably wouldn't though.

Beth sighed. "I was always more of a Raphael girl but whatever." She flicked her wrist and a staff that looked like it was made of redwood appeared in her hand. She looked at it, did some flourishes ending with her tucking it between her arm and back in a ready position.

I silently thought to myself that I was going to die.

"Before we start," Beth said looking way too eager to beat my ass, "You should probably grab a helmet or some padding or something. Go grab something from the armor rack."

"Yeah, that's a good idea." I agreed.

I turned around to go grab some protection when I felt a push from behind, stumbled a bit and fell forward. I rolled over and saw Beth with her staff out in prime poking position with a smile on her face.

"Why would you turn your back in a fight?" she asked mockingly.

I tried to think of some type of comeback but nothing came to mind. I also realized I wasn't getting any type of protection in our little sparring match. I sensed a concussion in my future.

I stood up, brushed myself off, and readied my staff to fight. In my head I felt that I looked badass, but I'm pretty sure I just looked like a little kid with a branch they found outside pretending it was a weapon. Beth gave me a little smile.

"That stance is adorable," she said in a bit of a condescending tone that I hadn't really heard from her before. "Okay, I'm not going to swing at you, just yet anyway. I want to see how much work I have to do with you." Beth readied her staff. "All I'm going to do is block, for now. Just try to hit me." She gave me a smirk.

My pride a little hurt, I took a swing towards Beth's midsection that she blocked easily.

"Really? That was pretty weak." She said with an annoyed laugh.

I shrugged. "I didn't want to swing too hard." In my head I was thinking of always being told as a kid that boys don't hit girls.

"What, are you afraid of hurting me?" Beth stared at me, a tinge of anger behind her eyes.

"Well no, yes, uh I really don't know the right answer here." I was struggling.

She quickly took a swing at my head but stopped just short of hitting me. She brought her staff back and resumed her blocking position.

"Stop pretending to try to hit me and hit me!" I noticed Beth was getting a bit of a red glow around her, a faint light that seemed to be illuminating her from behind. Either I pissed her off or she was trying to show me that she could handle it. It was probably a little of both.

Okay, I thought to myself, *I'm really going to have to try to hit her or she's probably just going to fry me right here.*

I readied myself and tried again. This time I tried to go land a bit of a combo, at least that's what I thought I was going for. I swung for her midsection again and then tried for her head. I put more force behind the strikes and she blocked them just as easily. The glow around her was slightly brighter and she gave me a smirk as she blocked the second hit.

"Better, but I can feel that you are still holding back. Attack me again, like you have some balls this time." She meant it as an insult, and that's the way I took it.

Her voice was different, almost like it was last night when I first got brought here. It sounded almost otherworldly, like it had a natural echo. Her attitude had changed as well, she was definitely more brash. Was this an effect of whatever power she had?

I attacked a third time. I put everything I had behind these strikes and swung like I was trying to bash down a wall. I just kept swinging and she kept blocking and dodging. The glow around her was getting brighter and I swear I saw fire at the ends of her staff. I advanced on her and she stepped back.

I was getting a little winded by this point and took a big overhead swing down towards her head. She blocked it and smiled at me, with a bit of fire behind her eyes.

"That's what I like to see!" She yelled approvingly. Her voice seemed to vibrate through me. "Now it's my turn!"

Oh shit, I thought to myself. *Well, I had a good life.*

Beth swung at my head and I instinctively blocked. She nodded in approval, stepped back and swung high with the staff again, only this time she also kicked low with her leg. I wasn't expecting the low kick and stumbled. In one fluid motion she brought her staff down and swept my legs on the left side and I landed on my back. I was about to get up and was greeted with a staff pointed at my throat.

"Not bad, for your first time anyway." Beth's glow had started to subside a bit. Her voice was normal again too.

"Yeah," I said as I lay there, catching my breath. "You never forget your first time."

Beth rolled her eyes and turned to walk away. I saw an opportunity and I took it. I swung with my staff from the ground and hit her in the foot. She stumbled, fell on her ass and glared at me.

"Why would you turn your back in a fight?" I said, trying to match her tone from earlier.

She stared blankly at me, nodded and got up.

"We're done here, for now." She brushed off her dress. "Touch the gem on your wrist and think of where you want to go. Your rig has a gem like my necklace. Once a day use." She walked towards the entrance of the room.

"Hey!" I yelled towards her.

"Yeah?" She turned and looked at me.

"Sorry for the cheap shot, I saw an opportunity and I took it." I was a little sorry. I was mostly proud.

"Don't apologize. I let my guard down. I deserved it." Beth turned, left the room and closed the door behind her.

I couldn't tell if I had upset her or not, she was still really hard to read. It was almost like dealing with two different people, normal Beth and "Battle Beth". She didn't seem to be in a talking mood right now so I figured I would just let it rest. I also really wasn't looking forward to my fourth teleport in under twenty-four hours but I touched the gem, thought of a spot near the dorm and was there in a flash.

CHAPTER EIGHT

Over the next week life was pretty normal. The only reminder that my life was anything but was my new accessory that I never took off. Well almost never took off, who knew if my Rig was waterproof. I might have gotten this thing wet and get thrown back in time and space through the stone age; I definitely did not want to risk that.

I was getting the hang of conjuring weapons from it though. I was able to summon them a little faster from when I started, and Professor Cline seemed to be impressed at the speed that the Rig became attuned to me. Beth might also have been impressed, but it was really hard to tell. Since our sparring match last week, I hadn't seen her around campus much other than class. The couple of times we did talk she seemed very distant, almost like she was actively trying not to talk to me.

I hadn't talked much to Scott this week either. We occasionally would share a passing greeting in the morning, or if we happened to see each other on campus, but that was pretty much it. Maybe it was the fact that our schedules conflicted because he was on the soccer team and a few other clubs, while I really had nothing school-wise going on. Or maybe he was still annoyed that I left The Griffon that night to follow Beth. I hadn't really had a chance to ask him, but wanted to find out soon.

Halloween was Friday, which was tomorrow. Ever since high school we would wear costumes of some famous duo. We had done a lot from Laurel and Hardy, to Kirk and Spock, and we took pride in our costumes every year. We didn't really talk about it this year. I still hoped the tradition was going to stay alive.

I left the dorm and started making my way over to Astrology. I'd grown to really enjoy the walk, just throwing my headphones on and losing myself in my music (at the moment, Santeria by Sublime). This seemed to help with all of the mind bending craziness that has happened in the last few weeks. Between my music, the crispness of the air and the coloring on the leaves, this was starting off as a perfectly normal fall day.

I entered the planetarium and went directly to the Professor's room only to be greeted by a sign on the door that read 'CLASS CANCELED DUE TO EMERGENCY. PLEASE REPORT BACK TO CLASS ON MONDAY'. I immediately felt a sense of dread come over me. What could possibly cause him to cancel class for the next two days? Was everything alright?

I was snapped out of my thoughts when I heard "Hey."

I turned around at the sound of Beth's voice. Her normal attire of a dark scoop neck dress, dark tights and boots now added a dark red sweater as part of the look. There was something about that look, and her, that I really liked. She appeared normal, like there was nothing wrong, but she had a look that I couldn't quite figure out in her eyes.

"What's going on? Is everything alright?" I was a little panicked.

"Yeah, everything's fine. Cline's in his office, he needs us." She stated, plainly.

"Why?" I raised an eyebrow curiously.

"Not sure, he was a little hurried this morning." Beth turned to walk towards the office and I followed. "I got to class as he was putting the sign up and he told me to wait for you and come to the office as soon as you showed up."

"He didn't give you the slightest idea why?" I pressed.

"If he did I would have told you." She explained.

Her tone seemed a little off. I really wanted to know why she seemed to be avoiding me since our little sparring match, but I didn't think this was the time to bring it up. Did I piss her off with that late hit when I was joking around? No, I don't think that was it.

We reached Professor Cline's office and Beth opened the door. We walked in and I saw Cline's face buried in his laptop looking over some type of data. He looked up and seemed relieved to see us.

"Excellent, excellent." He said with a frenzied look in his eyes. His hair was uncharacteristically messy and he looked like he hadn't slept in a couple of days. His desk was littered with coffee cups and wrappers of various foods. I don't think he's left here in a while. "Please, close the door and have a seat."

I closed the door and sat in one of the leather chairs in front of his desk. Beth had already sat down in the one to the left. Professor Cline immediately turned his laptop around to show us what he was looking at. There was all kinds of data being displayed on the screen, but it was all surrounding a map that had a flashing blip on it. It was a map of an area I knew very well.

"Two nights ago," Professor Cline started, "There was some type of disturbance reported in the Hamlet of Wallkill near Bruyn Turnpike."

"A disturbance?" I felt a lump form in my throat. "What type of disturbance?"

"The local authorities thought it was maybe a blown transformer based on the loud sound that was reported," the Professor explained, "But nothing was found. When the disturbance occurred the readings on my monitors in the base started fluctuating on a level I haven't seen in a very long time. A long time." His voice seemed to trail off a bit like he was lost in thought.

I could see Beth shift in her chair a little. She looked bothered by the news, not mad or angry, but this was the first time I had seen her look a little uneasy.

"Do you think," she said, sounding like she was trying to process something, "it's a rift?"

I had a feeling my normal-ish week was finished now.

Professor Cline looked at Beth with a solemn look.

"Yes, Elizabeth." She looked very uncomfortable.

"Okay," I said, trying to break the tension, "So what does all this mean?"

Professor Cline turned his attention to me.

"What it means Mister Howard," The Professor explained, "Is that we may have a visitor from another Earth from a different part of The Multiverse."

Shit. I thought to myself. For some reason, I had a feeling that's what that meant.

Professor Cline reached into the drawer of his desk, pulled out a small device and placed it on the desk. It looked to me almost like Egon's EKG meter from *Ghostbusters* but without the antennas on the sides.

"I would like the two of you to go see if there was a rift opened there." He pushed the meter towards me. "This will help you find out if there was. It scans atmospheric frequencies to find any variances in our Earth's normal vibrations. If anyone has opened a rift, this will find where it was."

It was weird hearing someone say "Our Earth". It just rolled off of the Professor's tongue like it was a normal thing to say. I reached out and grabbed the scanner on his desk.

"Professor," Beth said with a tinge of nervousness in her voice, "I've never…" Her voice trailed off.

"I know, Elizabeth, you will be fine. This is what you have been training for." He looked at Beth sympathetically.

Beth took a deep breath and sat back in her chair.

"Mister Howard," Professor Cline looked at me with a look of concern, "This will be Elizabeth's first time in the field as well as your own. Please be careful."

"Wait, what?" My interest turned immediately into terror. I figured that after seeing Beth do amazing things over these last couple of months that she was this amazing battle goddess. I looked at Beth and she looked back and actually gave me a kind of weak smile.

Professor Cline cleared his throat.

"I don't want the two of you using a Gateway to get there. There's no need to bring any more attention to the area."

"I have a car." My nineteen eighty-eight Ford Ranger was parked in the student lot.

"Excellent!" Professor Cline stood up and we followed suit. "You two should get going." He looked at his watch. "It's about three o'clock now. You should go, but wait until close to sundown to approach the area. I want the two of you to stay as hidden as possible. Please be careful. If you come across anything that seems dangerous, do not engage."

Beth and I shared a worried look to each other and back to The Professor.

"Don't look so worried. There shouldn't be anything there." He said to try to reassure us. "Since the disturbance two days ago there have been no abnormal readings."

As we walked out of the office, Professor Cline told us to meet him back at the base if we found anything and we started our walk to the student lot. My head was spinning again with all of this new information and Beth was very quiet. She was walking with her arms crossed tightly, almost like she was trying to bear hug herself. I hoped that maybe she would talk to me on the drive otherwise it was going to be a long twenty five minute ride.

When we got to the student lot I saw my alpine green Ford Ranger looking as shiny as ever. I loved my truck, it was a gift from my grandfather as I was starting my senior year of high school. I didn't make any modifications or anything to it, I really wanted to get a CD player for it at some point, but at the moment I was a bit on the "broke college student" side of the money spectrum. We reached the truck and I opened the door for Beth. I think she mumbled "thanks" before she got in. She leaned over and unlocked my door as I walked around. I hopped in, said thanks and we were off to my hometown.

I rolled down the window and we pulled out of the student lot and headed south on Route 208 which was a straight shot, more or less, to where we were going. Living in upstate New York, especially this area, either Routes 208 or 32 were your main ways of getting around without hopping on the New York Thruway. Both connected to New Paltz but Route 32 landed you in Newburgh where 208 put you right in the heart of Wallkill. Plus, heading into New Paltz, Route 208 had an awesome view of the Mohonk mountains and the Skytop Tower. There was so much beautiful countryside to look out on during the drive, especially at this time of day. Sunset always comes quickly in the fall and the sun was already hanging pretty low, casting reddish-orange light over everything.

I glanced over to Beth who was staring out of the window, still kind of hugging herself. She looked really nervous, which was totally understandable since I was nearly shitting myself with the thought of possibly coming into contact with something from out of *this* world. I could kind of see her reflection in the window of my truck and she just looked blank, more difficult to read than normal. We had been driving for what felt like forever but, in reality, was only about five minutes and we hadn't said one word to each other and I guessed it was up to me to break the silence and try to lighten the mood.

"So", I cleared my throat, "Since this is our first time alone and we are going somewhere, would this be considered a first date?" I jokingly said.

"This isn't a date, this is serious." She kept looking out of the window.

"I know, I was just trying to lighten the mood a little. I tend to make dumb jokes in scary situations." I reassured her.

Beth continued looking out the window and I kept driving. After about a minute the silence was broken again.

"Hey," Beth sounded like she was trying to carefully choose what she was going to say next, "I'm sorry. I'm just really nervous."

"No worries, I am too. My life was perfectly normal a couple of months ago until you walked into me. Now I'm just one big ball of nerves," I confessed.

She turned to look at me for the first time since we started driving. I looked over at her quickly and in this lighting she looked stunning, her hazel green eyes picking up bits of orange from the setting sun.

"You walked into me," Beth insisted.

"No," I countered, "I think you had your head stuck in a book..."

"And you," Beth interrupted "were talking to that Scott kid."

"Then you walked into me." I finished my sentence and turned to give her a quick smile.

"I think I might have hit you on the head too hard when we were sparring," She said with a hint of lightness in her voice, "You seem to be remembering things wrong."

"Yeah about that," I figured this was my chance to apologize, "I'm sorry for that surprise hit at the end. It was a dick move but I was trying to be funny."

"Why are you apologizing for that? I said it was fine." This may have annoyed her.

I explained, "I don't know, it seems like you've been more distant than usual with me since then. I figured you were a little pissed."

"No," Beth said flatly, "I'm not mad about that."

"So are you mad at me about something? It seems like you are." I didn't want to start an argument, but I wanted to know.

"Nope." Beth said, then her tone changed. "Hey, do you mind if I turn on the radio?"

I said it was fine and she started scanning the stations. I normally stuck to a couple of rock stations or listened to cassettes. I figured I would just let her scan and see what she would find, maybe it would make her a little less nervous. Also, maybe it would give me some insight to her personality. I fully believe that you can tell at least a little something about someone by the type of music they listen to. I just hoped she didn't land on country, or some poppy N*Sync or Backstreet Boys bullshit.

I glanced over at Beth as she started to find a station. She tucked her hair behind her ear and her eyes were fixed on the radio numbers. The way the setting sun hit her profile gave her a soft glow a little less intense than when she's Battle Beth. She looked beautiful and whatever perfume she had on smelled like baked apples.

Before I could stop myself, I felt a word escape my lips, "Wow."

She turned to look at me and I instantly felt like I should pay a visit to the multiverse where I didn't say anything.

"Did you say something?" She asked, with an eyebrow raised.

"Nope, not a thing." I stared at the road ahead, afraid to make eye contact.

"I think you're lying," she continued fiddling with the knobs of the radio, "What did you say?"

"It's nothing," I started, "I just…"

She was staring at me and I was afraid that if I said the wrong thing that I would be roasted in my car. Did Beth have heat vision because I could feel myself getting super hot.

"The way the light hit you just now," the words just started stumbling out of my mouth, "You looked really pretty. That's all." Holy shit, that was the cheesiest thing I had ever said. I wanted to hurl myself out of the moving truck while I was driving. I just continued staring straight as if Route 208 was the most important road in the world.

"Oh." She sounded shocked. After a moment, "Wonderwall" came on the radio. "I love this song!" Beth sat back in her seat and looked out of the window again. I dared to steal a glance at her reflection and thought I saw a slight smile on her face.

"So," I said trying to change the subject, "I know you've never been, like, in combat or anything but have you been to any other Earths?"

Beth adjusted in her seat a little.

"Yeah, but just to see them as Cline was training me." She didn't seem comfortable about her answer.

I was curious. "Did you see anything super different? Like way different from this Earth?"

"Kind of." She explained. "Nothing like super different or dangerous. Like, there was one dimension where John Lennon was never killed and The Beatles still made great music. Then there was another that the entire government was run by women."

"Really?" Those sounded like cool places to be.

"Yeah," Beth said as she brushed her hair back, "Things seemed to run a little smoother."

"That actually sounds interesting." I was intrigued by the countless possibilities that were out there in The Multiverse, even if it was terrifying. "It's good that The Professor didn't send you anywhere dangerous."

Beth looked back out of the window. "There was one time, accidentally, that we wound up" she paused for a moment "somewhere."

I could tell by her voice that talking about this rattled her a little.

"What happened?" I asked her, but didn't want to press.

She took a deep breath and continued.

"One time Cline miscalculated or something and we wound up in like an almost barren, frozen wasteland." Her voice trembled a bit as she recalled the memory. "It looked like either the Ice Age never ended or that it started over again. Like, all of the buildings were still there but they were like a ghost town type of empty. As soon as we got there I felt this sense of dread, like something was watching us or wanted us there."

I could see Beth nervously playing with her bracelets. She sounded truly scared, I had never seen her like this. She took another breath before continuing. "Cline worked as fast as he could to get us back but there was something happening with the thing we were using, like interference or something. It was the most scared I've ever been in my life, like I was frozen in fear. I couldn't do anything, no spells worked, nothing. But Cline got everything working and pulled us back. That was the last time we visited another place."

I tried to come up with something relevant to say, I asked, "How long ago was that?"

"Maybe a year ago? I've tried not to think about it much." I'm sure she does indeed think about it. Probably all the time, I know I would.

"Wow." I could tell it took a lot for Beth to tell me that and figured that I would let it go. Wherever she wound up really seemed to really freak her out so I figured I would try to switch gears a little. Luckily we were approaching my old high school, Wallkill Senior High, and thought maybe giving Beth a little tour on the way to our destination would lighten the mood again.

I pulled onto Robinson Drive which ran along the school and almost directly near where we were going. As we passed my old school and told her some stories of my time there; Lazer Tag battles in the hallways after classes, Homecoming bonfires and carnivals, Having a friend of mine and Scott's tailgate surf (and subsequently fall off) in my truck, the Senior Lockdown Night Jell-o slip and slide after graduation. There were a lot of fun times here when classes didn't get in the way. I hadn't really been back here since graduation, some of the memories seemed like a lifetime ago.

Beth seemed to enjoy the stories. I got a couple of chuckles and head shakes because either she thought they were funny or that I was an idiot, probably a little of both. I asked about her high school life but she didn't really want to talk about it or would ask me more questions about mine. I decided not to pry.

The sun was still setting and The Professor wanted us to get to the site when it got dark but I was getting a little hungry so I asked Beth if she wanted to grab something to eat before we went over. She said that she wasn't really hungry but she really hadn't eaten anything since this morning so I insisted and she agreed. I parked the truck on Main Street, grabbed my old, green, patched up army jacket from behind my seat because the temperature had dropped a bit but decided that I was fine with just my flannel, I left it on my seat and we walked over to the place that fed me all through high school, and where I learned all of my Street Fighter II skills, Rob's Pizza.

Rob's had the best pizza in town and the owner, named Rob obviously, used to hook up Scott and me with free food every now and then all through high school because when we had our licenses we would help him out with deliveries. In return we kept the tips and he fed us, it worked well.

We walked in and I saw Rob behind the counter flipping dough and someone was on the phone taking orders, it might have been a nephew or younger brother because he looked just like a younger version of Rob. Rob was a bear of a man in his mid forties and one of the friendliest guys I have ever known. As we walked up to the counter he turned and saw me.

"Jake!" he bellowed as he made his way around the counter, dusting his hands off on his apron. For a big man he was deceptively quick and before I knew it I was wrapped in a rib crushing bear hug. I heard Beth snicker as Rob asked "How've ya been man?"

"Good, till just now." I was able to say with the little bit of air I had still in my lungs. Rob put me down, clapped me on the shoulder and turned towards Beth.

"What's a beautiful girl like you doing with this schlub? Did you lose a bet?" He laughed and extended his hand. "I'm Rob."

Beth returned the handshake and introduced herself. He turned back to the kid behind the counter.

"Benny!" Rob yelled over to him, "Whatever these two lovebirds want is on the house!" He stepped back behind the counter and Beth looked at me with an amused look. I shrugged, asked her what she wanted and went up to order while she grabbed a seat.

I told Benny what we wanted, one plain slice, two ham and pineapple and 2 Cokes, and Rob approached me from behind the counter. I had a feeling I knew where this was going.

"She's cute, man," Rob said in a quieter tone, "How long you two been dating?"

"We're not, we're just friends." I protested.

Rob shook his head.

"Listen Jake," Rob leaned in closer to me, "I get a feeling about people and my feeling is that there is something there. You know I'm never wrong."

"Never?" I cast him a knowing look.

"I may be wrong with other bullshit in life, but when it comes to people, I'm usually dead on." Benny brought over our slices and Rob threw me a wink.

I brought our food back to the table and had a seat. Beth was looking out of the big window in the front. From here you could see Bruyn Turnpike, a bridge that went over the Wallkill River, and where we had been sent. She turned away from the window as I sat down and directly looked at my two slices of ham and pineapple pizza.

"Why?" Beth had a look of concern.

"Why what?"

She pointed at my pizza with her straw and asked, "Why do you have fruit on pizza?"

"Because it's great. Have you ever tried it?" I didn't look at her while I said this. I was pulling paper napkins from the dispenser on the table.

"No." She unwrapped her straw.

"Well, here," I pushed my plate towards her a bit, "Try it."

"No." She pointed at it again with her unwrapped straw.

"Well, do you like ham?" I asked.

66

"Well yeah." she stated as she placed her red plastic straw in the soda.

"How about pineapple?" I quizzed her.

She replied, "sometimes." I had gained an inch of ground!

"Well then try it. What's the worst thing that could happen?" I did my best to be compelling.

Beth looked down at my plate with a look of disgust and trepidation. She looked back at me, back to my plate and then back to me. I smiled and pushed the plate a little closer. She took a deep breath, grabbed one of my slices and took a small bite, enough to get some ham and pineapple in there. She sat there chewing for a bit in silence. I looked at her face for an answer.

She stared directly at me, still chewing. She swallowed, grabbed the slice and took a second bite. I smiled.

"See! It's great!" talk about small victories, this was a big one!

"It's really good," Beth said in agreement as she wiped some sauce from her mouth, "I'm keeping this one." She pushed her plain slice towards me. I laughed and said it was fine.

After we finished our pizza the sun was low enough that we shouldn't attract any attention if we continued over to where the disturbance was. I got up and tossed our plates in the garbage and thanked Rob for the free food. As I put two dollars in the tip jar, he gave me another wink and mouthed the words "never wrong."

I walked over to Beth who was waiting by the front door and she gave Rob a little wave, Rob waved back and we traveled down Bruyn Turnpike to see what Professor Cline had sent us here to see.

CHAPTER NINE

From Rob's it was a short walk, only about a block or so, to Bruyn Turnpike where Professor Cline said the disturbance occurred. I have no idea how Bruyn Turnpike got that name. The roads up here have always had names that made no sense, highways and turnpikes are very much normal country roads, not big multi-lane roads you would expect by those names while travelling state to state. Bruyn is just a road that connects the Wallkill to some other countryside, where the houses have enough land where you could film two movies on their properties simultaneously, and never have one interfere with the other, and has a small bridge that goes over the Wallkill River.

My friends and I always called the river 'The Mighty Raging Majestic Wallkill River' because on one of the many routes from Wallkill to New Paltz there is a section that looks like something pulled out of a white water rafting brochure. Big jagged rocks poked up from it and it just looked daunting, but this section was pretty tame. It's just a gently flowing river with a small landmass a little to the north of it. It made my town look like a quaint, typical picture of Americana.

The temperature dropped in normal upstate New York in fall fashion on our way over to the bridge but the cold rarely ever bothered me. I've always tended to run a little hot, Mom would always yell at me for not wearing a jacket in the winter. Even my Dad was the type of guy that would always drive with the car window cracked open a little because he was always hot. We're built like that, I guess.

As Beth and I were walking, there wasn't much conversation from either of us. I'm not sure how she felt, but it was probably the same as I did, nervous as hell. The butterflies in my stomach had turned into the sci-fi monster Mothra, trying to pull me back from what we were going to investigate. I glanced over to Beth and she seemed like she was trying her best to look strong, but there was a noticeable hint of fear on her face. After a few minutes of walking, she put her hands in front of her mouth like she was going to blow in them for warmth. Instead she seemed to whisper in them and her hands started faintly glowing red. She put them in the pockets of her sweater and kept walking.

"That's one way to stay warm." I said.

"It comes in handy," Beth replied and turned to me with a bit of a smile, "Especially when I want some popcorn."

I stopped walking and looked at her in shock.

"Did you just make a joke? At a serious time like this?" I said in a mocking tone trying to mimic her deadpan nature she has at times.

"Yeah," she said, nodding her head, "I've clearly been around you too much. But, really, I did try to make a bag of microwave popcorn by just using my hands once a couple of years ago and nearly burned down my fort." After saying that I saw the look on Beth's face change, like she recalled a memory she didn't want to remember,

"Are you okay?" I asked her. I thought that maybe she wasn't.

She turned and started walking again. "I'm fine, let's go."

She one hundred percent did not seem fine, but I decided not to press the issue and walked silently beside her. We reached an area where we could follow a path down to the riverside and walk under the Bruyn Turnpike bridge. I took out the scanner that The Professor had given us. I pressed the button at the top corner of the device and the green and black screen came to life. It reminded me of my old Gameboy, but the screen was very crisp, and it showed that there was some type of blip a few hundred feet ahead.

The sun was just about completely gone at this point and the only light came from the distant street lights and the occasional ambient light given off from a passing car above. I did have a little flashlight on my keychain so I turned it on. The faint light helped a little but it was still quite dark as we passed under the bridge to follow the device's plotted course. We followed the blip to the edge of the river and realized that it looked like our destination was the small raised sandbar in the middle of the river. There was only a sliver of moonlight shining down on the river from what looked like a fingernail in the sky.

"It looks like we have to get out there." I pointed to the small island that could barely fit two people on it set about fifty feet up the river.

Beth knelt down next to the river, stuck her hand in it and quickly pulled it back.

"It's freaking freezing!" She stepped back towards me and wiped her hand on her sweater. "I really hate being cold."

"Can't you just, like, space heater yourself to stay warm?" I was genuinely curious and I noticed her hands had lost their glow from earlier.

"No, not really," she said, "I just tend to run hot so I don't get cold as easily but, when I do finally get cold, it sucks and I hate it."

"Me too, but we really don't have a choice." I walked up to the river's edge and shined my tiny flashlight at the water. "This part is kind of shallow, we could probably cross here without too much trouble."

I stepped one foot into the water and was immediately happy that I decided to wear my boots instead of my Converse. My foot would have been soaked instantly but at least the boots gave me a couple more seconds of warmth before they filled with water. Well, I thought to myself, there's no turning back now so I stepped into the water with my other foot and turned to Beth.

"It's not too bad actually!" I lied through a forced smile.

"You're a terrible liar." Beth saw through my sad attempt at deception and stood at the river bank with her arms crossed.

"Yeah, but like I said, we really don't have a choice." I stuck my left hand out towards Beth. "Come on, it's pretty shallow."

She stepped toward me a couple times, her boots stopping just short of the water. She let out a little whine and I stepped a few feet towards her, my feet still in the water, and moved my hand towards her again. She looked at me with a look that reminded me of a time when my brother was hesitant to jump off the diving board at the pool but found himself stuck. He either had to jump or climb back down the ladder through the line of waiting people, so he just jumped. After he jumped the first time, we couldn't keep him off the damn thing every time.

Beth took a deep breath and grabbed my outstretched hand. The moment her warm hand touched mine, I felt my heart flutter. For what seemed like an eternity I just held it and stared at her. I swear on my life I heard "Happy Together" by The Turtles playing in my head. I shook off whatever I was feeling to focus on what we had to do.

I asked her, "Are you ready?" I did my best to sound normal, but my heart was racing. My soaked feet were squishy inside my boots. That's exactly how this moment felt to me.

She nodded, took a step into the water and I could tell that she immediately regretted her decision of joining me in the Wallkill River for our little stroll. Her grip on my hand tightened with a force that would have probably left me with permanent damage if I didn't have so much adrenaline pumping through me.

"Shit!" Beth shrieked at me as both of her feet met the water. She took a couple of quick steps towards me and I felt my hand get a little warmer. I couldn't tell if she was heating up or if my hand was just unreasonably warm.

I let out a nervous chuckle and we started walking towards the isle ahead of us. With every step that we took deeper into the river, I heard her mutter curse words under her breath and I had to stop myself from laughing. Fifty feet doesn't seem too far, but when you are wading through just above freezing water, it might as well be one hundred miles. As we walked, the river got a bit deeper. At its deepest the water was just above my knees and almost mid-thigh on Beth. The hem of her dress and the bottom of her sweater were floating in the water, and I'm sure her soaked stockings were doing very little to keep her warm.

"I swear if we came out here for nothing I'm going to kill Cline." Beth said through chattering teeth as we reached the shore of the tiny island.

She waved her left hand and a small ball of flame appeared in it to light up the area and gave us a small source of warmth since we were both freezing. She removed her hand from the ball of flame, and it stayed suspended in the air. We warmed ourselves by it for a moment. I took the radar device out and it looked like we were right on top of the blip. I looked around and didn't see anything remarkable.

"Do you have any idea what we are looking for?" I asked Beth as we explored the tiny island that now had two inhabitants that could barely fit on it together. "According to the radar we should be right on top of it."

"No," Beth said while doing her own investigating, "I guess just see if anything is around here doesn't seem normal." I watched her make some kind of motions with her right hand in the air.

"What are you doing?" I asked.

"Trying out a spell. I've only used it once before to find Cline's keys."

A small light that looked like a firefly appeared in her hand and started fluttering around the island. After a few seconds it zoomed to a spot about fifteen feet in front of us near the center of a slightly wider part of the landmass. We looked at each other with a shared nervousness and rushed over to see what the firefly found. We looked down where it was buzzing excitedly, and saw something sticking out of the ground. Beth knelt down and moved some of the dirt and mud from around the object and picked it up. She stood up, dismissed the firefly with a flick of her wrist, and I watched as it evaporated into the night. Beth turned to me, and held out the object she found.

In her hands was something that almost looked like the adapter thing you would put in an old .45 record single to play it on a turntable, but this was a little bigger. It had three shiny metal crescent shapes that met in the middle that seemed to be connected to some type of clear blue gem. The crescents had some type of black etchings on them that reminded me of some type of circuit board layout but not quite.

"What is it?" I wondered aloud, not necessarily asking Beth.

"I'm not sure." Beth said as she looked it over. "It really isn't from this Earth though." She reached around to her backpack purse and placed it carefully inside. As she did, we felt the ground rumble. I looked at her and saw a look of terror on her face.

"Beth," I said as calmly as I could, "Please tell me you did that."

She shook her head and her eyes grew wide.

"I think we have to get the hell out of here." Beth said as she reached for the crimson gem on her necklace.

The ground shook again and Beth lost her footing, fell into me and we both fell to the damp ground. Another tremor followed that and we saw something appear in the river ahead, and it seemed to be heading right for us. As it came closer to us through the river, it seemed to grow in size until it reached the shore where we saw what looked like a nine foot tall giant in front of us. I couldn't wrap my head around what was happening.

This creature was massive and looked like it was made of some type of crystal. It was almost as wide as it was tall and its body shape reminded me of a He-Man figure blown up to an insane level and covered in jagged spikes that started from its shoulders down to its hands. It was featureless, I couldn't make out any eyes or a mouth or anything. The two things I did know was that it definitely wasn't from around here and that a huge club was forming in its hand as it got closer. The club looked to be made of the same material as the thing holding it, a barely translucent monster.

I was scared shitless. What the hell was this thing? As we got to our feet I looked over at Beth for some answers and could tell she was just as freaked out as I was. Her hands were glowing red but the look on her face looked like she was a scared child that had just gotten caught doing something that they weren't supposed to do. It was like she wanted to fight, but also recognized the smarter option was to get the hell away from here.

"Beth?" I said as this hulking monster got closer. She seemed to physically be frozen in fear and I needed to snap her out of it. I yelled her name again and she blinked and looked at me, eyes still wide with terror but her hazel eyes slowly starting to turn a reddish orange.

The giant got closer and I could feel the temperature drop a little as it approached. It brought it's club slowly up over its head with what must have been the intention to turn us into paste. As the club came down I pushed Beth to one side and dove to the opposite side. Cold water and mud from the river splashed me in the face. I looked back and saw that the club hit the ground, missing Beth and me entirely, but now we were separated by a huge walking wall of ice. My first thought was that I should have dove to the side with her; it probably would have been better to stay together.

The monster slowly raised its club from the ground and turned towards the side where Beth was. I could see her getting up from the ground, thankfully from me pushing her and not from getting hit with what was a club the size of a Buick, her hands still glowing but not in full Battle Beth mode yet. Her hazel-orange eyes looked towards me as she threw a ball of fire at the big thing between us. The fireball struck the creature in its chest and Beth moved back a step.

It didn't appear to faze the monster one bit and it continued to follow Beth.

Instinctively I flicked my wrist and the first weapon I thought of appeared in my hand. I looked down and saw a war mallet, something like what a paladin would use in Dungeons and Dragons and a kite shield formed over my Rig. I didn't have time to appreciate how cool that was and I charged towards the monster that lumbered towards Beth like Michael Myers.

The mud splashed under my feet as I raced to help Beth. She was still hurling fireballs and backing up. She called her red blade sword that she had shown me when I first got the Rig, and she was off the island and about calf deep in the river. She still didn't have that 'battle glow'. What the hell was going on with her?

The giant raised its club again and Beth dove out of the way as it came splashing down into the river bank. She was soaked from head to toe as I reached my target and took a swing. I had never swung anything like this and my intention was to smack this thing directly behind the knee.. I had to try and slow it down. Instead, I hit it in what would be its thigh and it looked like I might have dented it a little. Some crystals broke away, but the dent re-formed itself.

The giant didn't turn its attention away from Beth but motioned its hand in a backswing and spikes rained off of its arms towards me. I raised my shield and stumbled back a little from the force of the contact they made. A couple of the crystals landed next to me and I could see that while they were spikey, they were actually icicles.

I ran towards Beth as the giant raised its club again. I reached her just in time to grab her arm and pulled her behind the rocks on the island's shore. Hopefully this would buy us a couple of seconds.

I looked at Beth's wet, muddy face and saw that her eyes were no longer glowing. She looked at me with tears forming in her eyes and just whispered two words. "I'm scared."

I looked at her and mouthed 'me too' as I saw the monster turn in the direction where we were. It walked towards us with a methodical pace.

"Listen," I said softly to Beth, "I'm going to try to distract it, but it seems really focused on you. Hopefully I can buy you enough time to get out of here."

She shook her head violently.

"No!" Beth said as she stared at me with panic in her eyes. "We both have to get out of here, NOW!"

She grabbed my arm and once again went to touch the gem on her necklace but, before she could touch it, the giant smashed the rock we were behind and sent Beth sailing down the river.

I looked in horror at the spot where Beth was. The giant's eyeless gaze didn't follow Beth down the river. Instead, it moved its head down towards where she just was and my eyes followed it where it was looking. Lying in front of me was the object we just found, the very thing that caused the weird ice monster to come after us. It must have fallen out of Beth's bag after-- suddenly I realized that while I was focused on my own scene, I had no idea what happened to Beth!

I looked back quickly and didn't see any sign of Beth in the river. I didn't know what to do. All of me wanted to dive in and find her, but trying to find anything in a dark river is nearly impossible. As I considered all of my options I could feel a rage growing in me. I didn't know Beth's status, but I did know that she wasn't here, and this big fucker was responsible for it.

As the giant reached down for the device I snatched it from the ground, stuffed it in my pocket and slid between its legs to get behind it. As the monster turned to face me I started wailing on whatever parts of it I could with my war hammer. Everything I could reach was fair game; hips, knees, shins, even its freaking toes were all about to meet the business end of my implement of rage. With each hit that connected chunks of what I now knew to be ice were breaking off and slowly reforming. I kept swinging at this thing that, for all I know, might have just killed Beth.

Its club swung down at me and I barely dodged out of the way and it shot another barrage of icicles at me. The force of them hitting my shield sent me stumbling backwards again and I wound up on my ass. The club was raised in the air again and I didn't have time to move. I raised my shield and it nearly doubled in size to block the blow. It worked, but holy shit was that a lot of force. I could feel myself sink a little into the muddy island as another hit followed, and another, and another. The vibrations of the club hitting my shield were intense and I didn't know how much longer I could take this barrage.

Of all of the ways I thought I would die it wasn't by getting smashed by a giant ice monster in the river of my tiny hometown in upstate New York. There was no doubt in my mind; I was not going to make it out of here. This was the end and whatever this thing was that Beth and I found, was the cause of our demise. I knew that my body, even though my shield was blocking all of the hits, was not going to be able to handle much more of this.

I could feel myself getting weaker and, just as I was sure I was about to receive the final hit that would end me, I saw a gust of flame shoot out of the river. The beatings stopped and I could feel the giant step away from me a bit while a sound like a flamethrower filled the air. That's when I heard a familiar, terrifying voice that I was glad to hear.

"Jake!" Beth screamed, "Get up and hit this asshole in the head!"

I lowered my shield to see Beth, in full on Battle Beth mode, sitting on top of the ice giant's shoulders, shooting fire directly into both sides of its head. The orange glow around her was brighter than I have ever seen. Her hair was blowing back like on the poster for *The Craft*. Her eyes were full orange without a trace of her normal hazel color and she let out a scream that would have made Xena jealous. The giant was down on one knee trying to grab at this fire-spewing creature on its back, but couldn't get the proper angle to reach her.

I smiled, placed the head of my warhammer on the ground and Beth lept off just in time for me to deliver a huge uppercut. In my head it looked like the kind of thing that Rock from Soul Blade would deliver, I'm not sure how it looked in reality, though. The hammer connected, the giant's head flew up off of its body like a cork leaving a bottle, and landed behind it. As its body fell forward, Beth rolled off to the side and onto her hands and knees.

I ran over to Beth and her entire body was smoldering. Steam was rising from her clothes, her sweater and stockings full of holes. There were some minor tears on her dress and a pretty big gash on her side. My flannel was shredded so I took it off and ripped some of it to wrap around her to maybe help with the wound. I tossed the rest of it into the river and watched it float downstream.

Beth was still on her hands and knees and facing the ground almost gasping to catch her breath. Her glow started to die down but her body was still giving off a lot of heat. I gave her a moment but then I started to hear sirens. I brought my hand to her face, and she grabbed my wrist and looked at me.

"Beth?" I said with trepidation in my voice. "You with me, Beth?"

She looked at me and I could see the orange in her eyes start to go back to hazel.

"I'm so cold." She said through chattering teeth. Beth's whole body was shivering and quaking hard.

I could hear the sirens getting closer and could see red and blue police lights reflecting in the night sky. She looked at me, grabbed my hand and touched the gem on her necklace. In a moment we were back at my truck and she leaned on the hood for support. I opened my door, grabbed my jacket, put it over her shoulders and helped her into the passenger side of the truck. I got in the driver's side, saw some police cars racing to where we just were, and we drove in the opposite direction towards New Paltz. I checked my pocket. Yes, the weird crescent object that almost got us killed was still there.

We kept driving for a while without saying a word. Beth pulled my jacket around her tight while the heat was on full-blast. I didn't turn the radio on, we just drove in silence. About half way back I pulled into a general store and she looked at me with a bit of worry in her eyes. I assured her I would be right back and a moment later I returned with two hot chocolates, I handed her one.

Beth took a sip and we sat in the parking lot for a while in silence. What happened tonight was unbelievable. Ice monsters, weird looking devices, magic spells, what the hell had my life become this year? I sure as hell did not expect any of this when Scott and I got in a dorm together. I wished I could tell him everything that was going on, he would love all of this shit. I really needed to talk to him, things have been really strained between us, but this all felt like something I couldn't tell him. I sat there, feeling all of this weight on me and took a sip of my hot chocolate that, at the moment, was the most normal thing in my world right now.

After a few minutes I heard Beth chuckle. I looked at her and she tried to muffle it but she did it again, this time a little louder while she was rubbing her ribs. She looked at me and just started cracking up. I raised an eyebrow and she was almost uncontrollably laughing.

"I didn't spike that hot chocolate, did I?" I asked, jokingly.

"I don't think so." she said with tears rolling down her cheeks as she wiped them away. She almost calmed down and started laughing again, holding her ribs with a little wince of pain. I cracked a smile.

"Okay so what's going on?" I was laughing a little just due to the fact that she was almost losing it next to me.

"We almost died!" Beth said through the tears. "Like, I don't know how we made it out of there."

Her laugh was great, just the kind of laugh that is so genuine and pure that it is infectious. The absurdity of what we just went through hit me and I started laughing along with her. Tonight did not go how I expected at all, but so far nothing has since I'd met the girl sitting next to me.

"That was the scariest thing I've ever been a part of." I calmed my laughing a bit to take a sip of my hot chocolate.

Beth nodded and tried to stifle her laughter.

"We should get back," Beth said wiping tears from her eyes, "Cline is probably ripping his hair out wondering what's going on."

I agreed and we pulled out of the parking lot and headed to The Griffon. After a few minutes I pulled into the street by The Griffon and we got out of the truck. As we were approaching the gateway to the base, Beth turned to me.

"Hey," she said to me wrapping my jacket around her, "It's getting late and Cline is going to have a ton of questions, that's how he is."

"Yeah?" I responded, rhetorically.

"So," she continued, "If you want to take off and we can meet up in the morning that's fine, otherwise it's going to be a long night."

I shook my head.

"Beth, we nearly died for whatever *this* is tonight," I said, in utter disbelief, as I held the funky crescent-moon disc thing. I stared into her eyes and got so caught in them I almost lost my train of thought, "I want to know what this is."

She nodded and we stepped through the gateway. Once we emerged on the other side we did see Professor Cline, but he was asleep in his chair in front of the massive computer. Beth put her finger to her lips and motioned for me to step to the side a bit.

"He's sleeping thankfully, which is good, because I'm beat." Beth whispered. "Almost dying does that to you." She gave me a little bit of a smile.

"Yeah, it does." I gave her the device. "I guess I should go."

Professor Cline stirred in his chair and we fell silent.

"Hey," Beth whispered as she got closer, "Thanks for the hot chocolate, and you know, helping me defeat a nine foot tall monster tonight."

I smiled. "Anytime, but next time maybe without the monster."

She pulled my jacket around her and smiled. Every ounce of me wanted to go in for a kiss, but I didn't. I had no idea how to read the situation and I didn't want to make things weirder than they already got tonight. To diffuse a little of the tension, I did feel the need to crack a joke though.

"So, I think I'm going to consider this the weirdest first date ever."

"This wasn't a date," Beth smiled at me, "but if it was, yes, this was the weirdest first date ever."

Beth looked like she was going to walk away but instead moved closer to me and gave me a hug. She still smelled like baked apples but mixed with a little bit of dirt and mud. As I was about to pull away she gave me a little peck on the cheek.

"You're pretty cool." Beth said as she started to walk away. I was a little speechless but found my words after a moment.

"You too." I said in an unintentionally louder tone. The Professor stirred in his chair once again and Beth gave me a look that basically said '*Don't you dare wake him up.*'

I motioned to the gateway, Beth waived and I stepped through. As I emerged on the other side in the basement of The Griffon I thought about all of the craziness of the night. Yeah, we almost died, but I seemed to make a real connection with Beth and was practically floating to my truck as I drove back to the dorm.

CHAPTER TEN

I woke up in the morning aching from head to toe, assuming this is the proper way to feel after fighting a giant ice monster from some other Earth. My eyes were open but my body sure as hell wasn't ready to move yet, my limbs each feeling like they weighed a hundred pounds. I felt like, in a word, shit.

I slowly sat up in bed and thought about last night, more specifically the parts without Frosty's older brother. This was the first time Beth and I actually spent a lot of time alone together and we seemed to have a genuine connection, I just didn't know how genuine it was. It's totally possible this could be the start of something real but it's also possible that everything that happened at the end of the night was just an adrenaline high from saving each other from turning into paste. This was a conversation that needed to happen, but that scared me more than the fight last night.

Since Shelly and I broke up I hadn't really felt a connection to anyone. I was head over heels for her, I even considered proposing at one point, but the way everything ended messed with my head pretty bad. Spending time with Beth last night, through everything, felt great. I was already crushing pretty hard on her before, but even just thinking of her now I could feel a smile growing on my face.

I kept replaying the last few minutes of last night after we got back to The Griffon. Should I have leaned in for a kiss to see what would have happened? Was she going in for a kiss and just decided on a kiss on the cheek and a hug? As these thoughts ran through my head I was taking a moment after each one to consider what multiverse would have spun out of each of these scenarios. My brain almost started hurting as much as my body did after trying to figure out all of the possibilities.

I reached over to turn on my clock radio that was telling me it was 10:15 A.M. and one of my favorite songs, "Girlfriend" by Matthew Sweet, was playing on the campus station. I shook my head and smiled. I swear that sometimes when you turn on the radio, it knows what you are thinking and loves to play just the right song at the right time. It's also totally possible that I'm crazy and it's just a coincidence. I laid in bed when I realized that today was my favorite holiday, Halloween.

I've always loved Halloween since I was a kid, dressing up in costumes and eating candy is always a good time in my eyes. One of my earliest costumes I could remember was one that I didn't even wear to go trick or treating. When my sister was born, I had a wicked flu and couldn't leave the house to go out on Halloween night. I was devastated because I had finally gotten the costume that I had begged my Mom for, a cheap plastic Batman costume with a plastic mask that said Batman across the forehead. It didn't matter that in the comics it didn't say his name on his forehead like a moron because I was about to be The Night!

The problem was that I was sick as hell. My dad was at work and my Mom had just come home from the hospital with my new baby sister, so I was on door duty. I handed out candy to kids that got to enjoy Halloween-time but I looked badass (or so I thought) in my Batman costume, dispensing justice one fun-sized Snickers at a time.

That was really my only negative Halloween memory. Every other Halloween I've had so far has been a blast. I always had a great Halloween party from eighth grade through high school, and my costumes were always great. I always won the costume contests in high school because I never phoned it in, I put maximum effort into my costume every year.

Scott and I have worked together the last few years on duo costumes, Halloween has always been one of my most anticipated days every year.

I sat up in bed and felt every muscle in my body protest. My mind was ready but my body was not about getting up and moving today. I remembered that I told Beth I would catch up with her later, but I needed to talk to Scott first. I really hoped we were still doing something tonight but we hadn't had a chance to talk about any Halloween stuff at all. As if he knew what I was thinking I heard Scott's drum roll knock on my door. I said, "come in," and he entered the room holding a giant box. He dropped it on the floor next to my bed and sat in the desk chair.

I felt I owed Scott an explanation. Since that night at The Griffon a couple weeks ago I hadn't really seen him much either through our schedules conflicting or maybe he was trying to avoid me. Either way, honestly, I missed hanging out with him. I just knew that I couldn't tell him everything going on right now and I hated hiding something from him. Scott grabbed a Jolt from my mini-fridge, took a sip and sat back in the chair.

"So," Scott said in a tone that I couldn't quite read, "what happened last night?"

I internally panicked.

"Huh?" I said, trying to sound like I didn't just fight an ice monster from another Earth in our hometown last night.

"Well," Scott said after taking another sip of Jolt, "I woke up this morning and saw a trail of muddy footprints leading to your room so I was wondering what happened."

"Oh shit, I'm sorry man," I stammered out while trying to think of something believable, "I went to my parents yesterday because Dad needed help with some stuff in the backyard and I stayed for dinner and came back really late." I hated lying to him.

I looked at Scott with the most sincere look I could, which came with some unintentional grunting from my aching body. He looked at me and nodded and then flashed a smile on his face.

"I got our costumes for tonight!" Scott started to open the box like a kid on Christmas. I'm glad he remembered and that any stress between us wasn't going to interfere with our tradition, I just hoped he picked something cool.

"What's in the box?" I said, trying to channel my inner Brad Pitt at the end of *Se7en*.

"Just wait," he said as he started cutting open the tape, "My uncle hooked us up this year."

Scott's uncle owned a costume shop out in Wappingers Falls so for the last few years we got our costumes there and they are pretty high quality. I remember in high school, when we first started doing this, Scott showed up with totally movie accurate Batman and Joker costumes from his uncle's shop and won the school costume contest that year. I swung my legs out of bed and slowly bent over from the edge of my bed to help Scott and take a peek inside. I gasped in excitement at what I saw.

"Han and Chewie!" I exclaimed. I was excited!

"Yep!" Scott pulled out the Han Solo costume and tossed it to me. "Here, I know you've wanted to be Han for years, I don't mind being Chewie."

"You sure, man?" I asked, but I was really happy that I was going to be Han. That Chewie costume looked hot as hell, I didn't think I would be able to wear that all night, especially in my achy condition.

"Totally," Scott said as he put on the Chewbacca mask and let out a mighty roar. "Besides, look how furry it is! Girls are going to want to pet the ol' walking carpet all night!" He shot me some finger guns, while still wearing the mask.

I shook my head and let out a laugh that made my ribs hurt a little. Truth be told, I missed hanging out with Scott. I wanted to tell him everything that had been going on for the last few weeks, but once again decided against it. I was just on the edge of knowing what was happening myself, I didn't want to bring him into it and complicate everything more.

Scott stood up and walked toward the door, but before he reached the knob, I started, "Hey man, I just wanted to say I'm sorry we keep missing each other."

"Yeah," Scott looked at me and nodded, "It seems we've both had a lot of shit going on."

"It's been pretty nuts lately," I agreed, "but tonight should be fun."

"Yeah man." Scott left the room and turned back towards me. "Meet here at like nine?"

"Sounds good." I replied.

I gave Scott a thumbs up and a couple of seconds later I heard the front door of our dorm close. I considered laying back down in bed again for a bit, but I did tell Beth I would meet up with her, and I really wanted to see her sooner rather than later. My clock was telling me it was 10:40 A.M., which sucked, because McDonalds stopped serving breakfast at 10:30 and I was really craving an Egg McMuffin. I'm sure I would think of something to grab on my way to The Griffon, but first I needed a shower.

I got to the gateway under The Griffon at about noon, with a terrible egg sandwich from the corner store that was totally *not* like an Egg McMuffin. I took a deep breath before stepping inside. I wondered what that thing was that we found last night, and did that thing create the ice giant that almost killed us. I also was a little nervous about how Beth and I were going to be interacting with each other. Would things be awkward? Weird? Totally fine? Only one way to find out.

Last night was nice. I had her laughing a handful of times and she seemed a little lighter than her normal dark and brooding self, at least for a little while. My heart started beating faster just thinking about Beth. Either this was an epic level crush or I was falling way too hard and way too fast. I could almost hear Goose from *Top Gun* yelling at me to pull up!

I stepped through the gateway and saw Professor Cline typing furiously on his computer, his back to where I just appeared. I looked around and didn't see Beth anywhere. My heart sank a little bit as I approached The Professor's workstation. Without looking up, he greeted me.

"Mister Howard!" The Professor said as he was reading over figures on the half dozen monitors in front of him. "Please, have a seat."

I sat in the chair next to him and he turned one of the monitors towards me. The screen looked like the worst kind of math that can be imagined. I had no idea what any of this meant at all. I think he saw my eyes glaze over and he turned the monitor back towards him a bit.

"Beth's not here?" I asked, trying to sound as nonchalant as possible.

"Elizabeth is still sleeping, I believe." Professor Cline said, still fully engrossed in whatever he was working on.

"Oh, okay." I sat there for a moment before saying anything again. "So, does Beth live here? Like in this cave?"

"Not exactly," he said, his eyes still fixed on the screens, "We both live in the Mohonk Mountain House. They have been an ally of The Conclave for hundreds of years."

I let that sink in for a moment. The Mohonk Mountain House was a secret base for a protection agency that had existed for hundreds of years? That was some really heavy knowledge to just drop in a conversation. I always thought there was something up with the place. It looked really old and cool, there's a rumor that Stephen King wrote *The Shining* after staying there with his family on vacation so there was always an air of mystery about the place. I guess this confirmed that there was more to that place than meets the eye.

I looked over and noticed the object from last night on The Professor's desk and that he had hooked various wires into it. The gem in the middle seemed to be faintly glowing, a dim blue light trying to find its way out. It was definitely not doing that last night, it was just a clear blue gem. I guessed that it had to do with everything Professor Cline had hooked to it.

"So," I said trying to change the subject, "Do you have any idea what that thing is?"

"I have some theories," he said, "But I would like to share them with both of you so I would prefer to wait until Elizabeth is here also."

The door on the far side of the room opened just then and Beth started making the long walk over to Professor Cline's workstation. I felt my heart flutter as I looked at her coming toward us, she looked stunning. She wasn't wearing anything crazy, just jeans (which I had never seen her wear) and a Liz Phair tee shirt from the 1995 tour. Her hair was in a ponytail instead of down and loose like I had seen every other time I had seen her. She wasn't wearing any makeup, it looked like she had just gotten up or got out of the shower. She didn't need any makeup anyway, she was perfect.

Beth looked at me when she got closer to me, gave me a little smile and sat in the chair next to mine. I smiled back and was about to ask her how she was feeling when The Professor turned his chair toward us with a very stern look.

"As much as I appreciate the two of you recovering this device," Professor Cline began in a stern tone that matched his glare, "It seems you caused quite a disturbance last night."

The Professor tossed a copy of The Times-Herald Record at us, and Beth and I looked at the headline on the front page. Yikes.

EXPLOSION NEAR THE WALLKILL RIVER CAUSES LOCALS TO TEMPORARILY EVACUATE

"What happened?" Professor Cline folded his arms and sat back in his chair, waiting for an answer.

Beth and I looked at each other wide-eyed after reading the page. I guess we didn't realize the power that Beth released by going supernova. I don't remember hearing any explosions, I'm guessing the explosion that was being reported was actually Beth, but I do remember the streets had been dark.

"Well," I began carefully, "After we left here yesterday we got to Wallkill early so we grabbed some pizza."

"Yeah," Beth chimed in, "The place was pretty close to where we were going so…"

Professor Cline looked over the top of his wire framed glasses. "I don't care about the pizza," he quipped with an unflinching look at the both of us, "What happened where you found the device. Stop stalling."

I looked over to Beth and saw her clench her jaw. She took a deep breath and continued.

"So, we got to the spot in the middle of the freezing river that the radar was pointing us too and we found... that." Beth pointed at the object on Cline's desk.

"Yeah," I added, "And after we found it, a monster showed up."

Professor Cline's eyebrows raised, "A monster?"

"It was huge," Beth picked up the story where I left off, "It was like eight or nine feet tall and it looked like it was made of some type of crystal but then it shot icicles at Jake and started charging towards me."

I looked at Cline and something about him changed. He was still mad, but there was something different about the look he was giving Beth.

Beth continued, "I hesitated and the thing knocked me downstream into the river…" Her voice trailed off a little so I continued our harrowing tale.

"I grabbed the device and the thing started chasing me," I continued, "And it started beating on my shield pretty much pounding me into the ground. That's when Beth literally flew out of the river, on fire, and melted the things head enough for me to smash it off with my hammer and when we got the hell out of there because we heard sirens."

Beth spoke up again.

"I ported us back to the truck and then we got back here kind of late."

There was a period of silence that seemed to last forever. Professor Cline stood up, massaging the bridge of his nose with his thumb and forefinger, and paced back and forth, muttering to himself.

"I shouldn't have sent you out there." He looked at Beth, to me and then back to Beth. "You weren't ready."

The Professor was getting increasingly agitated and I looked over to Beth. She was staring intently at him, jaw re-clenched. Her eyes were following him as he began ranting.

"I told the both of you that if there was any danger to get out of there immediately!" Professor Cline was getting very angry, I hadn't ever seen him like this. He was usually very calm and calculating.

"There was no time to run," Beth said as she watched Professor Cline pace back and forth, "As soon as we touched that thing that monster showed up."

"Regardless!" he continued, "You were not equipped to handle anything like that. You know what type of dangers are out in The Multiverse, Elizabeth! You obviously need more training before you go out in the field again."

Beth stood up in her chair so fast that it fell over on its side and clattered to the floor. She balled up her fists and glared at Professor Cline.

"More training?" She began through clenched teeth. "More training? All I've done since you showed up on my fucking doorstep seven years ago is train!"

The Professor interrupted.

"Elizabeth, language please." Beth ignored him and continued.

"I wake up, I train. I go to school, I study. I come back, I fucking train again! I can only train so much. If there are threats out there that I am 'training' for I'm not going to be able to do anything training in this fucking cave!"

"Elizabeth, calm down please."

Beth's hands were starting to glow a bit as she continued. She was pissed and I don't think I've ever heard her curse this much before, if ever. I guess the filter comes off when she's angry.

"I'm not going to calm down!" She continued. "You barely ever let me out of here! Even that night at The Griffon when Jake showed up," Beth pointed at me, "You were giving me shit about studying different multiverse bullshit in public. No one was even

90

paying attention to me, it was fine! It's just a fucking bar as much as everybody knows, nobody knows anything else about it. Me reading a book in the corner while having a fucking drink LIKE A NORMAL COLLEGE STUDENT wasn't going to attract any attention toward me. I just wanted to be around some normal people my own age for a little while instead of being kept here like some fucking princess in a castle! I'm just so sick of you treating me like some porcelain doll that is going to break at any moment!"

I could feel the heat Beth was giving off from where I was sitting. Professor Cline was standing strong, staring Beth directly in the eye and it didn't look like either of them were about to back down. I stood up and tried to position myself between them, I wasn't sure what was about to happen but I wanted to at least try to diffuse the situation a little. I looked in Beth's eyes and they were reddish-orange, that was probably not a good sign.

"With all due respect Professor," I began, "Beth was pretty great last night. After the initial shock of a giant ice monster showing up she, well we, both held our own against it and if she hadn't gone all supernova we probably wouldn't be standing here." I turned my head from side to side, like a tennis match. to look at both of them.

Beth looked menacing, her eyes were glowing like a sunrise and her hair bellowing behind her from some supernatural breeze that wasn't felt by anyone but her. Professor Cline was just staring at her. I couldn't get a read on what was going on with him, whether it was anger towards Beth having been in danger, or something else. I looked back to Beth and her eyes locked with mine. I heard Professor Cline clear his throat.

"Elizabeth," He began in a bit of a softer tone than before, "I understand your frustrations."

Beth's eyes moved from mine and stared back at The Professor.

"I know you didn't ask for any of this," he continued, "but this is a weight that unfortunately has fallen onto your shoulders.

91

I've promised to protect you but, perhaps, I have been a little too obsessive in keeping my word."

I saw a tear roll out of Beth's now slightly dimming eyes. Professor Cline continued.

"Maybe the time for training has ended. I have tried to prepare you for any situation I could think of, maybe to your detriment, because in doing so I have limited your exposure to real threats in The Multiverse."

Professor Cline walked towards Beth, who was no longer glowing. Tears were streaming from her open eyes, but she wasn't sobbing. Her face was as statuesque as she could muster, although her chest was heaving in and out as she was doing her best to keep her composure. I stepped back a little to make room for Professor Cline and he put his hand on Beth's shoulder. She met his gaze.

"It seems you might be ready, but Elizabeth, as prepared as you think you are, and as much as I have taught you, there are still many unknowns in The Multiverse. There are things that I have yet to encounter and I have been doing this for a long time. The training may be over but the learning never stops. You must always be prepared for the countless dangers that The Multiverse can possibly throw your way."

Beth nodded, wiped the tears from her face and sat on the edge of Professor Cline's desk. She looked at me, mouthed the words "thank you" and gave me a weak smile. Professor Cline went back to his chair and I stood there looking at the both of them, making a note of the questions forming in my head.

"Is everyone good now?" I asked.

"Yes, Mister Howard." The Professor responded.

"Yeah." Beth said as she looked over to the computer screens.

"Cool." I said as I approached the screens. "So, Professor, you said that you found out some stuff about that thing?"

"Ah, yes, Mister Howard." Professor Cline cleared his throat and turned a monitor to a better angle for Beth and me to see. I still couldn't make out the jumbled mess on the screen but, when I looked over to Beth, I saw her eyes widen like she was scanning over each line.

"Are these coordinates?" She asked The Professor.

"Yes," The Professor said as he nodded his head, "except that the coordinates don't match up to our Earth, not exactly anyway. The degrees are slightly off."

"What does that mean?" I asked, lost.

"Essentially, Mister Howard," he began, "this device can rip a hole in The Multiverse, allowing someone or some… thing to come through therefore creating a rift in the tender thread holding all of these realities together."

"Okay…" I said, following along.

The Professor continued.

"The problem is when a gateway to another Earth is opened, the origin of that gateway is easily accessible to The Conclave for the purpose of keeping order in The Multiverse. No matter what I have done to this so far I can't find where it is from because the origin coordinates keep changing as if something is encrypting, or blocking, the information."

"So it's like someone 'star sixty-sevened' a gateway?"

Professor Cline looked blankly at me and Beth let out a slight chuckle.

"Yeah, Jake," Beth said with a smile, "that's pretty much the idea." She looked at Professor Cline. "Star sixty-seven is the code you use on a phone to block your number from someone's caller ID."

"Ah, yes, Mister Howard." Professor Cline said with a nod.

"So then what coordinates is this Rift Ripper thing showing?" I asked.

"That's a great name." Beth said in approval.

"It just came to me." I smiled slightly.

Professor Cline looked at both of us and shook his head in dismay.

"I see Mister Howard has a penchant for naming this like you do, Elizabeth."

"Well, yeah," Beth said. "It makes it easier than just saying 'this thing' or 'that thing'. You can only call so many things 'things' before things start getting confusing." Beth used her fingers to accentuate quotes each time she said "thing."

"I suppose." Professor Cline said before refocusing on the question. "The one set of coordinates that are constant show where you found it, give or take a couple of degrees. The other set fluctuates with seemingly no pattern. In the time I've been experimenting with it the coordinates have bounced from Tokyo to England to Melbourne to New York City to Dubai to Brazil to right here in New Paltz. Sometimes they are city specific, sometimes they are just general country coordinates. It makes no sense."

"So then what does that mean?" I asked looking toward Beth, who shrugged. Apparently she didn't know either.

"What it means, Mister Howard," he started, "Is that I have a lot more work ahead of me, too, to figure out the origins of this 'Rift Ripper', as you call it. I will let the both of you know if and when I find anything else out. For now, there's not much that the two of you can do."

"Oh, okay." I got up to get ready to leave and turned to Beth. "Hey, can I talk to you for a minute."

She nodded and we walked up the stairs to where the gateway in the room opens up. As we were walking, I saw Professor Cline look at us from over the top of his glasses. We got to the gateway and I got lost in her eyes for a moment.

"What's going on?" She asked with a smile.

"Well," I started, "I just wanted to let you know that, since tonight is Halloween…"

"Yeah?" Beth raised an eyebrow quizzically.

"Well Scott and I are going to a party tonight," she rolled her eyes at the mention of Scott, "It's like the biggest party on campus, and I love Halloween, so I was wondering if maybe you wanted to go."

My heart was beating so hard in my chest that I was sure she could hear it. I was glad this cave was a little cool because I could feel the sweat coming. This was stressful as hell.

"I don't know Jake," Beth protested, "I really don't do parties and I'm willing to bet that there are going to be a lot of douchebags there."

"Yeah, probably," I agreed, "But that's why it would be cool if you were there. It's not really my crowd and I'd like to spend some time with you, like, not almost getting killed by an ice monster."

Beth laughed a little and smiled and I continued my sales pitch. I gently reached my fingers out to meet her hand, almost without realizing I was doing it.

"You did say that you wanted to spend some time with normal people. What's more normal than hanging out with some probably drunk college students in costume at a Halloween party?"

Beth looked at me and smiled slightly. I got lost in her eyes again.

"I'll think about it." she said, "I don't really do costumes though."

"Then don't and just tell people you're 'dark and brooding'." I tried to make my face look solemn and sad. That got another chuckle out of her. She took a couple of steps closer to me and my heart almost flew out of my chest.

"I'll let you know." Beth said with a smirk and then opened a gateway behind me and shoved me through.

CHAPTER ELEVEN

The rest of Halloween leading up to the party was uneventful. It was Friday and my classes were already over for the day so I decided to catch a movie. I loved going to the movies and, even more, I loved going to see movies alone. That's not to say I hated going with people, but when you go to a movie alone you can actually concentrate on the movie and not have to answer any questions in hushed tones to someone that is watching the exact same thing as you are. Sometimes it's just really great to get lost in what is unfolding in front of your eyes.

The New Paltz Cinema was my favorite little theater. The movies were cheap, five dollars anytime or two for five on Tuesday Date Nights, but they're always first-run movies the weekend they came out, not something that has been in theaters a month before they hit our little town. The manager, Lou, was a good guy and hired me on the spot after I left the McDonalds across the parking lot on my one year anniversary there. I hated smelling like a grease pit after a year, so I left and walked right in, and boom, Lou hired me. In fact there is only one tarnished memory I have from working there, it's where Shelly and I went all the time.

The summer before my Freshman year at SUNY New Paltz, Jen met Shelly and introduced us. She was a cute little dirty-blond haired girl who was also starting her first year at SUNY and I, as I tend to do, fell hard and fast for her. She was from Belmar, a town I had never heard of in New Jersey but was apparently about a half-hour north of Point Pleasant, a town I had been to a couple of times. She was bubbly as hell, a former cheerleader, and had the bluest eyes I had ever seen. They were blue like the most blue summer day that you could imagine, and

I'm a sucker for pretty eyes, so I was a lost cause from the first day. To me, she looked like Alicia Silverstone in *Clueless*, a movie she was obsessed with. In hindsight, that should have been a huge warning sign because she actually kind of acted like Cher, Alicia's character. A lot like her actually, to a disturbing degree. I didn't know any other girls from New Jersey, I just thought that they must all act like that. I blamed the beach air. In addition, she was really pretty, and I was a hopeless idiot, so I tolerated it.

I tried to get the memories of Shelly out of my head as I paid my five bucks and went in to see *I Know What You Did Last Summer*. I'm not the biggest horror movie fan, but I actually loved *Scream* and this looked like it was in the same vein, as that so I gave it a shot. I grabbed my popcorn and nacho cheese to dip it in (my favorite movie watching combination) from the concession stand and settled in to get lost in some teen slasher cinema for a couple of hours. The movie was actually pretty good. I did check the bed of my truck a few more times than I would like to admit on the way back to the dorm just to make sure there were no fishermen with hooks waiting for me.

I got back to campus a couple of hours before the party and walked briskly back to the dorm very quickly, keeping an eye out for any fishermen that didn't belong to our little village. I have always had an overactive imagination, but I was still on high alert. When I saw *IT* on T.V. a few years ago I couldn't look at Ronald McDonald straight for like three years. Did that play a little bit into me quitting McDonalds? Maybe, Ronald's statue on the bench next to the play area was always a little creepy. That miniseries did mess with me hard though, at least until the end when they fought a giant space-spider or something. But I watched it because I love Tim Curry. He's a treasure and brings greatness to nearly everything he touches, even that really bad movie that my sister loves, *The Worst Witch*.

I got back to the dorm before Scott and laid on my bed for a bit before getting ready for the party. I was still pretty sore from fighting the ice giant but it was at a manageable level at the moment. I closed my eyes just contemplating what the hell I'd gotten myself into in the span of two months. In a million years I couldn't have predicted that I would meet a girl and wind up getting wrapped up in protecting a multiverse against an ice monster.

I reached over to hit the power button on my stereo and was greeted with the sounds of "Today" by The Smashing Pumpkins. I liked this song so much, and again, it was fitting. Today is a great day. It's Halloween, I'm getting to dress like Han Solo while my best friend is Chewbacca and there is a small chance that Beth will come to the party. I don't know for sure, but I am really hoping that she does.

My mind wandered to thoughts of Beth. I could feel myself falling for her, hell I've probably already fell, but after Shelly I've been so gun-shy about getting into a relationship that I really haven't allowed myself to open up to another girl. I've just kind of felt numb inside, like there was some type of hole in my heart that just can't be filled. Beth is the first girl to make me feel, well, anything since Shelly and I split up. From the first day that we bumped into each other, I felt something. I can't even imagine not following this path, wherever it is leading, but apparently there is some Earth somewhere in The Multiverse that we just bump into each other and go our separate ways. Wherever that Jake is, he's an idiot.

I heard the front door of the dorm open and I opened my eyes. Scott poked his head in my room to let me know he was back and to get ready. I must have drifted off for a bit, I sure as hell needed the rest. I felt a little energized from my apparent cat-nap so I got up to start getting ready for the party. A short time later, Han and Chewie walked out of DuBois Hall ready to enjoy the night's festivities.

From the looks of things it seemed that everyone on campus was on their way to some type of Halloween party. The whole place was buzzing, even though it had to be no more than thirty-five to forty degrees outside. I'm really glad Scott grabbed

98

Bespin Han for me, the jacket helped a bit. It was almost as heavy as my Dads Carhartt jacket and really toasty. I was wearing the traditional Han solo vest underneath because I knew that I would not be able to wear this jacket all night, I would absolutely be melted into a puddle if I did. It was a short walk over there anyway, like maybe less than a half mile, so we wouldn't be out in the cold that long anyway.

A group of girls dressed as sexy nurses passed us as we made our way to the party and Scott let out his best wookie roar. They gave us a little smile and wink and kept walking as I wondered if they were going to get hypothermia at the cost of being dressed in as little as possible when Scott gave me a little friendly shove.

"Dude," the Wookiee next to me said, "You should take a shot at the blonde one."

"The blond what?"

"The nurse, man!" He motioned to the girls walking away from us. "She was really hot. I'd like to check her pulse, that's for sure." He let out another disturbingly accurate wookie sound.

"Oh, yeah." I responded absentmindedly.

"Are you okay man?" Scott asked, taking off the Chewie mask. "We haven't really seen each other, like, at all. You seem really out there. You good?"

Was I good? Yes and no. I really felt like I couldn't tell Scott everything that was going on, but I felt really bad not sharing this huge part of what's going on in my life lately with my best friend. I figured the best thing to do at the moment was to kind of tell him what was up, but not really.

"Yeah, man, I'm good." We continued walking towards the party. "I've been working on, something, with Beth for Astronomy so that's why I haven't really been around much."

"Beth? Oh, you meant Witch Hazel!" Scott laughed.

"Don't call her that man." I said sharply, a little sharper than I meant to, actually.

"Calm your shit, dude, I was just kidding." Scott seemed a little annoyed. "It just seems like you are throwing yourself against a wall with her. She's fucking weird man."

"You don't even know her dude." I was starting to get a little mad. I could feel myself getting really warm under this jacket, even in this chilly weather. "She's actually pretty cool if you would actually get to know her."

We reached the party and Scott stopped walking. I walked up the couple of steps onto the patio and turned to look at him.

"You coming?" I asked.

Scott didn't say anything for a minute, he just looked at me.

"Hey," he started, "I'm not trying to get into your shit or anything, I just get a weird vibe from her. I'm just looking out for you."

"I appreciate it, but I'm good man, I swear." I was getting tired of saying this to him.

"If you say so dude," Scott put his Chewbacca mask back on, "Let's go."

Scott let out a mighty Wookiee howl and we headed in for a night of costumed shenanigans. Well, he was, parties weren't really my thing.

As soon as we opened the door, I was assaulted by smoke from a dry ice machine and Dee-lite's "Groove is in the Heart". People were everywhere. There were plenty of guys and girls all over, and apparently the "sexy" costumes weren't just limited to the girls as there were a lot of guys, jocks and frat boys mostly, dressed in whatever would show off their muscles. Most of the girls were dressed in sexy anything. There was everything from sexy teachers to sexy mechanics to even a sexy Where's Waldo, which was pretty much a girl in a red and white striped bikini and a hat.

I wandered around for a bit saying hi to some familiar faces I've seen around but hadn't really interacted with much. I don't think of myself as an antisocial person, but I also don't really go out of my way to meet new people, either. I'm content with just knowing who I know and if I meet someone new along the way, that's fine too. Maybe it was because I really didn't go out much in my high school days, or maybe it was just because I wasn't really into what most people were into at my age.

Most twenty-one year olds are all about getting drunk and getting laid, especially around college. I was never into any of that. Like, yeah, sex is great don't get me wrong. I just don't want to sleep around for the sake of sleeping around though, I've always been a long term relationship kind of guy. In high school I dated a girl named Jess for like two years till I got grounded Homecoming weekend of my senior year after she bought her dress so she broke up with me. She wound up hooking up with some guy and got pregnant shortly after. She didn't even graduate, but she got her GED a year or so later. After Jess was Shelly, and I've already talked about how that turned out.

Drinking wasn't a big thing for me either. I didn't mind being the designated driver because I'd rather know what was going on than make some stupid decisions and blame it on the alcohol. Scott could hammer them down like nobody's business, which I'm pretty sure he's doing right now. He always calls himself a 'functioning drunk' because unless you really know him it's really hard to tell when he's hammered or not. Scott can have a full on coherent, intelligent conversation with you while he's drunk enough to make Sam Adams jealous.

I grabbed a can of Coke and started talking to a group I recognized from some of the game nights at the dorm. A couple of the guys were drunk already so they were babbling to each other, while Nick and Krissy, a couple from my Astronomy class, were chatting each other up. Nick had her laughing and he seemed to be trying to get something started with her so I excused myself and waded through the sea of various drunk people.

The small talk with various people continued as I made my way around the bash. I looked at my watch and saw it was around ten-thirty. We got here like an hour and a half ago but it seemed like forever, and I haven't seen Scott since we got here. I was pretty much ready to leave. I was tired, still kind of sore and more than a little bummed that Beth decided not to come. I really thought for sure she would be here, maybe things weren't as clear cut as I was hoping they were. I went off to look for Scott but he spotted me first as I was passing the kitchen. He let out a great Wookiee howl and lumbered over to me. This was one of the tells that he was pretty smashed already, his movements were just different enough that to the naked (sober) eye he looked fine, but I knew he'd be sleeping in tomorrow.

"Dude!" Scott said as he slung a furry arm around my shoulder. He wasn't wearing his mask so I got a full whiff of his breath. Yeah, that was totally tequila. Tequila was Scott's kryptonite, the one thing that could make him go from 'functioning drunk' to 'scooping him off the pavement with a spatula'. "I haven't seen you since we got here man!"

I took a slight step back because I was pretty sure I could get contact buzzed from the hot breath that was coming at me.

"Yeah man, I think I'm gonna go." I shouted to be heard over the crowd and thumping music.

"What! Why?" Scott pulled me closer, he seemed a lot stronger when he drank. "This place is a blast! Why do you want to leave? We gotta find you a chick, that'll make you stay."

Scott called over to some girl in the corner, a pretty attractive girl with dark brown hair who was dressed like "Carnival" Sandy from *Grease*. She waved and winked, but then went back to talking to her girlfriends.

"I met her before, man," Scott said into my ear, "She's super hot and her friends are cute too. Let's go talk to them." He started to pull me along with him and I snaked out of his grasp. He took a couple of more steps before realizing I wasn't with him and he turned back to me with a puzzled look on his face.

"I'm just gonna go man, I'm beat." I turned to walk away when Scott grabbed my shoulder.

"What the hell is your deal, Jake?" Scott questioned loudly. A couple of people turned their heads towards us and then went back to their conversations. "We've barely hung out anymore! I saw you more when we didn't share a dorm!"

"I've been busy man, I don't know what to say." I replied. If I was going to tell him what was going on, this was totally not the right time.

"Busy? Or busy wasting your time with witchie-poo."

"Dude, seriously, stop calling her that."

"Why? Is she gonna turn me into a frog or something." Scott wiggled his fingers in my face and I slapped them away.

"Seriously Scott, cut the shit with that. You don't even know her." I turned to walk away and he grabbed me by the shoulder again and spun me around. I pushed his hand off my shoulder and he took a step back. "Scott, we can talk about this tomorrow. I'm leaving."

"Fucking whatever Jake. Go waste your time with witch face and get some blue balls over a girl that is probably going to sacrifice you on some altar somewhere in the woods."

"Seriously, stop!" I said as I gave Scott a shove. Scott looked stunned and for a split second I thought he was going to take a swing at me. We've never had an actual, physical fight before and I wasn't about to try to fight him tonight. A few more people turned towards us, now interested in a pending fight that might break out. He just stared blankly at me for a moment and put his Chewbacca mask back on.

"Whatever," Scott muttered as he slid the mask into place, "Doesn't fucking matter anyway."

"Yeah, why's that?" I said, clearly agitated.

Scott motioned toward the door.

"Looks like your girlfriend's here." He turned and stumbled back into the kitchen and I turned towards the front door and saw a sight I didn't expect to see.

Framed in the doorway of the house was Beth dressed as Batgirl from that god-awful *Batman and Robin* movie. That is the only movie that I've walked out on in the theater, it's that terrible. Alicia Silverstone was Batgirl, Alfred's niece, not James Gordon's

103

daughter like she's been since the beginning of time, but that was the least of the problems with that movie. It was also the furthest thing from my mind at this point.

Other than earlier today when I saw Beth in jeans and a tee shirt, she's usually been in a black dress of some sort with some dark stockings. But this costume clung to every piece of her. She wasn't a stick figure and her curves were on full display. She looked amazing, like I'm pretty sure my brain shut off at some point and was looking for the right words to let me know how to feel. She saw me and jockeyed the people in the hallway I was in as I struggled to not seem like I was a babbling moron with a heart-stoppingly massive crush.

"Hey," Beth said, her eyes looking slightly up at me from behind her domino mask, "I thought about what you said and decided that a party might not be the worst thing in the world." She gave me a little smirk and my knees got weak.

She smelled like baked apples and for a moment I got lost in her hazel eyes again. I could hear my brain screaming at me to say something and not just stand here like a giant dolt. I felt my mouth go dry.

"I...I'm glad you came." I stammered out, trying my best to sound normal and trying not to stare too much at her. "I thought you didn't like costumes?"

"I don't, usually." She pulled at the fabric on her midsection a little. "I hate the fabric that they're made of. And I had to settle on this one since it's Halloween and this was like the only thing left at Ames in my size." Beth looked at my costume and pulled the lapel of my vest. My heart jumped.

"This is a nice Han Solo costume." she said with a smile.

"Uh, thanks," the words were coming a little easier to me now, "Scott's uncle owns a costume shop in Wappingers so he hooks us up every year. He came as Chewbacca."

Beth rolled her eyes at the mention of Scott's name.

"Is he still here?"

"Yeah, he's drunk somewhere." I didn't want to rehash the argument we just got into so I tried to change the subject. "So, fan of Joel Schumacher's work?"

Beth gave a little laugh that made me feel all warm and fuzzy.

"That crap movie? Hell no! That movie was so bad."

"I know, right!" I agreed, "It's like the man never read a Batman comic in his life!"

"Yeah!" Beth pointed to the mask on her face. "Like, why doesn't Batgirl wear the full cowl except for the motorcycle helmet for one scene? And why isn't she…"

"Barbara Gordon?" I finished her sentence for her and she smiled.

"Yeah, that was so dumb!"

"I have no idea," I said, "the whole movie was stupid." I reached into my pocket, took out my wallet and showed Beth my bank card. "The Bat Credit Card…"

"Don't leave the cave without it!" We finished the infamous American Express TV ad quote in unison, then giggled about it.

This moment felt like we were the only two people in the room. I really started to feel at ease. Beth was getting easier to talk to and I just loved spending time with her the more I got to know her. It's taken a couple months, and I am convinced that she hated me when we first met, but now I feel that just seeing her smile can get me through anything.

The party was in full swing and this place was getting crowded quickly. Beth and I tried to find a quieter place where we could talk so we each grabbed another can of Coke and went out front to sit on the patio. There wasn't a lot of people out here because it was probably about thirty degrees or so but I think just being around Beth made me feel warm. It was either that, or maybe she was throwing off heat like a space heater. We found a bench and had a seat.

"I really thought you weren't going to come," I said, feeling a little more calm than before, "I'm glad you did."

"I wasn't going to." Beth said, taking off her domino mask. "After you left I went back to Cline and we had a talk."

"About?" I was curious.

"Well, first, I did apologize for freaking out on him." She kind of chuckled to herself a little while playing with the mask in her hands. "I'm usually able to keep my emotions in check and I think after everything that happened over the last day it just, like, came out. You know?"

I nodded. "Yeah, not what I expected to start off Halloween weekend with, that's for damn sure."

Beth laughed again and gave me a little smile before it faded away.

"You know, my mom and I used to share Halloween as our favorite holiday, too." she said solemnly. "Since Mom died I haven't really celebrated it. Cline kind of convinced me this year that she would have wanted me to enjoy it, not just sit in my room and mourn like I've done for the last seven years."

"I'm sorry." was all I could manage to get out.

Beth raised her hand to her chest and grabbed something under her costume. She stuck her hand in the neckline and pulled out her necklace with the red gem on it. Beth reached behind her neck and unclasped it, held it in her hands and pressed a small button on the side of it. The gem swung open and underneath there was a picture. She inched a little closer to me to show me what was inside. I saw a little girl being hugged from behind by a pretty woman that looked a lot like Beth.

"This is my Mom, Peggy. This is my favorite picture of us together." Beth said smiling. "I was ten years old and I had just rode my first roller coaster at Great Adventure. I was so excited and Dad took this picture of us."

"You look just like her." I felt so lucky that she trusted me with this.

"She was beautiful." Beth said and rubbed her thumb on the picture a bit. She closed the locket and clasped it back around her neck. "Losing her seven years ago is the hardest thing I have ever been through."

I haven't had the experience of losing a parent, or anyone in my family really, so I had no idea what to say. I could see Beth was getting a little upset so I put my hand on top of hers that was on the bench. The warmth it gave off immediately filled my body. She looked over to me and smiled.

"She had a great voice too." Beth said smiling at the memory. "When I was little I wasn't sure what my mom did for work, but I know she went away every couple of months or so for business trips. Before she would leave she would always sing me that song "Beth" by Kiss."

"That's a nice song." It was one of the few songs by Kiss that wasn't directly about sex or drugs I think, just a really pretty song.

"Yeah," Beth wiped a tear from her eye and continued, "it turns out her business trips were actually her and Cline protecting The Multiverse. Dad apparently knew all about it, and hated that she did it, but understood the responsibility. I had no idea."

"Oh wow." I didn't have any idea what to say about that. What do you say?

Beth continued. "The last time Mom left, her and Dad got into a huge fight about it. He never liked when she left but this time was different. There was, like, a different feel in the air or something. Eventually the argument settled, I had been listening through the vents but couldn't really make out much. It was late and I was supposed to be sleeping, so when I heard the fight settle down and footsteps on the stairs I jumped back into bed and pretended to be sleeping. She knew I was awake." Beth got a little choked up and took a sip of Coke.

"Mom came in," Beth continued, "and brushed the hair to the side of my face, gave me a kiss on the forehead and sang me my song. There were tears in her eyes, I don't know if it was from the fight with Dad or if she knew something else. That was the last time I saw her."

Beth turned her hand over and squeezed mine. We sat there in silence for a moment. I really was at a loss of what to say. I looked at Beth and she was looking straight ahead, not making eye contact with anything. She wiped more tears from her eyes and told me more.

"A couple of days later Uncle Bryan, well Professor Cline, was sitting in the living room with my dad when I came home from school. Dad was distraught, his head was in his hands hunched over on the couch and Cline was sitting next to him trying to console him. Dad looked up at me, tears pouring from his eyes, and I just knew. I knew she was gone." Beth took a deep breath.

"I ran to my treehouse in the backyard. I hadn't been up there in a while, probably like two or three years at that point. I was angry, so angry. I felt a rage burning in me that I had never felt, ever. I started just hitting things, my sleeping bag, a stuffed animal, my posters of New Kids on The Block, everything. The last thing I punched, the wall, burst into flames."

"Oh!" I exclaimed. I wasn't expecting that.

"That was pretty much my reaction too." Beth chuckled a little, tears in her eyes still. "In seconds my entire treehouse was in flames. Dad and Cline rushed to the back and put out the fire with a garden hose. We had a ceremony for Mom a couple of days later. Since then I've stayed with Cline and he's been training me. Dad wasn't happy about it at all, but it was really out of his control. Once someone is handed down a gift, as The Conclave calls it, they need to be taken in and trained."

I sat there for a moment, not knowing what to say. Finally, I thought of a question: "Do you still get to see your Dad?"

"Yeah, he lives in Westchester." Beth nodded. "I go see him as often as I can, holidays mostly. He's remarried. She's nice but, like, she'll never replace her. Even Dad knows that."

"Hey, listen," I said inching a little closer to Beth, "I understand if you don't want to answer this but, how did she die?"

Beth took a deep breath and looked at me. Her eyes showed grief, pain. A look that I hadn't ever seen her have. I felt her grip on my hand get a little tighter.

"I know she died fighting," Beth started, "She ran off alone to stop some kind of invasion, ahead of Cline. When Cline got there, my Mom was already dead. He opened a gateway on Mohonk Mountain and brought her back to the cave. It's been seven years as of the beginning of October."

Beth stared at me wide eyed, tear stains on her cheeks. I stared back at her, processing what she just told me when, suddenly, it was like something in my brain clicked. I felt my own eyes widen and Beth nodded her head.

"You were there the day my mother died."

CHAPTER TWELVE

We sat there in silence for a while and I tried to process the news Beth just dropped on me. I looked over to the door of the house and saw various costumed students coming and going from the party, while I attempted to get my head around this new information. Luckily, Beth broke the silence first.

"That's the reason I was really weird around you after the gateway in The Griffon didn't close that night. I've never seen that before. And then the blood test that we did…"

"Showed that there was something in my blood that reacted with it." I interrupted.

"Yeah," Beth said, "Cline said it was an enzyme or something, but that was just for ease of explanation."

"So, then, what is it?" I was still a little shaken, but I wanted some answers.

"Basically, Cline's gateway closed in a certain unexpected way after he found Mom that it let off some type of discharge. He called it," Beth stopped for a minute to think of the right words that Professor Cline used, "Interdimensional Dark Matter Residue."

I looked at her blankly and Beth let out a slight chuckle.

"That's why Cline said 'an enzyme', Interdimensional Dark Matter Residue is a nightmare to say. It's not, like, dangerous or anything," she continued, "It just means that you have a better connection to The Multiverse than most normal people."

I snickered when she said normal. "I don't even remember what normal is anymore."

"Yeah," Beth sighed as she held my hand slightly tighter, "I don't either."

I locked my fingers in her hand and looked for an explanation in her face. She stared straight ahead, maybe lost in thought of what a 'normal' life might look like. In some Multiverse out there, maybe she does have a normal life. No gifts, no fighting, just Beth living her life with her family. Maybe we would meet, maybe we wouldn't. But the fact is that, right now, we met, she has gifts, and there is definitely something that is brewing between multiverses. There might even be something brewing between us.

I moved over a little closer to Beth. I wanted to kiss her. I've wanted to kiss her since last night but this situation is murky at best. I didn't want to seem like a creep that was making a move on her when she was vulnerable but I felt like this was THE moment, like the perfect moment in every movie I've ever seen.

"Listen, Beth, I…"

Beth let go of my hand and held it up in a 'talk to the hand' motion.

"Wait." she said staring in the direction of the Science Hall. "Do you hear that?"

At the moment, all I heard was my heart pounding, but I looked in the direction she was staring in. I didn't hear anything, but I saw a flash of light. We looked at each other.

I gasped loudly, "What was that?"

"I'm not sure," Beth said, "But I feel weird. Like Spidey-Sense or something."

Beth stood up and started running towards the Science Hall, her cape blowing behind her, internally thinking about what multiverse would have Han Solo and Batgirl investigating a disturbance. I took off after her. With the cold air in my face, I caught up to her in no time, we were a short distance away from the building. Beth motioned for us to duck behind a hedge across from the building.

In front of the sidewalk leading to the Science Hall was a gateway. Its blueish-green light lit up the immediate area. There was no one around it, at least not yet, just a lone gateway. I looked to Beth in amazement and she shrugged. I pointed to my feet and mouthed to her, "Should we stay hidden?" and she nodded. A few seconds later I was glad she said yes.

111

Three shapes emerged from the gateway, two medium sized and one larger one. The big guy wasn't as big as the ice monster from last night, but still pretty big. The other two were more slender. All three beings seemed human in shape, but not quite exactly. They wore cloaks like old druid robes.

We watched carefully from behind the hedge as one of the monks knelt down on the sidewalk in front of the Science Hall and touched the ground. Blue light emanated from the spot where it was and ceased just as quickly as it began. The monk stood up, turned towards the other two figures and held something in front of them. I couldn't quite make it out because of the way it was facing, but I'm sure it wasn't something friendly.

The monk placed the item on the ground again and within seconds lightning bolts stretched from the portal and started crawling towards the item on the ground. It was almost like the lightning was searching for the thing, like a craving.

I turned to Beth again to ask her what to do now, and she was gone. I had a mild panic attack as I looked over the hedge and saw her crouched behind a bush on the other side of the street. I have no idea how she got over there so fast, or so quietly, but she saw me and waved me over.

I quickly, and quietly, dashed over to Beth as she was peeking around to get a better look. I put my hand on her shoulder, so she knew I was there, and looked over the top of the bush. From here I didn't have a better view of the monks, but I did have a decent look at the item as it was slowly being caressed by the lightning tendrils. It began to levitate a few inches from the ground.

It was a Rift Ripper.

I started to feel a warmth next to me and my hand got very warm. I took my hand off of Beth's shoulder and she turned to look at me, her hazel-sunset eyes now almost fully orange. There was no trace of fear in her face like last night, just determination.

"We need that Rift Ripper!" Beth whispered to me in an almost otherworldly voice. Before I could agree, she took off towards the trio.

I ran after her. Just from a math perspective there were three of them and two of us. I had no idea what they were, at this point I've decided not to try to predict anything. They could be people, ice monsters or tentacles in a humanoid shape. Who the hell even knew at this point. All I knew was Beth could not do this alone and I had to be there to help.

Beth lept into the air, aimed a fireball towards the hovering Rift Ripper and she landed on the back of the biggest of the trio. The Rift Ripper slid a few feet away, the electrical tendrils almost lost their grip on it and crawled to grab it again. The big guy now had a fire demon on it's back and started to melt into a puddle on the ground.

At least now we knew they were made of ice.

The two other monks, the smaller ones, turned around to see their former friend (do ice monsters have friends?) melted on the ground with a very angry Batgirl standing on its cloak, fire radiating from her hands. I caught up to her and flicked my wrist, and my Rig made the hammer and shield from the night before.

We stood there for a moment, looking at each other when the monks shed their robes and we got a good look at what we were fighting. They were mostly ice, but with some human pieces. The armor they wore under their robes showed us that these creatures were seasoned fighters. Here's what was really strange: They had human heads, and the guy had a human left arm and the girl's right arm was human. Everything else looked like ice, the guy was bald and the girl had short, bleached-white hair. They both had soulless crystal-blue eyes that just drilled into me.

"What the hell are these things?" I asked Beth. I was a little scared at what I was looking at.

"I'm not sure." Beth replied with an echo in her voice.

"Zombies?" I was whispering. Why was I whispering?

Beth didn't reply to me but kept her eyes fixed on the two creatures in front of us. The two ice zombies didn't move, they just kept staring at us. If we moved in the slightest way, their eyes would follow almost like they were studying our movements. It was a little unnerving. After a moment, Beth spoke.

"Where are you from?" She demanded.

The bald zombie guy turned his head to Beth while the white haired girl zombie kept her gaze locked on me.

"Where we are from doesn't matter," they both said in unison in a cold, hollow voice, "What matters is that soon we will all be one."

I cast a sideways glance to Beth.

"Beth, that doesn't sound good at all." Beth nodded in agreement. Feeling a little brave I asked a follow up question to the two creatures. "What the hell does that even mean?"

They shifted their gaze so now the girl was looking at Beth and the guy was looking at me.

"It means the end, and the beginning." they both replied, robotically.

The fact that they were still talking in unison was freaking me out. It reminded me of those two little girls in *The Shining*, and I did not like that movie at all. It freaked me out as a kid and I still can't watch it. All I knew was my name was not Danny and I really did not want to play with these two.

Beth sent another mini fireball towards the Rift Ripper to knock it further from the lightning coming from the gateway. The electricity curled away from it and the two zombies let out a haunting, hollow shriek.

"You can not prevent what is coming!" they yelled out and charged at us. As they ran toward us I saw their icy arms turn into sharp points. Before they could reach us, Beth said some words and moved her hands, and before I knew it we were surrounded on all sides by a six- or seven- foot high wall of fire.

"Hopefully this buys us a few seconds." She looked at me intensely. "Are you ready for this?"

"Fuck no," I said quickly, "But I haven't been ready for any of this."

Beth gave me a little smirk.

"Just keep moving and keep the Rift Ripper away from them. I want to bring it back to Cline if we can."

I nodded as I saw these two figures leap over the wall and land in front of us. As soon as their feet hit the ground, they charged at us. Bleach made a beeline toward Beth while the Baldy charged at me. They were both unnaturally quick and their movements were a little erratic and unpredictable.

I saw Beth produce her red-bladed sword from her rig and the blade of it burst into flames. "Ha! I knew it!" these words flew from my mouth as I turned to face the icy bald man approaching me with a quickness. I had a sneaking suspicion from the very moment she showed me that blade, that it would catch fire. I need that. Like NOW.

Baldy ran at me with a shoulder tackle but my shield took the brunt of the impact. He pushed me back a couple of feet. He did a backflip off of my shield like a ninja and landed in a stance like a runner and dashed at me again, this time with his icy jousting arm straight ahead like a javelin. I sidestepped before he got to me, towards the Rift Ripper and took a little swing at it to knock it away. It didn't look like the lightning was creeping towards it anymore, but the lightning was still sparking out of the gateway. The fact that I could see the gateway now meant that Beth had dropped her shield and I took this moment to glance over at her since Baldy overshot me.

Beth and the Bleach were locked in an intense battle. Beth looked a lot stronger than she did the night before (when we almost died), but then again Bleach was about the same size as Beth, not a towering giant. I saw Baldy running back toward me out of the corner of my eye just as I saw Beth cut off Bleach's ice arm. Bleach grabbed the spot where her arm used to be then Beth wrapped her in something like a fire whip and then Bleach was evaporated. Baldy must have seen this, too, because he turned like a *Tron* lightcycle and headed straight toward Beth.

I ran as fast as I could after him but this thing was super fast. Beth dodged out of his way but Baldy had another plan. His ice pick arm turned into a hook and snatched Beth by the cape and dragged her quickly towards the gateway. Beth dug her sword into the ground to try to slow him down. It worked, but I didn't know for how long.

While I was running, I thought of a dagger. My sword and hammer combo disappeared and a dagger showed up in my right hand. I reached Beth and did the only thing I could think of. I slid next to her and started to cut off the cape of her costume. I didn't take much of a cut, a quick slit was all it needed and the cape tore off of the costume and Baldy ran through the gateway with a cape, and part of the upper shoulders of Beth's costume, and the gateway closed behind him. Beth lay on the ground a little out of breath, slowly returning back to Regular Beth and I sat next to her making sure Baldy didn't come back. I looked at her and said the only thing I could think of: "Happy Halloween."

Beth looked at me and let out a little laugh as I helped her to her feet. Her costume was shredded; some cuts on the leg and midsection, and the shoulders and upper back were pretty much ripped off. In the cold air I could swear I saw steam rising from her now bare shoulders. She looked down and around at her costume and looked at me.

"At least it was a shitty costume." Beth let out a little chuckle and we started to walk towards the Rift Ripper on the ground a few yards away from us.

This Rift Ripper looked kind of like the last one, a small three curved-pronged disk with a gem in the middle, but it was a little bigger and more intricate. Unlike the other one we found, though, this gem was glowing bright bluish-purple, not a faint glow like the other one. I reached out to grab it and Beth held my arm back. She kneeled down and waved her fingers in front of the Rift Ripper and created something that looked like that fire bubble from Sonic the Hedgehog around it and hovered it in the air in front of us.

"I don't think it's safe to touch this one," Beth eyes were firmly focused on the ripper, "I can feel a lot of dimensional energy coming off of this thing."

I nodded in agreement. I felt a little weird about it too, but I didn't know if maybe it was the sensitivity that Beth said I have or that I was coming off of the high of an adrenaline rush.

"So what's next?" I asked.

"I'm bringing this back to Cline," Beth said flatly, staring at the ripper encased in the fire bubble, "I have questions for him." She looked at me. "When we were telling Cline about the ice monster we fought yesterday, didn't he seem to get, like, really uneasy for a minute."

"A little, I guess," I replied, "Like before you blew up at him."

Beth said uneasily, "I have a feeling he's holding something back, like there is something he's not telling me."

"Do you want me to come back with you?" I prodded.

Beth shook her head. "No," Beth touched her necklace and a gateway appeared, "If Cline isn't telling me something, I think he might be a little more open if it's just me and him."

"Oh, ok." I really wanted to know if Cline knew more than what he was letting on, but if Beth felt that she needed to ask him on her own I wasn't going to push.

"Hey," Beth grabbed my hand, "For what it's worth, I'm glad I came out tonight."

"I am too," I said as I fell into her eyes again, "I just wish that every time we would get together we weren't fighting some type of monsters."

"Yeah," Beth laughed a little, "Maybe next time."

I felt my ears perk up a little. "So what you're saying is...." I was pleased to hear her refer to the possibility of a 'next time'.

117

"That we will talk about it later." Beth gave me a smirk and turned towards her gateway. "I want to get this talk with Cline out of the way first."

I smiled, said ok and the gateway closed behind her as she stepped through.

CHAPTER THIRTEEN

I barely slept as I looked at my clock and saw that it was 7:00 a.m. I think I got in at maybe two or three o'clock and just spent the rest of the night tossing and turning. These last forty-eight hours had been so mentally and physically draining that I needed to try to sort everything out. I was overwhelmed by all that had been told, or had happened to me so I decided to get up and go for a walk into town to grab some breakfast.

When I got out to the living room, I saw that Scott's door was wide open and his bed looked like it wasn't slept in. He probably hooked up with someone or just crashed on a couch at the party. My mind started retelling the fight we had the night before. I know he was drunk and I maybe could have diffused the situation a little differently, but that didn't change the fact that we needed to talk. I went to grab my jacket but couldn't find it, so I threw on a poncho and left.

I went outside and saw toilet paper streamers on most of the trees. I smiled a little and shook my head before the cold hit me sending a shiver down my spine. It was bitter cold today, but after dealing with ice creatures over the last few days I was ready to pack it up and transfer to Florida for my senior year. The campus was eerily quiet, probably because it was the Saturday after Halloween, at like quarter after seven in the morning and everyone was either passed out or still drunk.

I put my headphones on and traipsed into town. "Why I'm Here" by Oleander came through my ears, a great song that was just moody enough to let my mind wander while I walked. I really didn't know what I could say to Scott, but I really wanted to try to sort out this whole deal. Should I just tell him everything? Maybe I would just casually go up to him and say 'Hey dude, Beth and I are protecting The Multiverse. See ya later!' and leave it at that. I'm pretty sure he would have some questions.

The fact that he didn't like Beth at all really was sticking with me. Scott had, at times, some questionable choices in women, but I was there for him every time he made a mistake. One of them actually tried to stab him with a carving knife because Scott and I went to my Grandparents house on Long Beach Island for a couple of weeks in the summer of our senior year. The nut, I think her name was Carla or something that, was convinced that Scott cheated on her while we were gone. He did not, in fact we hung out at the beach and the arcade the whole time. She lunged at him, he dodged and we got the hell out of there. As it turns out, she got committed for being actually clinically insane.

But the point is I was there for him. I supported him through his good and not so good choices. Beth and I aren't even "a thing" yet, but I think we might be a thing soon though. He is giving me such shit about her that I am kind of starting to resent him for it. Even though he was drunk last night, I know in his mind there was some truth behind what he was saying. They say alcohol is like an amplifier, and last night, he was turned up to eleven.

Then my mind wandered to Beth. She didn't like Scott because he kept calling her a witch, which is fair I guess, but the two of them haven't even ever talked. I felt like that might be something that needs to happen, maybe if they would talk they might start to get along, maybe even like each other! That would be the best case scenario, I guess the worst case would be that she sets him on fire. Yeah, I might have to work them both over slowly to get that idea going.

I got to the little breakfast shop in town, ordered my sandwich and my *cafe mocha*, and grabbed a window seat while I waited for my order. I stared out of the window and just took in the quietness of the town this morning. There weren't a lot of cars coming through, barely anyone on the streets, it was just really peaceful. I think since I first met Beth this is the first time I've actually been able to take a breath and just relax a little.

The semester would be winding to a close soon, Thanksgiving break was a couple of weeks away and then after that Christmas break. Amazingly, even with the amount of insanity I've been through, I'm still passing. Barely, but it counts.

A cute girl I recognized from campus brought over my breakfast and I made no notice of my food. I took a bite as I looked outside. I needed to talk to Scott, but I really wanted to know what Beth meant when she said we would talk about maybe going somewhere later. Like how soon was later? With the bombshell she dropped on me last night I just didn't know when the right time to approach her for a maybe-actual date would be. I should probably just play it cool today and see if she found out anything from Professor Cline.

"Wonderwall" came on the cafe speakers and I couldn't help but smile a little, it made me instantly think of Beth again. I really wanted to tell her how I feel, scream it from the top of Skytop Tower, but deep down I knew it was a bad move. We seemed to get closer when we didn't mean to, not by me forcing the issue, but just through conversation. In my previous relationships I always bared my feelings too fast. I think with Shelly I told her I loved her like two weeks in or something crazy like that. I made a decision to actively not do that this time, even if what I was feeling was even stronger than before. Hell, we're not even together! I really have to watch to not ruin anything before it even starts.

The little chime on the door rang as I continued my morning breakfast and deep thinking when a voice snapped me out of my thoughts.

"Hey." Scott said as he stood next to the chair across from me. I don't know how I missed him arriving; he walked past the window I was staring out of.

He looked rough, and was surprisingly not in the Chewbacca costume. I figured he'd still be drunk and sleeping in it. He had on the darkest sunglasses I had ever seen, they reminded me of Tom Cruise's in *Risky Business*.

"Hey." I said through a mouthful of sandwich. I could feel the tension in the air and I hated it. I pushed the chair away from the table with my foot, and motioned with my open hand for him to sit. Scott sat down across from me and let out a big breath.

"I went back to the dorm and saw you weren't there," Scott sounded really distant, "I figured you were either still out with her or you were here." The cute waitress dropped off Scott's coffee and pancakes and gave Scott a little wink.

"I got in late last night," I replied, "We spent the whole night talking."

Well it wasn't a complete lie.

"Talking." Scott repeated as he took a sip of coffee. "Listen, about what I said last night…"

I stepped in, "You were drunk man, I get it."

"Let me finish." Scott said with kind of a harsh tone. "Yeah, I was drunk, but I meant most of what I said. She's trouble. There is a really weird gut feeling I'm getting," Scott took off his sunglasses and stared at me through bloodshot eyes. "And I feel like there is something you're not telling me."

Oh shit, I thought to myself as Scott continued.

"I'm not sure what it is, but there's something off about you. It's not like with Shelly, you were just like blindly in love with her even though I kinda saw it coming. I even told you I had suspicions about her and you always had an excuse as to why Shelly was faithful to you." Scott practically inhaled a huge chunk of pancake. "This time it's almost like, I don't know, there's just something different. Like you are trying to get hurt."

"What do you mean?" It didn't seem like he was going down the path I thought he was going to go down.

"After Shelly, you were a wreck. You cut yourself off from everyone because you poured your heart out to this girl really early on and she took advantage of it and shit all over you." He took a sip of his coffee, as punctuation. "You locked yourself in your room listening to Bush and Stabbing Westward on repeat until Jen and I had to drag you out of there. I just feel like you're falling for a girl that you have no chance with because you think it's safe. It's not."

It's not safe at all, I thought to myself, *but not for the reason you think.*

"Being into someone and not having them feel the same way about you sometimes hurts more than actually getting hurt while you're actually in a relationship with them. Trust me it's happened to me and it sucks, I just played it off really well. You wear your emotions on your sleeve, it always gets you hurt and then you get super defensive when someone calls you out on it. Before Shelly there was Jess, before Jess there was Christine and the list goes on. Shelly was the one that hurt you the most, by far, but it's almost like you are trying to force this thing with what's-her-face, Beth, because of some type of challenge and it's going to lead to you broken again. I know it."

I felt myself get annoyed. I'm not sure why, most of what Scott was saying about my past was true. I am the type to fall hard and fast for a girl, it's just who I am. A lot of the time, I was blind to the clear signs in front of me that either the girl was using me, cheating on me, or just done with me. Damn, thinking back I guess I really have had a run of shitty luck, but this thing that might be starting Beth was different. Besides that, Scott was way off with why I haven't been honest about Beth anyway.

"Scott, listen," I did my best to stay even tempered, "I hear what you are saying but, trust me when I say this, you are dead wrong about Beth. Yeah I may have had some blinders on in the past, and thanks for pointing out all of my failed romances by the way, but Beth is really different. Yes, she didn't really seem to like me when we first met, but if you actually would take a few minutes to talk to her you would find that she's actually really great. She has her…" I paused for a second and took a sip of coffee, "demons that she is working through, but so does everyone! Besides, I would rather pour my heart out to a girl in hopes that there is something there, and I'm not saying I've done that with Beth by the way, than do a Tarzan dick-swing from one meaningless relationship to another."

I regretted what I said as soon as it came out of my mouth. I shouldn't be attacking Scott, I should be telling him what is actually going on, but at this moment I guess I was more annoyed at how badly he was misjudging what was going on with Beth. What's worse is I knew it was all my fault for not telling him everything, but I couldn't, not here and now anyway.

Scott stared at me for a minute, processing what I just said. He shook his head and let out a little bit of a grunt as he stood up to leave. I guess what I said hit a nerve somewhere.

"Scott..." He held up a finger to cut me off.

"Jake, you're a big boy." Scott's tone seemed a little condescending, "You can make your own decisions on who to waste your time with. I'm not going to hold your hand while you crash and burn with her." I started to tell him to wait but he cut me off again. "If you feel like not being a dick about this, we can talk more tomorrow after I get back from my cousin's, but all I'm going to say is that sometimes it's better to do things like I do them. It keeps the hurt to a minimum."

Scott picked up his coffee and left, I knew better than to chase him. In the few times we had argued during our lifelong friendship, it was always better to just let us cool off and we may or may not talk about this later. Sometimes it meant things wouldn't get resolved, but most of the time it would work out fine.

I felt like shit though, I should have just told him at least some of what was going on instead of getting super-defensive about Beth. The problem is that I really don't think Beth wants Scott knowing anything about what she is or what we are doing. Maybe I should talk to her about it, hell, it couldn't hurt anyway just to ask her or Professor Cline.

I looked at the clock on the wall and saw that it was just about eight thirty. It was probably too early to head over to the cave, I really didn't want to go back to the dorm yet and then I remembered that today was the first of November. I think there were a couple of games coming out today for Playstation so I decided to visit the Poughkeepsie Galleria to pick them up early. Maybe I would even get a chance to play them before my world would inevitably be turned upside down again. Games usually helped me and Scott get past whatever disagreements were happening too, so this was a win all around.

I got back to campus at about one in the afternoon. I would have been out a lot sooner but after I bought Crash Bandicoot 2: Cortex Strikes Back, the guy at the counter had me try this really weird game, Parappa the Rapper. It was about a cartoon dog that was in love with a flower and battle rapped an onion and a moose to win her love. I don't know, it was nuts, so I bought that too and then spent a couple of hours in the arcade. The arcade had a couple of cool new games in it, Top Skater which had you almost actually skateboarding, and Virtua Fighter 3, which was probably the prettiest fighting game I have ever played. They also had Street Fighter III, which I tried but it just didn't feel like Street Fighter to me for some reason. The graphics seemed to look sloppy somehow and the timing of the moves seemed off. I decided that I would stick to Super Street Fighter II for a while longer.

The walk back to the dorm was a chilly one, the cold was really hitting early this year. It wasn't freezing but it sure as hell wasn't comfy out either. It was bugging me that I couldn't find my jacket, no matter what the temperature was outside it was always perfect. The last time I remember seeing it was in my truck and then I remembered where it was, Beth had it. I could feel a really goofy smile form on my face from the memory of her in my jacket. Was Scott right? Was I falling too hard for Beth with nothing to show for it? No, I really think there is something there but I've also been known to think I see something there when there clearly isn't. I decided that I needed to find out for sure, I had to just straight out ask her.

I rounded the corner to DuBois Hall and looked up at my window. Scott had probably left by now, at least I hoped he had. Not enough time had passed yet, I've known him long enough how long he takes to simmer down after an argument. He really wouldn't be in a talking mood until tonight. Maybe tomorrow I would grab a pizza and we'd talk, play the new games and move past our disagreement. As I was playing out scenarios in my head, a friendly voice snapped me out of my daydream.

"Hey."

I turned as I saw Beth standing in front of my building. She was wearing her normal dress and stocking combo with a new addition, an army green jacket with various patches on it. My jacket. It looked great on her.

"Hey," I replied, trying to fight back the goofy smile I had earlier when I thought of this very picture, "I was wondering where my jacket was."

"Do you want it back?" Beth gave me a look that would have turned me into a puddle if I didn't already like her.

"Oh no!" I stammered out. "It's cold out, wear it! It looks better on you than it does on me anyway."

Beth smiled and brushed her hair away from her eyes before shaking her head like she remembered why she was here in the first place. "Cline wants to see both of us."

"I'm guessing it's not for happy news?" Now I was cold *and* nervous.

"Yeah, I don't think so," Beth shook her head, "I told him what happened last night and he got really concerned."

"I don't like when he gets concerned," I said, "That means trouble."

"Yeah," she said solemnly, "I filled him in about last night and he seemed to get really, just, weird again. Something about these ice creatures is unsettling him."

"Then we should probably go see what's going on." I wanted to know what was happening, and what our roles were in this whole thing.

I followed Beth back around the corner of Dubois Hall and in a flash we were in the cave. Over the last few months I guess my body has settled into gateway travel, I had no side effects anymore which was really nice. When we popped in I saw The Professor working on his computer with both devices hooked up to it. A quick look at the monitors showed letters and numbers that I couldn't make any sense of. He spun his chair around as we approached.

"Mister Howard!" He said as we approached. "I see Elizabeth has found you, good."

"Yeah." I was so anxious. I was careful not to sound sarcastic, but really, what kind of response did he want? I mean, obviously she found me. I'm here, right? Cut to the chase, Professor Cline! Did I sound sarcastic? Geez. It came out snarky, didn't it?

"Elizabeth told me that she also filled you in on the results of the blood test." The Professor was all business today. That was a relief.

I nodded and Beth moved to her spot near the corner of Professor Cline's desk.

"I wanted you both here," he said as he turned back to the computer, "because after the information that Elizabeth told me last night, and the fact that we now have a second one of these devices, I am developing some major concerns."

Professor Cline had more wires hooked to the newer ripper. This one had a lot more intricate detail than the first one and came apart. Pieces were sorted neatly on The Professor's desk, and the gem in the center was flashing like a blue light special at K-Mart. The old ripper had wires hooked to it again, but was a more solid construction than its newer, bigger brother.

I felt a wave of nerves come over me and Beth and I shared a look.

"These devices, the Rift Rippers as you call them," Cline began, "seem to not do much on their own. I am just able to pull random coordinates off of them, more so from the one you both found last night. However, would you both back up a little please."

Beth and I stepped away from the desk and Professor Cline stood up. He moved the dim Rift Ripper to one side of the desk and the other one to the other side. He spun both of them slightly, hit a button on his computer and a beam of crystal blue light formed between them and began pulsing. We looked at each other and back to the beam and when the beam started pulsing faster Professor Cline hit the button again and the beam disappeared.

"Whoa." Beth said in amazement.

"Was that beam dangerous?" I asked.

Professor Cline moved the Rift Rippers out of alignment with each other.

"At the moment, no, but potentially yes." He looked at Beth and I with concern. "From what my calculations can gather, that line represents a joining of multiverses."

I didn't know what that meant but I saw Beth's eyes grow wide. "Does that mean…"

Professor Cline nodded his head but I was still confused.

"Um, can someone fill me in?" I asked both of them.

"Mister Howard, what that means is that someone or something from another multiverse is trying to join multiverses together for some reason. The problem with doing that is that there can only be one instance of a multiverse in any given space. Trying to join multiverses together will lead to the destruction of one, or more."

None of that sounded good at all.

"This is what The Conclave was formed for, to prevent this." Professor Cline continued. "For centuries, people have been trying to do something like this and we have prevented them. This, this is the closest anyone has ever come to actually accomplishing it." Professor Cline sounded a little shaken with that last statement.

There was a long pause before someone spoke.

"So," Beth spoke first, "did anything happen there, between those two points I mean?"

"No, Elizabeth, not to the best of my knowledge." Cline stated. "I was able to make it a closed environment so there would be no repercussions. However, I do not want both of these here together any longer than they need to be." He turned to me and I felt a sense of dread come over me. "Mister Howard, I would like you to keep the inert one somewhere away from here."

"What? Why?" I did not want to be responsible for that crazy thing.

"Uh, yeah, is that a good idea?" Beth agreed. "That thing seems really dangerous."

"Perfectly." the Professor started. "Right now the only way to get that reaction here is for me to actually activate it. The problem is that if they are in close enough proximity to each other, they might be able to be activated remotely somehow and that can be catastrophic. They need to be apart and by Mister Howard keeping this somewhere, we still have eyes on it in case something happens with it. With the distance to Mister Howards dorm and the mass of this mountain itself, it should be safe from being remotely activated. I have told The Conclave about the newest device and I am going to be sending it to them first thing in the morning. Half a world away should be a good enough distance." Professor Cline gave a bit of a nervous laugh.

Beth began to protest and I grabbed her hand to stop her.

"If you think it will be safer that way, and you can guarantee this thing isn't going to kill me in my sleep, then fine. I'll keep it in my dorm." I agreed.

Beth's grip on my hand tightened.

"Are you sure?" Beth clearly wasn't.

I nodded, Professor Cline handed me the Rift Ripper and I put it in the pocket of my poncho.

"Thank you Mister Howard." The Professor turned his attention to Beth. "Elizabeth, since you already used your personal gateway for today please bring Mister Howard to the Griffon Gateway. I need to contact The Conclave and tell them of my findings."

Beth nodded and in a few moments we were in the basement of The Griffon. She looked a little shaken by what we had just witnessed.

After a quiet moment, I asked Beth, "Are you okay?"

She nodded. "In training, Cline would tell me the theory of things like this. I just figured I would never actually witness it. It's freaking me out a little. I'll be fine though."

"Okay." I pulled the Rift Ripper out of my pocket and looked at it. The gem in the middle was faintly glowing blue. "I'm going to keep this in my room, buried somewhere to add even more space between this and the other one. Maybe I'll dig a hole and bury it as deep as I can go."

Beth chuckled a little. In the face of everything that we just heard, at least I could still get her to smile. I took a deep breath and decided to take a shot.

"Hey," I could feel my heart pounding and was sure Beth could hear it.

Beth raised her eyebrow and gave me a curious look.

"So I was thinking," I was still mentally forming the words I wanted to say, "The last two times we've been out somewhere and started talking things have tried to kill us."

"Yeah I noticed that." Beth laughed.

"So, like, if you're not doing anything later do you want to come by the dorm and like eat and talk and watch a movie?" I heard my brain ask myself what the hell I was doing.

"Like, a date?" Beth asked, and raised her eyebrow again.

Even in this cold basement I could feel the sweat starting to pour out of anywhere it could.

"Yeah! Well, no." I stuttered. Then the words spewed forth in a torrent as quickly as I could think of them: "I consider a date, like, actually going somewhere. I just figured we could get a pizza or something and maybe rent a movie and just, like, relax and talk." Then I caught my breath. "Hopefully nothing will break into my dorm and try to murder us."

This is it, I thought to myself, *this is what death feels like.*

"I don't think Scott will be happy with me hanging out in your dorm, not that I really care about that anyway." That wasn't a 'no,' but it wasn't a 'yes,' either.

"He's not around tonight. He's up in Ithaca to celebrate his cousin's twenty-first birthday." I was happy to report this news.

The silence lasted for a while, at least it seemed that way. After seventy-two years, or in reality maybe twenty seconds, she smiled at me. "Sure. I could use a normal night after the last few days."

I nearly fainted.

"Oh, okay!" I was a little surprised. "Uh, do you want to come by around seven?"

Beth hesitated. She was probably thinking of backing out.

"Only under one condition." She said after a moment.

"What's that?" I hoped I could oblige.

Beth took a step towards me, looked slightly up into my eyes and gave me a smile that would make me do anything for her. I'm such a sucker for a pretty smile. And pretty eyes. And, well, her. "I get to pick the movie."

I laughed nervously, said okay and told her to ring the bell for room 402.

"Okay then!" Beth smiled at me and couldn't help but smile back. I was ecstatic. "I'll see you later, at seven." She stepped back into the gateway and I left feeling happier than I have in a long time.

CHAPTER FOURTEEN

I practically floated the whole way back to the dorm after leaving The Griffon. The fact that I actually got out of my own way and asked Beth to a "not date" was a big step for me; and the fact that she said yes was an even bigger one.

As soon as I walked in my door, I put the Rift Ripper in my nightstand drawer and went in full cleaning mode, like the kind of cleaning when you are expecting your parents to come visit. I was a whirling dervish of arms and legs scrubbing, wiping, stowing and storing everything to make this place look great. Scott and I weren't slobs by any stretch, but we were two twenty-one year old guys, and cleaning wasn't at the top of our priority list. If this was a movie montage in some romantic comedy, "Friday I'm In Love" by The Cure would probably be playing over scenes of me cleaning my little heart out. I cleaned, left to pick up chips, drinks and pizza, I got back at 6:45 PM. It was beginning to snow a little as I got inside. I freshened up a bit and waited for Beth to show up, patiently, with my heart in my throat.

I know I said this wasn't a date, but this sure as hell felt like one.

The buzzer rang at a couple of minutes past seven and I don't think I've moved faster in my life to answer anything as quick as I did to buzz Beth up. As she came upstairs I glanced over to my reflection in the mirror and gave myself a simple command. "Don't fuck this up and rush things, stay cool." I said aloud. My subconscious needed to tell me that.

I think I played out every possible scenario as she was heading up to my room. This is something I would have normally done. At times I tend to overthink things, but this was different. Knowing that there is a Multiverse out there, that every decision essentially spawns an alternate timeline that plays out differently, suddenly put a huge weight on what was supposed to be a night of talking, hanging out and watching a movie with a girl that I really liked.

Beth's knock at the door snapped me out of my multiverse-induced, momentary daydream. I opened the door and nearly didn't recognize the girl standing in front of me. Beth was wearing her boots, I'm pretty sure I've never seen her in anything else, a pair of slightly ripped jeans, a SUNY New Paltz sweatshirt, my jacket and her hair was in a ponytail again. She looked like a normal college student, not a defender of The Multiverse, and she looked perfect. She gave me a smile as I invited her inside.

"It's freezing outside," Beth said as she brushed some snowflakes off of her- I mean my- jacket, "I had no idea it was supposed to snow, it started when I was halfway here."

"You walked?" I asked as I slung the jacket over a chair.

"Yeah, I had to." Beth pointed to her necklace, "I can't use it till after midnight and Cline went out and took his Jeep."

Beth looked around and nodded her head. "Nice place, how did you guys get a suite?"

"Scott," I said, "He's lived on campus since he was a Freshman. I just moved in this year because his roommate just left, we think he cracked during finals last year or something."

There was a little bit of an awkward silence as we just stood there. Suddenly Beth reached into her sweatshirt pocket and pulled out two VHS boxes.

"So," Beth looked at me and smiled, "You said I could pick the movie. I rented two and am leaving the decision up to you."

"Okay," I said nervously, "What are my choices?"

I noticed we were still standing.

"Hold on," I said, "Why don't you go sit down and I'll bring the pizza over and then you can tell me what my choices are."

Beth sat on the futon and I brought the pizza to the coffee table. I sat down as she spun to face me and sat cross-legged with a serious look on her face.

"Jake," she said in a serious tone, "This is a very important decision. The movie you pick will alter the very fabric of time and space and determine what happens in countless multiverses."

I felt all of the blood rush out of my face and instantly felt clammy. Beth looked at me and just started laughing.

"I'm kidding." Beth said before adding, "But there is one movie I really want to see over the other one. I'm wondering if you will pick the right one."

I let out a sigh of relief and shook my head to clear the anxiety. "Do you have any idea how much you freaked me out just now?"

Beth smiled at me in a way I haven't seen before, like a playful way.

"I know, I'm sorry, that was mean." she said as she laughed again. "Listen, I don't want to talk about multiverse stuff tonight so I just wanted to throw that out there, just kind of get it out of the way so maybe we can hang out and hopefully nothing tries to kill us."

"A perfectly normal sentence." I laughed.

"I know, right," she giggled in agreement.

Beth put both VHS boxes between us.

"Pulp Fiction and The English Patient." Beth said. "One of these I want to watch tonight and the other one I don't."

I knew for sure that I did not want to see *The English Patient*, that movie sounded boring as hell.

"Do I get a hint?" I asked.

"Nope." Beth leaned back and smirked.

I've seen *Pulp Fiction* a hundred times and love it. I asked Beth if she had seen either one and she wouldn't even answer that. I put my hand on one box, and then the other and looked at Beth. Her expression didn't change, she had a pretty good poker face. Finally I made my decision.

"Pulp Fiction." I decided confidently.

Beth looked at me with a solemn look. "You chose," Beth looked me dead in the eyes and smiled, "wisely."

"Did you just quote Indiana Jones at me?" I joked.

She smiled and nodded. I replayed the words in my head reminding me not to rush things and confess my love right then and there.

"Truth be told," Beth said, "I love Pulp Fiction. I've seen it so many times."

"Me too!" I said, "It's such a great movie!"

"I know!"

I opened the pizza and saw Beth smile when she saw I ordered half ham and pineapple and half plain. We both grabbed a slice of each and I glanced out the window. The snow was really coming down hard and part of me hoped this wasn't going to be the start of an ice monster attack in my dorm.

"So what would have happened if I picked The English Patient?" I asked before taking a bite.

"Looks like we'll never know." Beth looked at me and smiled. "I really didn't want to see that anyway, I'm not big on wartime romances. I just picked it up to see what you would do."

A piece of molten pineapple stuck to the roof of my mouth (of course) so I started fanning my mouth and took a big swig of Mountain Dew. Very smooth, I thought to myself as Beth chuckled.

We started talking about anything but The Multiverse. I told her about my family and she told me about hers. We talked about relationships. She dated someone last year, Donnie, and it didn't work out, and I went into a shortened version of my whole thing with Shelly. I got into some more stories from high school that probably should have resulted in grievous bodily harm, and had her laughing. Her laugh was intoxicating and with every smile I had to keep reminding myself to play it cool. Beth mentioned that she was going to her Dad's in Westchester to visit tomorrow and she would be back Monday afternoon. *Hopefully everything wouldn't go to shit by then,* I thought to myself.

A couple of hours and an entire pizza later we decided to put the movie on. Both of us have seen *Pulp Fiction* way too much because we were quoting lines as it went on and adding in our own commentary. During the dance scene I stood up and grabbed her hand. She knew exactly what I was thinking and we started dancing along with the movie and nearly collapsed laughing afterwards. Later, as Butch went down the stairs to save Marsellus Wallace from the basement I looked over to Beth.

She was fast asleep.

I studied her for a minute and two thoughts popped into my head. She's sleeping because either I bored her to death or she just felt really comfortable with me. I was pretty sure it was the latter reason, we seemed to have a really good time. I had a decision to make though, do I wake her up and take her home or just let her sleep here.

I got up, looked out the window and made my decision. It looked nasty out there, I really didn't want to drive in that.

When I turned around I looked at Beth again. Apparently she moved and was now laying down on the futon, her feet where I was previously sitting. Just being here, looking at her got me thinking. She's smart, funny, beautiful and I knew that I've been in love with her for a long while.

I walked into my room, grabbed a blanket and gently laid it over her. She made a sound, just a little breath or something, and stirred a little. I decided to go into my room before I did anything stupid and tried to go to bed, knowing the girl of my dreams was asleep one room away from me.

When I woke up the next morning I was blinded by the reflection of the snow outside. The clock read nine and my eyes took a minute to focus on the world around me. My feet hit the cold tile and I walked out to the living room to see if Beth maybe wanted to go grab some breakfast somewhere.

The futon was empty. The checkered blanket I put on Beth last night was neatly folded and there was a note laying on top of it.

Jake,
Thanks for last night, I had a great time.
I didn't want to wake you up so I just left, thanks for the blanket.
We need to hang out again, or maybe go somewhere.
See you Monday,
Beth

I plopped down on the futon, re-read the note more times than I care to admit and replayed the previous night. That was the first night in a long time that I felt, well, great. My heart actually felt normal, it's really hard to explain. It's like I've had this empty space in there since Shelly that I just haven't been able to fill with anything. Now I felt like my heart was bursting. I really think this might be the start of something real. A proper date might actually be in order soon, as long as The Multiverse can keep its shit together and stop attacking us.

I looked out the window and saw that there was a good foot of snow on the ground. Scott wasn't going to be around until probably seven or eight o'clock tonight since Ithaca probably got more snow than here. Beth wasn't going to be around until tomorrow and it's Sunday and I have no classes, so this was the first day in a long time that I had literally had nothing to do. I decided to crack the cellophane on Crash Bandicoot 2 and settled in on the futon, that vaguely smelled of baked apples, and proceeded to have a very 'do nothing' type of day.

Scott got home around eight that night, saw that I was playing Crash 2 (still) and sat next to me on the futon. We didn't say anything other than hello for a while, he sat and watched me play and then after I died I handed him the controller and he took a stab at it. That's pretty much how our relationship works.

After a couple of hours Scott got up and went into his room. As he got to his doorway he stopped and turned around to talk to me.

"I just want to get this out there," Scott said, "I still think that Beth is trouble but, if you think there's something there, I am willing to give her a shot."

I paused the game and looked at Scott.

"Like, you'd be willing to hang out with her, or us?" I needed clarification.

"Not like tomorrow, but yeah," he replied aloofly.

"Cool." I didn't know what else to say.

Scott went into his room and closed the door. That was actually a pretty big deal for him to say that. Saying he'd be willing to hang out with Beth was basically Scott apologizing to a point. Anytime Scott changed his mind about something, it was a pretty big deal. Sometimes he can just be a stubborn ass, but he's like a brother to me. There's nothing I wouldn't do for him.

I got up off the futon and my muscles creaked and felt stiff, probably from sitting in one spot for nearly ten hours. I old-man-hobbled my way over to the Playstation to shut it off and decided to head to bed. As I started to get tired, my mind wandered to thoughts of Beth, and a wave of warm feelings helped me fall asleep.

CHAPTER FIFTEEN

The next couple of weeks were perfectly normal, it was kind of nice. No invasions, no unexplained things happening, nothing. Just classes and everyone winding down until Thanksgiving break. A couple of my professors were doing their midterms before Thanksgiving to get them out of the way before Christmas which was a nice ball of stress, but amazingly, I think I am prepared for them.

Scott and I put the past couple of months behind us and things were seemingly back to normal, it was nice to get that part of my life sorted out. We were hanging out, hosting tournaments in our room, it really felt like old times. Well, not really old, but before I found out about multiverses and before I met Beth.

Beth and I have hung out a few times in the last couple of weeks and we've been getting a little closer. We're not dating, but we are *almost* dating it seems. We haven't kissed, we have long talks and she hasn't stayed over since that night. I honestly don't know if she is into me or not. I think she is, at least I *hope* she is.

I thought we were about to at least kiss after we went to see *Titanic*. It was the second time we hung out after our *Pulp Fiction* night. We sat through this slog of a movie, the only reason we went to see it is because it was all campus was talking about, and holy hell did it drag. We sat in that theater for nearly three hours only for that old lady to throw her necklace in the ocean. And she was greedy with that floating door! There was more than enough room for her and Jack instead of having him sink to the bottom of the ocean.

It was pretty late when we left the movie, because it was long as hell. Winter came early this year. I held Beth's hand to keep her steady on the icy lot. She slipped a little as we reached my truck. I caught her as she held onto my shoulder really tight and looked up at me.

"I'll never let go, Jake." Beth said with a smile.

One of my weaknesses with Beth that I've discovered over the last couple of weeks is that when she randomly quotes a movie to me I really dig it. I feel something in me stir, maybe it's that I've never been with a girl that has done that.

I moved my other arm to brace her from falling and looked into Beth's eyes. I felt the moment, this was it. Every part of me told me to kiss her, it was time. Beth looked back at me with a smirk and a raised eyebrow and...

I panicked. My plan was to spin her around and dip her like I was fucking Fred Astaire or something but, because it was icy, I slipped and fell on my ass. I started laughing which made her start laughing and she slipped too and fell on her ass in front of me. We sat there for a few minutes, both of us with freezing asses, laughing on the ground because we couldn't get up and every time we were about to we would laugh harder.

It was a fun night, but I killed the moment.

I honestly don't know why this was so hard. I know I'm in love with her, no question. It just seems that every time something might happen, I hesitate. Maybe I'm still hurt deep down, making me really gun-shy when it came to Beth. I need to get out of my own head.

On the morning of Thanksgiving Eve I woke up and heard the ping from my AOL Instant Messenger to me and Scott.

```
Guys!
I'm HOME! What are we doing tonight?
It's been too long!
I miss you two!
Love ya,
J
```

Scott was probably still sleeping but I hadn't left my room yet. I wrote back.

```
Jen,
We miss you too! How about The Griffon
at like 9?
I might have someone I want you to
meet.
Jake
```

Within seconds Jen wrote back to me.

```
Jake!
IS THERE A NEW GIRL???
I WANT TO MEET HER!!
```

I wrote back that yes, maybe there was a new girl. She replied back with a string of exclamation marks and that she was happy for me and that she couldn't wait to meet her. I sat back in my chair and figured I should see if Scott was up.

Scott was studying in the living room, eating a bagel and drinking coffee. I saw that there was a second coffee where I normally sit so I grabbed it and took a sip. The sweet cocoa-coffee hit my lips and I said thanks.

"You check your IM?" Scott asked, not looking up from his book.

"From Jen? Yeah, I just wrote her back." I replied, thanking Juan Valdez and the Swiss Miss in my head for the coffee I was drinking. "I asked her if she wanted to go to The Griffon and she was into it. She wants to meet Beth."

I saw Scott take a deep breath. He put his notes down and looked at me.

"Beth is going?"

"Well, yeah, hopefully." I said, "I mean, I have to ask her."

Scott made a sound like a grunt.

141

"And besides," I added, "You said you would make an effort to get to know her and the three of us haven't hung out. Maybe with Jen as a buffer and being at The Griffon it will be easier for you."

Scott leaned back on the futon and let out a breath.

"Fine," he said with a mouth full of bagel. "I told you I would give her a chance. For you I will try. I will be on my best behavior." Scott put his hands together like he was praying and batted his eyes at me.

I shook my head and grabbed the Playstation controller. I was meeting Beth for lunch later and would pitch this to her. Scott was a surprisingly easy sell, hopefully she would be too.

A couple of hours later, Beth was staring at me blankly.

"So you want me to, like, willingly hang out with Scott tonight?"

"Well, yeah," I explained, "It's not like it's just Scott. Jen's awesome, I've known her forever. Besides, what else are you going to do tonight?"

Beth took a bite of pizza and wiped sauce from her mouth.

"Well, I mean, I am going up to my Dad's for Thanksgiving. I was going to leave tonight," Beth looked at me and smiled, "I guess I can leave in the morning."

"Awesome!" I said.

"I'll do my best not to set him on fire." Beth joked about Scott.

I looked at Beth with some concern and she put her hands in the air.

"I'm kidding. I'll be on my best behavior." She said.

"That's exactly what Scott said," I laughed, "Well, besides the 'setting someone on fire' thing."

We sat there finishing our lunch and talked about our Thanksgiving plans. Her Dad and Stepmom lived out in Westchester so she was going to take Professor Cline's Jeep and go up there tomorrow morning. Professor Cline didn't have any

142

family close by and since Beth's Mom died Beth's Dad didn't really want Professor Cline at the house. They haven't talked in years but apparently they were really close friends a long time ago.

On the way from My Hero to The Griffon I was really glad that I decided to drive instead of walk. This November was the coldest I remembered in a while and the wind was howling. It had snowed a couple of times already this month and the forecast called for this to be the worst winter in a while for the Hudson Valley. I pulled up behind The Griffon, got out of the truck and opened Beth's door. She got out, thanked me for lunch, gave me a quick hug, told me she'll meet me here at around nine, and descended into the basement to port back to the cave. I stayed there for a minute, leaning against my truck and wondering if Beth and I were ever going to be an actual thing or not.

Even after all of these months of knowing each other, I wasn't totally sure if she was into me in that way. Sometimes she seemed to be, other times she didn't. Maybe I'm just an idiot and can't pick up on cues. Like just now she kind of hurried inside but at the movies, before I ruined it, I was one hundred percent sure we could have kissed. I need to flat out just ask her what we are but, honestly, I'm scared to have that conversation.

I drove around for a little while before going back to the dorm to clear my head. By the time I got back there it was about six o'clock. Scott's 'beauty regimen' was in full swing so I just poked my head into his room to let him know I was back and decided to get a couple of games of Mortal Kombat Trilogy in before we left.

Scott and I drove separately because he was driving up to Kingston tonight since Thanksgiving was at his Grandparents this year and he planned on going up tonight. The backup plan was that if he was too drunk to drive tonight I would just bring him back to the dorm and drive him to his car tomorrow morning.

Thanksgiving Eve, or "Weds-giving," I've heard it called, was an event in this town. There were so many bars on the main strip that people spent most of the night hopping from one to

another just getting hammered, I'll usually just have one or two
and call it a night.

Scott and I walked into The Griffon at about ten minutes to
nine, before the big crowds would be there, and saw Jen standing
at the bar talking to the bartender. In a flash, Scott made his way
over to her, grabbed her from behind and gave her a big hug. She
instantaneously screeched, spun around, and hugged him back, and
then ran over to me and gave me a giant hug as well. Just seeing
Jen put a smile on my face, she's so full of life that you can't help
but feel happy around her.

Jen grabbed us by the hands and brought us to a booth,
weaving through the growing crowd like a shark looking for her
prey. The cover band was playing "Santa Monica" by Everclear
and if I didn't know better I would think it was the actual band, not
a cover. She sat next to Scott, across from me, and seemed to stare
directly into my soul.

"What is her name and where is she?" Jen asked with a
smile. She looked like a kid that was expecting to get a puppy for
Christmas, I could feel her excitement.

"Her name is Beth," I said with a smile, "And she'll be here
soon. I told her around nine, she's usually punctual."

"So how long have you two been together?" Jen rested her
chin in her hands and waited for the story.

"We're not, really," I said sheepishly, "I like her, I think
she likes me, but I haven't made a move. She hasn't either. It's
complicated."

The waitress brought over our drinks and some nachos
while Scott made a grunt.

"Problem?" Jen asked Scott with a raised eyebrow.

"There's something off with her." Scott said as he reached
for his Corona. "Since the first time this fool bumped into her he's
been obsessed with her. I get a weird feeling."

I looked at Scott sharply. "You said you would behave."

"I'm going to. It's not like she's here yet." Scott used this
loophole-style thinking often. I don't like it.

"I usually, with the exception of Shelly, have a good sense of people. I'll tell you if she's weird. Besides," Jen grabbed a nacho, "I'm just happy Jake 'may have' (Jen used air quotes with her fingers) found someone new after the mess that he was stuck with before. I'm still sorry by the way, Jake."

Scott let out another grunt and went to take a drink from his bottle when it nearly slipped out of his hands. I hid my smile behind a napkin, feeling Beth was here and a couple of seconds later I saw her maneuver her way over to us. I gave a knowing look at Beth and she gave me a little shrug and a smile. I mouthed the words 'be nice' and she smirked at me. She looked great. She was wearing her regular attire, a black dress with all of her normal accessories, but she just looked amazing. She was also still wearing my jacket which Jen noticed immediately and shot me a surprised look.

I said hi and scooted over to make room for her and she sat down while I introduced her to Jen. Scott gave Beth a little nod, and Jen immediately switched into inquisitive sister mode.

"So!" Jen enthusiastically asked, "What are you drinking tonight?"

"I don't know, I don't really drink too much." Beth said and motioned towards Jen's drink. "What are you having?"

"Long Island Iced Tea. Do you want a sip?"

Jen put her drink in front of Beth for her to try. Beth's eyes got wide and she nodded approvingly. Jen called the waitress over and ordered two more.

"So, important question," Jen said as she grabbed Beth's hands, "How did you two meet."

"They literally bumped into each other." Scott said and motioned for another Corona.

"Quiet you," Jen mockingly scolded Scott, "I asked Beth."

"Well," Beth said as the waitress placed down the drinks, "Scott's not wrong. Jake wasn't paying attention and he walked right into me."

"To be fair," I added, "You were walking with your nose in a book."

"Well you should have watched where you were going." Beth smiled at me and felt myself melt inside. She turned back to Jen and added, "As it turns out we were heading to the same class."

Jen and Beth hit it off super well. They were chatting up a storm and at one point I looked at Scott and he just rolled his eyes and went back to drinking. Every now and then I would try to jump in the conversation but their little chat train just kept rolling. If Scott would say something negative Jen would just wave her hand or shush him and if I saw his drink teetering I would nudge Beth under the table and it would stop. I felt like I was juggling live grenades while Jen and Beth talked like they've known each other for years.

A couple of hours later Jen asked me to come up to the bar with her to close out our tab and wander to P&G's up the street. I really didn't want to leave Beth and Scott alone, I lost count of how many drinks in Scott was and I'm pretty sure he was close to the point where his brain, and his filter, would be off. I looked at Beth and quietly asked if she would be okay. She nodded, and Jen and I went up to the bar.

While we waited for the bartender, Jen grabbed my arm like a vise.

"I love her!" Jen said enthusiastically. "She's funny, so pretty and so into you it's not even funny."

"Is she?" I glanced back at Beth. I couldn't see Scott from where I was standing but Beth looked like she was talking to him.

"Are you an idiot?" Jen looked at me blankly. "Did you not notice how she would look at you or like slightly touch your arm or anything? Also, she's wearing your jacket! You didn't even like me wearing your jacket!"

I looked back at Beth who noticed and smiled at me. "I think I love her." I said to Jen quietly.

"Whoa cowboy, hold up a minute." Jen said, "I love that, Jake, I really do but pump the brakes a little. You have a habit of saying that really early. Do NOT do that this time."

"I know." I said, "You have no idea how hard I have been fighting to hold those words in."

"I get it, I really do." Jen said as she glanced back at the table. "Sometimes you just have to keep your mouth shut until the time is right. It sucks, but hopefully the wait makes it worth it."

The bartender came over, we paid the tab and walked back to the table. The first words I heard Scott say to Beth when we got back to the table were something along the lines of "Why are you being so bitchy?" and I knew that trouble was brewing.

"Is everybody playing nice over here?" Jen reminded me of a fairy or something with the tone that she took. "We're paid up, ready to head to P&G's?"

I took one look at Beth and could see she was seething. Scott was sitting there still drinking. I'm pretty sure he was past the point of no return already.

"Actually I think I'm gonna go," Beth looked at Jen and me, "I have a bit of a drive to get to my Dad's and I was thinking of heading up tonight."

Beth started to stand up and I looked at Scott, he didn't look back at me.

"Beth, wait a second." I put my hand on her arm while still looking at Scott. "What happened?"

Scott sat there silently drinking. I could feel Beth's arm twitching and I knew what was coming. Scott's drink fell out of his hand as he went to put it to his lips and he responded with a loud curse.

"Scott I think you've had enough already." Jen looked really concerned and she looked at Beth. "Beth, is he being an asshole? He tends to get like that when he drinks a little. Or a lottle."

"Yeah, go hop on your broom and get out of here!" Scott slurred towards Beth.

Shit, I thought to myself. I could feel the heat coming off of Beth's arm and gently squeezed it to keep her calm. We locked eyes and I quietly mouthed 'stay calm' to her. Jen looked lost.

"Am I missing something?" Jen asked. She looked back and forth between Beth, Scott and me.

"It's nothing." Beth said. I felt the heat coming off of her die down a bit.

"I better not make her mad, she might put a curse on me." Scott said and laughed while he wiggled his fingers. I saw the bottles on the table start to slightly sway so I bumped the table a little and squeezed Beth's arm slightly again.

"Scott thinks Beth reminds him of a witch." I felt Beth go a little tense at the word but I hoped she knew why I said it.

"Like spells and stuff?" Jen looked at Scott and shook her head. "Scott, I think you may have played too much Dungeons and Dragons."

Scott got to his feet and started to the door.

"Whatever," he shouted towards us, "I'm going to P&G's. If you, Jake and Witchie-poo want to come, fine. If not…"

I felt Beth's arm twitch again and in a moment Scott tripped over his own feet in front of the bouncer. I looked at Beth and she was clearly not happy. Jen rushed over to Scott and, with the bouncer's help, got Scott up and out of the bar.

"Beth!" I was starting to feel like I was losing control of the situation.

Beth started walking toward the front door and I followed close behind. She was pissed and I wanted to make sure she didn't do anything crazy. When I got outside Scott was sitting on the stone quarter-wall around the outside of The Griffon and Jen was tending to him to see if he hurt himself. Beth walked over to them and I quickly followed.

"What happened?" Beth asked with a little concern in her voice. I don't know if it was genuine or not.

Scott stayed quiet, mostly because Jen shushed him. Scott did look kind of dazed from either the fall or just being drunk.

148

"It looks like he hit his head, he's got a cut." Jen put something from her purse on it and Scott kept waving her off. "Stop being a baby Scott, It's not going to burn."

Scott finally gave in and let Jen treat his wound. He winced a little when she finally put the tissues on his head and then Jen placed his hand on it to hold them in place. Scott didn't say anything, but he wouldn't take his eyes off of me and Beth.

"Maybe we should call it a night," I said to Jen before turning to Scott, "You want me to bring you back to the dorm."

"No." Scott gave me an icy glare and slurred, "I'm going to Kingston tonight."

"The hell you are!" Jen looked at Scott with an intensity that I rarely saw. "You are way too drunk to drive."

"No I'm…"

"Yes, you are." Jen was very stern with Scott, she knew how to deal with him better than I did at times.

"Well," Scott continued and never broke eye contact with me. "I'm not going back to the dorm with him, that's for damn sure."

I could feel myself about to reach my breaking point. If Scott didn't run his mouth, we'd all still be having a good time. I shouldn't have left them alone. My gut told me not to, but I knew Jen wanted to talk. I looked at Beth and she aimed her eyes elsewhere.

"Fine," Jen said to Scott, "You can crash on my parents couch and I will bring you back here in the morning. Does that work?"

Scott nodded and Jen helped him to his feet.

"It was really nice meeting you Beth," Jen gave her a hug, "I'm sorry the night ended like this. Sometimes Scott is a handful but I really want to hang out next time I'm in town, maybe over Christmas break?"

"It was nice meeting you too," Beth said, "Yeah, that sounds good."

Jen loaded Scott into her car and gave me a hug. "You got this," she whispered in my ear before she got in her car and drove away. I turned to talk to Beth and saw she was already at the end of the block, rounding the corner. I ran to catch up to her. She got to Professor Cline's Jeep as I caught up to her.

"Beth, wait," I shouted.

I saw Beth's shoulders tense up and she turned around to face me. She looked upset.

"Jake, I'm sorry, I really am." She had her hand on the door of the Jeep. "That word sets me off and he was really being a jerk,"

"What was he saying?" I pleaded.

"At first I thought he was just trying to make small talk so, like, it wasn't just an awkward silence while you and Jen were at the bar." She bit her lip a little. "He started off asking things like 'are you a cat or a dog person' and 'do you prefer the city or the woods'. I realized where he was leading when he started asking if I had been to Salem or ran into any houses made of candy in the woods. Then he just was being an asshole." Beth made a sound of frustration.

"Did he say anything else?" I walked a little closer to Beth.

"I kind of tuned him out after that just because I was getting so pissed and I was trying to stay calm. That's when you guys came back."

"I know it's no excuse, but Scott can be an asshole when he drinks. And.." Beth put her hand up and cut me off.

"You don't have to defend him Jake," she said as she opened the car door, "He was being a dick and I lost control. I tried to be the better person and just go with it because he's your best friend, but I reached my limit with his bullshit. I knew I shouldn't have even come tonight. I should have just gone to Westchester."

She started the Jeep and closed the door.

"Then why did you come?" I yelled at the window in frustration.

Beth opened the window and looked at me through glassy eyes. "I don't know."

I stood there in silence as Beth pulled away and left me there wondering how everything went so wrong so quickly. A light snow started to fall as I reached my truck and drove back to the dorm. I just wanted to get some sleep and forget this night ever happened.

CHAPTER SIXTEEN

I walked into my dorm, and I was more upset than when Beth left me in the parking lot. I had big hopes for tonight; Scott and Beth maybe getting along, hanging out with Jen, maybe seeing if Beth and I really did have something and in a flash it was all gone. The last words Beth said to me rang in my head. *I don't know.*

That sounded like there was more to it than not knowing why she came out tonight. Did Beth not know about me? Did she not know about us? Did I even know anything about us? Jen said that Beth seemed really into me, but now I don't know. If Scott had decided to not be a dick, maybe I would have answers, but now I'm in emotional limbo until Beth comes back from her Dad's and that's not even taking into account dealing with Scott when he gets back.

I threw my keys on the table and yelled out of frustration. DuBois Hall was pretty empty tonight, people were either still out (like I would have been) or were already home for Thanksgiving. I decided to take advantage of the near emptiness of the building and play some music a little louder than normal since it was after midnight.

Stabbing Westward's "Save Yourself" came through the speakers as I threw myself down on the futon. I didn't feel like playing anything, watching anything, nothing. My current plan was to just stew in the pot of shit this night turned out to be, watching the snow fall and wondering how things could have gone differently. My gut told me I shouldn't have left Beth and Scott alone, but I did, and now have to deal with the consequences.

My stewing continued and I heard a knock at the door. Someone was probably coming to bitch at me about the music being too loud and I really did not feel like dealing with it so I took a couple of extra seconds to sit. By the time they knocked on the door a third time I was ready to lay into whatever asshole really felt like getting in front of me at the moment. I stomped over and swung the door open with a loud "WHAT!"

It was Beth.

"Oh!" I was surprised to see her.

"I'm sorry, I should go." Beth looked surprised and turned to walk away.

"No wait!" I knew she had to be here for a reason. "I thought you were someone else. Come in, please."

Beth walked in hugging herself from the cold and stayed in the entryway for a bit.

"It's freaking freezing outside," she said as she rubbed her arms, "I'm so tired of this winter already."

"Yeah, it's sucked so far." I was happy to see her, but still angry about everything at The Griffon. "I'm surprised you're not wearing my jacket. Where is it?"

"I left it in the car like an idiot. Sometimes I don't like to drive with a jacket on. I feel, like, constricted."

"Yeah. I get that." I figured I would just get to the point. "So, why are you here, or do you not know that answer either?"

I sounded like an asshole, I knew I did, but I didn't care right now. Beth saying 'I don't know' really stung me. It's just such a vague response in an argument that just clarifies nothing and just prolongs whatever situation is going on.

"I deserve that," she sighed and looked at me with some sadness in her hazel eyes, "Listen. I'm sorry. I am. I know why I left and I know why I'm back."

"Well I really would like to…" I began.

Beth continued, "I like you, Jake," Beth said, "Like a lot. And it kind of scares me."

I didn't know what to say. Beth said just what I wanted, but I was too stunned to speak. Beth moved two steps closer.

"It's been a long time since I felt this way and I've been having a problem dealing with the feelings." she said with a drop of sadness in her voice. "I have trouble with that sometimes."

"I get it." My ability to speak came back, so that was nice. "I feel the same way. I haven't been into someone in a long time but," I felt the words flowing out and there was no way to stop them, "I've been in love with you since we first met."

Holy shit, why didn't I just stay mute! I did the one thing everyone told me not to, it just flew out of my stupid mouth. Alarms were going off in my head like there was a fire truck driving around looking to extinguish whatever caused my brain to start short circuiting. I think I tried to babble something afterwards but nothing came out. I probably looked like a fish gasping, just slack-jawed and wide eyed.

Beth just stared at me, her eyes locked on mine. I honestly had no idea what was going to happen next, did I just scare her away? After a few moments she took another step towards me, embraced me and buried her head in my chest. I wrapped my arms around her and pulled her closer, she still felt a little cold but not as much as before.

Beth lifted her head up from my chest, put her hand behind my neck, pulled my face down to meet her and kissed me.

I know it's cliche, but I felt fireworks. It almost felt like winterfresh mints, like that little spark and pop you feel when you put one in your mouth. The sparks were real. Beth pulled away first and she looked up and gave me the sexiest smile I had ever seen.

"Do you mind if I change the music?" Beth asked as she bit her bottom lip. "Stabbing Westward is a little aggressive right now."

I think the word "sure" may have left my lips.

Beth took my hand, led me to the futon and motioned me to sit down. I sat and she leaned down towards me and gave me a small kiss on the lips. My heart felt like it was going to fly out of my chest and I got chills every time she touched me. I watched her

154

walk over to the stereo with a saunter in her step as she flipped through my CD collection.

"Oh, this is a good one." I heard her say as she bent down to change the music.

"#1 Crush" by Garbage started playing. Beth stood up while swaying her hips back and forth, it was hypnotic. She had my full, undivided attention as I watched her move. Beth placed her hands on the top of the stereo and moved her hips to the beat. As she turned around to face me she slid one shoulder out of her dress.

The only thought running through my head was *holy shit*.

Beth moved like a gentle breeze as she made her way over to me, removing her other arm from her dress and slowly pulling it down. She would tease pulling her dress down further and then stop and pull it back up a little. By the time she was about half way towards me her dress was half off revealing a lacy black bra.

I sat there like a deer in headlights while I, well, looked at her headlights.

"Uh, is this what a couple of Long Island Iced Teas does to you?" I joked.

Beth smiled as she got a couple of feet away from me and slowly pulled down the rest of her dress. The girl of my dreams stood in front of me clad in lacy black matching bra and thong and I was in total shock. I'm surprised I was even able to stammer out that. She looked beautiful, my eyes read her every curve like a book.

"No," Beth straddled me on the futon and whispered in my ear, "This is what you've done to me."

Beth started nibbling on my ear and laying gentle kisses on my neck.

"Take your shirt off."

The shirt came off and Beth started kissing and slightly biting her way down from my neck to the middle of my chest before she stopped and locked eyes with me. She leaned in and gave me a deep, passionate kiss. I broke away first and started kissing her neck and chest. Beth gently moaned and placed my hands on her hips.

Beth moved her hands up to her breasts and reached behind her back to unhook her bra.

"You take it off." Beth's sultry voice had me in its control.

I went to take my hands away from her, and she slapped them. I gave her a confused look.

"With your teeth."

I did as I was told. I moved my head down to her breasts and bit the middle of her bra.

"Slowly." I heard her whisper, as she cradled my head in her hands.

I slowly pulled my head back and Beth's arms moved to allow her bra to easily slide off. I dropped her bra out of my mouth next to me and took a moment to soak in everything. Beth must have known what I was doing because she just stayed on me motionless, her body just waiting for me to absorb every inch of it. She looked like a goddess, or like a statue you find in Greece. She didn't look like a model, she didn't look like an actress, she looked perfect.

I whispered, "Are you..." Beth put her finger to my lips.

"I feel like I've wanted this longer than you have, Jake," Beth continued as she leaned in and kissed my neck again, "And I can feel that you want it too."

She wasn't wrong. I gently pushed her back a little so I could kiss her bare breasts and slowly moved up to give her a kiss. As I did that, I felt her hands move down to unbutton my jeans.

I woke up alone on the futon the next morning, not completely sure if the previous night was a dream or not. If it was, it sure as hell felt real. Well, I was naked and I usually sleep in boxers, so that was a sign that last night happened.

I sat up and allowed my eyes to bring the room into focus. I noticed the whole place looked like it was ransacked, and I remembered that things may have gotten a little wild last night. If my memory serves, everything started off nice and sweet but by the end we were on each other like animals. It was a side of Beth that was definitely surprising, I guess Scott was right when he would say that the quiet ones are always the wild ones.

I threw on my shorts and noticed a note by my keys next to the answering machine:

Jake,
Thanks for last night. I needed that.
Love,
Beth

I sat back down with the note in my hand.

"She does love me." I said out loud. I felt my heart grow really warm and a smile grew over my face. I hadn't felt like this in a long time and it felt great.

The clock read ten in the morning so I hopped up, took a quick shower and went over to my parents to catch the rest of the Thanksgiving parade with my brother and sister, and to help Mom cook. Well, really, me helping Mom just involved me taste testing everything but traditions must be upheld. I also told myself not to smile like an idiot all day because I had just had sex with a girl I loved. I didn't want to have to answer questions.

Well I'm an idiot, and I walked in smiling like an idiot. I didn't think my Mom suspected anything but my Dad read my face and instantly gave me a knowing look. He definitely knew something had happened, but he wasn't the type to pry. My brother and sister came running at me, tackling me like I was trying to score a touchdown and I went in and gave Mom a big hug. I grabbed a pinch of stuffing, got smacked on the hand and went to watch the rest of the parade.

My grandparents and aunts and uncles showed up a couple of hours later and the house filled up quickly. I was in and out of the kitchen all day helping (snatching food) and beating my siblings and cousins asses and Street Fighter and Mortal Kombat. I

157

was fielding questions about school, how I liked living on campus, the girl situation and plans for after college from various family members. Truth be told I didn't really have an answer to that last one. I avoided the girl-related questions by talking about the library. Nobody cares about the library. That allowed the interrogators to change the subject.

But when she had a second to spare, Mom pulled me aside and asked me about the girl. I played dumb for a second but she read it all over my face when I walked in. I told her a little about Beth and that I hoped that she would get to meet the family soon. Mom told me that she was happy for me, and that she never really liked Shelly much anyway, and I assured her that Beth was nothing like Shelly.

After dinner and dessert I said goodbye to my family and continued my Thanksgiving tradition of going to the movies on Thanksgiving night. I started doing it a couple of years earlier and quickly realized that it was a great time to go. There is practically no one in the theater because a lot of people are home watching football. I don't care about football unless it's a Madden video game, so the movies became a great alternative.

I went to see *Mortal Kombat: Annihilation.* I loved the first one, this one was not good. They killed my favorite character, Johnny Cage, right at the beginning and I mentally checked out soon after that. They recast a bunch of people, the costumes looked mostly shitty and overall it was just really bad. I should have gone to see the new *Alien* movie instead.

I got back to campus at around ten that night and walked to the dorm. My thoughts wandered to the night before and I couldn't help but smile again. I didn't care about whatever was going to happen with Scott, it would work itself out I'm sure, but everything that was going on with Beth made me forget any problems I was having. I rounded the corner to DuBois Hall and noticed someone sitting on the bench in front of the building. I noticed a light flickering in their hands and realized very quickly who it was.

It was Beth.

I quickened my pace and she saw me coming. She extinguished the little flame ball she made and stood up. As I was walking up the path to her, I took a moment to take her in. She was wearing a pair of jeans, a nice black sweater and my jacket. She still looked perfect.

I wasn't sure how to play this. Do I go in for a kiss hello? Do I not? I figured I would play it cool and not just dive in. Beth smiled as I walked up, not like a huge smile, but just a sweet smile.

"Hey," Beth said as I approached, "I didn't know when you would be back so I just figured I would wait."

"I'm glad you did," I said trying to sound as nonchalant as possible, "I didn't expect you back till Sunday or Monday."

"Yeah, I didn't want to stick around. My Dad and Stepmom were bickering the whole time and I really didn't feel like dealing with it," She was looking for answers on her shoes, looking down.

"Well I'm glad you're back."

"Yeah," Beth said with a sigh, "Me too."

We stood there silently for a minute and then both decided to talk at the same time.

"Listen, Jake, about last night…"

"It's cool," I said, "I…"

"Jake," she said, "Just let me say this. I've been practicing it the whole ride back."

We both let out a little laugh and I told her to go ahead.

"Listen, last night at The Griffon I lashed out and I'm sorry. Even though Scott was being a dick, I shouldn't have messed with him. I didn't mean to hurt him and I didn't mean to hurt you. I knew why I was leaving and I knew why I was upset. I like you Jake, like, a lot."

"I know," I said with a smile, "You told me last night."

"I haven't liked…" Beth stopped talking and looked at me. "Wait, what did you say?"

"You told me this last night."

I took a step towards her. Beth took a step back and cocked her head slightly to the side.

"When did I tell you this?" Beth sounded really confused.

I instantly thought that I took advantage of her because maybe those drinks hit her too hard. I started to feel really bad.

"Last night you came by and told me that. Don't you remember? Oh my God were you drunk. Did I take advantage of the situation? I'm so sorry." The words were just pouring out of my face.

"Hold on a second." Beth looked like her head was spinning. "Last night, after I left The Griffon, I drove to my Dad's. I got there late, but I was there all night."

Something was wrong. I felt my stomach drop into my shoes.

"Did I dream everything that happened?" I said out loud softly.

"Jake," Beth took a step towards me and stared directly into my eyes, her hazel eyes starting to show flecks of orange, "What happened last night?"

My mind started racing so fast I couldn't form a coherent thought. I started to say everything that came to mind.

"You came by and said that you liked me, then you kissed me. You brought me over to the futon and sat me down and changed the music. Then you did like a strip tease, and then I took your bra off with my teeth and then we…"

Beth looked at me wide-eyed. "We what?"

"We…" that was all I could get out,

"I wasn't here last night Jake." Beth sounded freaked out and I felt myself start to feel the same way.

"Yes, you were." I quietly insisted. "If it wasn't you, then who was it?"

We didn't say anything for a few seconds. Beth looked like she was trying to piece something together.

"Jake," Beth's voice turned cold, "Where's the Rift Ripper."

"It's… it's upstairs in my nightstand." I affirmed.

"Are you sure?" She panicked.

"Yes?" I wasn't sure of anything at the moment.

"We need to go up to your room, NOW!" Her panic grew.

I threw the door open and ran up the stairs, Beth close behind. I had a pit in my stomach and I felt like I was going to throw up at any second. I had no idea what was going on. What the fuck even happened last night? I fumbled with the keys, finally got the door open and we ran right to my nightstand. I flung the drawer open where I kept it and found... nothing.

It was gone and in its place was a note.

Sorry Jakey, I needed this too.

My head started spinning and I sat on my bed. I was trying to get a grasp of the situation when Beth's voice broke me out of my trance. I looked at her and she was holding the note that she left me last night.

"Jake," her voice cracked a little, "I didn't write this."

"Please tell me you did." I felt my eyes well up a little bit.

Beth shook her head and I noticed that her mascara was running.

"Beth, I…" As I was about to say something she touched her necklace and vanished.

My head fell into my hands as I tried to piece together all of the possibilities that could have happened. I needed to talk to the Professor, and I'm pretty sure that's where Beth went. I didn't want to drive all the way to The Griffon, so I decided to try out the emergency portal on my Rig. It worked and in a flash I was in the cave. The Professor wasn't here yet, but Beth was. She was crying, I made her cry, and I felt like shit.

"Beth…"

Beth wiped her eyes and held up her hand towards me.

"Don't talk." She sounded harsh. "Cline is on his way and you can tell him your whole fucking story."

I sat in the chair across from her in silence, the sounds of her trying to suppress her crying echoed off the walls and hit me right in the heart.

Professor Cline entered the cave a few minutes later and asked what happened. I told him everything that happened the night before. I stayed vague with some of the more sexual bits, the hurt on Beth's face ripped into me with every look.

I thought it was Beth, I KNEW it was Beth.

I finished my story and the three of us sat in silence. After a few minutes Professor Cline took off his glasses, rubbed the bridge of his nose, walked over to the computer and started typing. He stopped for a moment and spoke.

"I know what's happening and I *know* who she is." He said with a solemn tone.

Professor Cline hit a key on the computer and a black and white picture of Beth's face was on the screen, only the name next to it didn't say Beth and it looked like she had lighter hair.

"Her name is Lizzie Davenport," Professor Cline said before looking at Beth glassy eyed and adding, "And she killed your mother."

CHAPTER SEVENTEEN

The silence in the air felt like a thick fog as I looked at Professor Cline's computer screen in disbelief. The person on the screen, Lizzie, looked just like Beth right down to her cute little smirk. I didn't know what to say and I looked over to Beth who seemed equally stunned.

"What… what are you saying?" Beth's voice cracked as she spoke. "You said that you found my mother dead on the mountain."

Professor Cline pulled his chair closer to Beth and sat down. He reached for her hands but then thought better of it and pulled them away.

"Elizabeth," he spoke softly, "there's a lot about that night that you don't know, that I neglected to tell you, in order to keep a promise. I was going to tell you when I thought you were ready but recent events show that I should have told you a while ago."

Beth noticed me looking at her and slightly turned her head away from me. I felt the dagger twist in my heart. I looked at Professor Cline who looked back at me and, as if knowing that I wanted answers too, gave me a sympathetic look and a slight nod.

"You know I had known Peggy for a long time." Professor Cline sat slightly forward in his chair as he spoke. "Your mother was the one that introduced me to this whole world while we were in college, after her handler had passed. I still consider her the best friend I've ever had, a sister even. After you were born she looked at me and said, 'Say hello to your niece, Uncle Bryan."

Professor Cline's voice caught slightly as he said that and Beth looked at him with such a look of sadness that broke my heart even more than it already had. She wasn't sobbing at the moment, but tears streamed quietly down her face. Beth wiped them with the sleeve of my jacket as the Professor continued.

"Your father knew what we did and was always sick with worry, especially after you were born. As you got older and he learned more about The Conclave, the legacy of Casters, and the power that can be passed from generation to generation, he became more worried. Not only concern for his wife, but for his only child as well. This led to a lot of arguments between your parents."

Beth nodded slightly, listening carefully to every single thing the Professor explained to her. I just sat and listened while still looking at the computer screen.

"I always promised your father that I would watch out for Peggy. I used to be quite the fighter and your mother was one of the most powerful Pyromantic Casters that The Conclave had. There weren't a lot of disturbances from other multiverses but when there was, no matter where in the world it happened, we were always in the leadership of the team they would call. From San Francisco to Dubai, we led many teams in protecting our Earth."

"That's great," Beth said as her voice trembled, "But what about Mom."

"I know, Elizabeth, I was getting to that." Professor Cline took a deep breath and continued.

"One night as I was monitoring our area, I noticed an anomaly appear on the mountain. I wasn't quite sure of the origin and Peggy was home with you and Nathan. The readings on what I was picking up were strange, nothing like we had ever come across. I drove out to Westchester to tell your mother, it was late by the time I got there. Nathan and Peggy met me at the door and your mother could see on my face that something was wrong. I told them everything and your mother was ready to pack up and leave with me right then to go see what was going on. Your father got upset and they got into an argument."

"I remember." Beth said softly, haunted almost, like she was reliving the moment.

"Nathan wanted her to stop doing this, the stress was making him sick. He had been asking for years to see if The Conclave would send someone else to protect this area, but Peggy was stubborn. She refused and said that this was her legacy, her responsibility. Your father threatened to leave if she didn't stop. She couldn't turn her back on it, she wouldn't. Nathan just shook his head in surrender and went to grab a drink while Peggy went up to check on you."

Beth's eyes grew wide with that revelation. I got the feeling that we were about to go into uncharted territory.

"Peggy came back down, glassy eyed, and told me that after tonight she would talk to The Conclave about a replacement. As duty bound as she felt, she didn't want to tear apart her family anymore. I understood wholeheartedly, she loved you and your father more than anything in the world. Nathan came back into the room shortly after that and she told him. They embraced, and your mother and I left."

Professor Cline stood up and took a deep breath. I watched as Beth's eyes followed him as he paced for a little bit before regaining his composure, sitting back down and continuing.

"When we got back here, the anomaly wasn't showing on my monitors anymore. We thought maybe it was a false alarm but Peggy decided to stay till the following night to see if it happened again. Luckily she did because the next afternoon it appeared again, stronger than the day before, near the top of the mountain on the way to Skytop Tower."

I immediately thought, *That's near where I had my first experience with a gateway, a day I will never forget.*

"Peggy got us near the area using her, well your, locket and there was instantly a chill in the air. Shortly after we arrived an ice creature, very similar to what you described to me in Wallkill, appeared in our way. We were able to see a gateway in the distance, but it looked different from our normal gateways that we would use. It almost looked like it was sparking at the edges. The bigger problem was the giant in front of us. We fought it and it

165

seemed almost entirely focused on me, so I decided to try to lure it away so your mother could investigate the gateway. I didn't realize what a mistake that would be until later."

Professor Cline closed his eyes and took a breath. Beth's jaw was clenched tightly, I don't know if it was out of anger, sorrow or just trying to stop herself from crying. After a moment, Professor Cline continued.

"I felt like I fought this monster for a while when, all of a sudden, it just dropped to the ground and melted away. I ran back towards where I left your mother and that's..." The Professor's voice caught again. "That's when I saw a sight that still haunts me to this day. I saw your mother, my best friend, lying on the ground with a large icicle in her chest and a girl that looked like you, *exactly like you*, standing in front of the gateway with an evil grin. I didn't know what to do, and I knew there was no way it could be you, so instinctively I made throwing knives from my Rig and threw them at the child. She waved them away and launched shards of ice at me. I dodged most of them, but a few of them landed in my hand and arm, causing nerve damage."

Beth's eyes were wide with horror as I looked from her to the monitor to Cline.

"The child went through the gateway, which let off an unusual discharge before it disappeared. I grabbed Peggy and used my Rig to teleport us back here, to the cave. She was gasping, clinging to life, as I held her in my arms. The icicle pierced through her, right through her heart, I knew that there was no way to save her. All I could do was hold her in my arms and she said 'Her name is Lizzie' over and over. In her last breaths she made me promise to protect you, do whatever I could to keep you safe. I grabbed her hand and I promised her that I would. I held her in my arms, on my lap, as she slipped away."

Professor Cline wiped tears from his cheeks as he continued.

"I contacted The Conclave as soon as I could and alerted them of the situation and they got right to work. The best Casters in the organization set out putting protective wards and security measures at various points of interest around the globe. The head of The Conclave at the time told me to keep an eye on you to see if you showed any signs of Pyromancy. Occasionally gifts skip a generation. I prayed so hard that they would skip you."

I watched as Professor Cline stood up and walked over to the computer. He hit a couple of keystrokes and a model of the Earth appeared showing where the wards were. One of them looked like it sat right above us.

"In the years since, while I've been training you, I've been trying to secretly gather information on your mother's murderer. It's difficult because the wards work both ways, we are invisible to her Earth and she is invisible to ours. I was able to spy on her, but soon after I did that, she was able to somehow lock on to us. She pulled us out of our gateway. That's how we wound up on her Earth, that frozen wasteland. I tried as quickly as I could to get us back here. I fear that by me doing that, I may have opened a bridge that she has been able to exploit."

Beth sat there in silence, I could see her processing what the Professor was saying.

"But why is she here?" I asked. It was the one thing the Professor didn't answer yet.

"I'm not entirely sure," Professor Cline said, "But I was able to deduce something with the help of The Conclave."

Professor Cline pulled up another graphic showing hundreds of Earths. It looked like about a third of them had a red "X" through them.

"Lizzie has been amassing power for at least the last seven years and has become an incredibly powerful Cryomancer, among other types of gifts." Professor Cline said with a dark tone. "She has been going to different multiverses and killing her bloodlines there if they show any traits of being a Caster. She started by killing off whatever version of Peggy had power, not all of them across The Multiverse do, but now it looks like she's going back after versions of Elizabeth. The more she kills from her own bloodline, the more powerful she somehow gets. No one in The Conclave has ever seen anything like this."

Professor Cline walked back over toward Beth and sat down. Beth looked at the floor as she wiped tears from her face. I didn't know what I should do, but I chose to keep my distance.

"Elizabeth, I am so sorry for keeping all of this from you." I could tell he was trying to comfort her. "I've never forgiven myself for the events of that night. One wrong decision in the past had such unfathomable consequences and caused me to try to protect you from everything, maybe too much."

Beth looked up and stared at Professor Cline with a look that made me shift in my seat. The sadness was still there but it looked like there was a good amount of rage that came along with it.

"You're sorry?" Beth stood up slowly while maintaining eye contact with the Professor. "You're sorry!? You've lied to me for the last seven years and all you can say is that you're sorry!?"

Tears were still streaming down Beth's face as she set her chair on fire. Professor Cline stood in front of her, unflinching, while I jumped behind my chair in case she felt like shooting fire this way.

She waged on, "All of these years you've been keeping this from me. All of these years just telling me that she was just killed in battle, while holding this fucking bombshell in until I was 'ready' to hear it and all you can say is that you're sorry?"

"It was a mistake…" Professor Cline started to speak when Beth cut him off.

"A mistake? It was a fucking lie of omission and you know it! I've trusted you all of these years and now what? Does my father even know the whole story?"

"To a point," Professor Cline said, "He knows she was murdered. He doesn't know it was from a version of you. I didn't think he would process it well when I told him the news originally and over time, as I saw him come to terms with your mother's passing, I chose not to tell him to help him with his healing."

Beth looked at the Professor and shook her head in disgust before turning to me. I felt an immediate sense of fear.

"Beth, I…" I didn't have anything planned to say.

"I don't want to hear it." Beth said as she took off my jacket. "I thought we had some type of connection or, like, something going on. Apparently I was wrong if you couldn't even tell it wasn't me and just decided to get laid."

"It wasn't like that…" I started to argue before she interrupted.

"Just stop Jake," Beth threw my jacket at me and it landed on the floor, "I came to you tonight to tell you how I felt, but it doesn't matter now. So take your fucking jacket back and maybe I'll see you around."

I wanted to tell her to wait but she grabbed her locket and looked right into my eyes.

Beth's eyes began to weaken with tears again as her bottom lip pouted out slightly. She said calmly, "I knew I shouldn't have let my guard down," as she said this, her eyes began to slightly glow orange.

In a blink, she was gone.

I slumped back down in my chair as Professor Cline pulled out a fire extinguisher and put out the remaining flames from where Beth was sitting. I rested my head in my hands, looking at the floor, as I watched tears fall from my eyes. In one night everything had gotten so fucked that I couldn't even make sense of it. I started to feel like I was losing everything. Beth, Scott, hell even my own goddamn mind. My brain told my body to just let it go and I just started crying. The sadness, frustration and anger at myself finally caught up to me.

After a couple of minutes I felt a hand on my shoulder and looked up to see Professor Cline. He pulled a chair over to me, sat down and handed me a box of tissues. I took them, wiped my face, and sat back to look at him.

"Mister Howard, Jake, will you be alright?"

I shrugged. I honestly didn't know if I would be. Right now I felt like throwing myself off of Mohonk.

"I know you didn't ask to be a part of this," Professor Cline began, "and I apologize for dragging you into this. I guess I saw a little of myself in you, but I feel that I failed to properly prepare you for what to expect as well."

I let out a slight sarcastic chuckle. "Can you really prepare anyone for this?"

"Maybe," Professor Cline tilted his head slightly, "maybe not."

"Where did she go?" I wondered if The Professor knew.

Professor Cline held back any emotion and shook his head. "I don't know, Jake." His voice sounded a little distant. "As badly as you think you hurt her, I fear I may have hurt her more. Elizabeth has only acted like this once before and she didn't tell me where she went then, I doubt she will now when she comes back."

"I honestly thought it was her," I said softly, "she looked identical. If there were any differences I just didn't see them. Maybe I didn't want to see them."

"Jake," Professor Cline removed his hand from my shoulder and leaned forward in his chair, "I know you care deeply for her, I've seen it since the first day. Elizabeth cares for you as well and, with enough time, maybe she will hear your side. Right now, she is not in a place to hear or deal with any of this. Between what I held back from her and the events with you and last night, she just needs some time. She will be back though and we can deal with all of this then. For now, we need to figure out what Lizzie is up to."

"I can't handle this tonight." My voice cracked as I spoke.

"I understand," Professor Cline said, "Go home, rest. Come back when you feel up to it."

I got up, sulked to the platform for The Griffon gateway, and passed my jacket lying on the floor.

170

Before I reached the platform, Professor Cline called out to me, "Jake, you're a good man with a good heart. Don't let this sour you."

I didn't know what to say, I just kept my back to him and walked through the gateway. It was a long, cold walk back to my dorm and I felt like I deserved it after the clusterfuck that I caused. I pushed Beth to the brink but the Professor may have pushed her over the edge. The fact that she actually liked me stung. The fact that her double told me the same thing was worse, but me telling Lizzie that I loved her stung the most. Maybe Beth was right, maybe I didn't even really know her at all.

It was nearly three in the morning as I got back into my room, I got into bed and tried to fall asleep. My body had other ideas and decided to break down in tears again. I guess I eventually fell asleep because before I knew it my clock read that it was two in the afternoon. I didn't want to get out of bed, but I knew I had to eat something. I shambled to the kitchen for a handful of dry cereal and went back to bed.

I didn't get out of bed, other than to go to the bathroom and put some type of food in my body, until Sunday morning.

That's when I heard a key turn in the front door. Scott was home.

I had no idea how this would go, but I couldn't feel worse than I did at the moment. I heard him go into his room and I decided to get out of bed to talk to him. My legs buckled a little as my feet hit the cold floor and as I hit my doorway he was coming out of his room. Scott looked at me, first with anger and then with concern.

"What happened?" He asked.

I shook my head and could feel myself getting choked up. I said the only thing that I could.

"I fucked up."

CHAPTER EIGHTEEN

I told Scott everything that had happened since the first day of class. I held all of this information in from him for so long that telling everything I had been hiding from him felt like such a relief. I paced around the room while Scott sat in front of me as I told him about the gateway I saw on that field trip, Beth, The Conclave, the hidden gateway under The Griffon, Thanksgiving Eve, all of it. I didn't want any more secrets between us. I just wanted, and needed, my best friend back.

I finished my story and Scott just stared wide-eyed at me. I felt like a hundred pounds lighter after unburdening myself, but I still felt like shit. I swear I could see the wheels turning in his head as he was processing everything I said. After a few minutes, he finally spoke.

"See, I knew I wasn't that clumsy," Scott smiled at me, "Beth owes me some drinks."

I sat on the coffee table, smiled a little and laughed.

"You're an asshole," I said, "I missed you man."

"Same here man, you should have told me all of this sooner."

"I know," I acknowledged my mistake. "I'm sorry."

"No worries man," Scott stood up and put a hand on my shoulder, "I don't know what I can do to help, but I'll try. This sounds like some end of the world type shit and I'd rather not have the world end yet."

"Thanks, but we can't do it without Beth," my voice caught a little, "and right now she's gone and not even Professor Cline knows where she is."

Scott pulled me to my feet, put his hands on my shoulders and stared into my eyes like he was looking for something. It honestly made me feel a little uneasy. "What are you doing?"

"Look," Scott was still staring at me, "As much as what happened with not-Beth, Lizzie, whatever, sucks, it sounds like there was pretty much no way for you to tell the difference." Scott let go of me while he continued. "And it sounds like you and Beth were kind of on the verge of something. If and when she comes back, you guys will deal with it but it sounds like, in my opinion, that even though you screwed her cosmic doppelganger that she may have overreacted given the circumstances."

"I still fucked up though." I surrendered.

"And you will probably fuck up again, it's part of your charm." Scott punched me hard in the arm.

"Ow, man!" Damn that hurt.

"Because," Scott smiled like the asshole that he is, "Maybe that will remind you to stop telling girls that you love them as your opening line."

"I seriously don't know what to do next." I might have felt better by telling Scott what's been going on, but I wasn't any less confused.

"I know, man," Scott sounded concerned, "Is there anything else you remember at all that might help?"

I told him that I didn't think so. Even though everything happened a couple of days ago, it really did seem like an eternity. I thought back to that night with Lizzie. Just thinking about it made me shudder in a mix of rage and sorrow. My heart actually hurt thinking about it. "I do remember that she didn't smell normal."

"She didn't smell normal?" Scott sounded confused. "What are you, a wolf now?"

"No, like Beth has a perfume or something that smells like baked apples," I explained, "Lizzie didn't smell like that. She smelled like, I don't know how to describe it, cold. Like you know how the air kind of smells when it's about to snow? She smelled like that, but I thought it was just because it was freezing outside."

Scott nodded as I continued rambling.

"She wasn't, like, super warm either. Beth gets warm really easily but she stayed at a cool to normal temp the whole time…" My voice trailed off a bit. How was I so blind to all of this before?

"You okay?"

"No," I was getting more upset at myself the more I thought about everything, "I missed such obvious stuff. I'm an idiot."

"Yes, you are," Scott was not helping my self esteem, "But being into someone makes you blind sometimes. Sometimes obvious things are overlooked and it sounds like she had just the right excuses to pull one over on you."

I shrugged my shoulders, stood up, and walked into my room, closing the door behind me. I just wanted to go to sleep again, I was still so mentally drained. Telling Scott everything helped, but realizing that there were obvious clues that I overlooked just felt like knives in my heart. Coupling that with the fact that I may, in fact, be responsible for the coming end of the world made me really tired all of a sudden.

For the next week Scott practically had to drag me out of bed to get me to go to my classes. My motivation was gone, but I sat through all of my classes like a zombie. I don't know how I absorbed any information and with finals rapidly approaching I didn't feel any stress. Why should I? The world would probably be ending soon so my grades probably wouldn't matter much anyway.

The one place I did go back to every day was the cave. Professor Cline seemed to appreciate that I was there, even though I don't know how much help I was actually being. Beth hadn't come back yet and he hadn't heard from her. The Professor sounded a little worried but was sure she was being safe and, most importantly, was still alive. My eyes would always drift to where she would sit, all that was there was my jacket that he hung on her charred seat.

I missed her so much.

Professor Cline was in contact with The Conclave a lot. I wasn't sure where the home office, for lack of a better term, was and he never disclosed it to me. I know that there was a constant string of emails between him and, I guess, the higher ups there. They were not happy that one of their Casters had gone missing and they definitely were not happy about the situation that I may have caused. The Professor didn't mention my name, or my part in the situation to the best of my knowledge, just that Lizzie had a device that could possibly destroy everything.

The Professor seemed to be getting more stressed by the day. We barely spoke when I was there but I know it gave me a little bit of comfort just being here and I hoped that he felt the same.

The Professor worked on something all week. I wasn't sure what it was exactly and when I asked all he would say is 'hopefully something that can help us'. I would hand him various tools and items that he would ask for and watched him build this thing that kind of looked like a clawed glove.

By the end of the week I was still pretty drained. Scott did his best to try to keep my spirits up but what really helped me feel better was just being here in the cave. I think it was less about feeling better and more about just wanting to talk to Beth if and when she showed up again.

Another week went by and we were starting to approach winter break. I was in the cave with the Professor and he was about to call it quits for the day so I got ready to leave. As he explained, sort of, what this thing he was building was when both of us heard the gateway open. We looked over and saw Beth appear on the platform. My heart skipped a beat when I saw her but when she locked eyes with me she looked away.

"Elizabeth!" Professor Cline exclaimed in what sounded like relief mixed with anger, like when a parent is glad you're home safe but so mad that you may have done something dangerous. "Where have you been?"

"Away." Beth avoided looking at me as she addressed the Professor.

"I was worried. You can't just disappear like that, especially now."

"Yeah, well, I had to." Beth looked directly into his eyes. "We all need to have our secrets, don't we?"

Professor Cline silently turned back to his work, not wanting to continue this conversation, at least right now. Beth still seemed super pissed at him. I had no idea how she felt toward me but given the conversation I just witnessed with The Professor, I didn't have a good feeling.

Beth walked over to the monitors and started looking at the various calculations that were on them. As she walked by me I caught a whiff of baked apples and closed my eyes for a moment, just taking it in. How could I have missed that with Lizzie?

I knew I had to try to talk to Beth. I needed to know if she was okay, if we were okay, if everything was going to be okay, or if everything was really as fucked as I thought it was. And what if I really had just caused the end of the world? I started to walk toward Beth trying to figure out what I was going to say. I knew I had to apologize, again, but I really didn't have a plan after that. I stood next to her as she looked at the screens and didn't say anything for a minute.

"Beth," I said softly, "I'm glad you're back."

Beth didn't say anything, she just kept looking forward. I saw her jaw clench a little so I at least know she heard me. I decided to continue to at least try to reach her.

"I'm sorry, I…" I began.

"It's fine." Beth continued looking at the screens.

"It's not. I just…" I kept on.

"Jake, I said it was fine." I got cut off again. "Besides, it's not like we were anything anyway. Now I just have to figure out how to stop the end of the world from happening because you couldn't control yourself."

I didn't know how to respond to that. I felt my face starting to get warm and my eyes start to get watery so I just turned around and walked to the gateway platform. I went through, left the basement of The Griffon and trudged back to the dorm. By the time I got there it was after midnight. I didn't realize how long I was in the cave.

I poked my head into Scott's room and he was sleeping. He had all kinds of textbooks and papers everywhere, I thought all of his tests were over, but I guess not. I really was hoping that he was awake. I wanted to talk to him and tell him Beth was back and ask how I should deal with it. He had more experience in dealing with pissed off girls than I did, that's for sure.

I went into my room and flopped down on the bed. I knew I had to sleep, but I couldn't. I just laid there, thinking of everything I caused and how I could even possibly try to make it better. As I lay there torturing myself I finally drifted off to sleep.

I dreamt that Beth and I were walking along the Wallkill River, near where we found the first Rift Ripper. We were talking, but I couldn't make out the words. As we were walking, it started to snow and we stopped to watch it. I started to walk again and couldn't move. I looked back to Beth.

She was an ice statue.

I let go of her hand and touched her face. She was solid ice, not like a frozen person, but almost see through ice. The snow was still falling and I was starting to panic when I heard a voice that went right through me.

"Aww, what's the matter Jakey? Is your girlfriend freezing you out?"

I turned around quickly and saw that standing about six feet in front of me was Lizzie. She looked like she could be Beth's twin, but with electric blue eyes and blond hair. She was dressed in something that reminded me of an outfit a biker would wear. A leather looking low cut top, leather pants and a long, midnight-blue coat. She seemed to stare directly through me.

I felt a wave of fear ripple through me. I knew I was dreaming, but she was a terrifying sight.

In the blink of an eye Lizzie appeared up close in front of me and I stumbled back a couple of steps. The ice statue of Beth was gone, it was just Lizzie and me.

I said the only thing I could think of, "This is a fucking nightmare."

"Is it?" Lizzie sounded amused. "I thought you would be happy to see me. We had such fun last time." She started to run her fingers down my chest and I pushed them away.

"I thought you were Beth."

Lizzie snapped her fingers and instantly looked like Beth.

"Does this make you feel better? This weaker version of me?" Lizzie looked just like Beth. Lizzie made a mirror out of ice in her hand to look at herself, made a face of disgust and snapped her fingers again to go back to her normal look.

I looked around and saw that we weren't on the bank of the Wallkill River anymore. We were standing on Mohonk Mountain, a few hundred yards from Skytop Tower. I looked around, a little unsure of what to expect.

"I've been watching you for a long time Jakey," Lizzie's words rang like icicles in the air, "Since that night in Wallkill when you found one of my toys. You and the little firestarter made quite a team once she got out of her own way."

"You wanted us to find that." I said softly.

In a blink Lizzie was behind me and whispered in my ear. "I did."

I nearly jumped out of my skin and Lizzie laughed.

"So jumpy," Lizzie said as she walked around to stand in front of me, "Nothing like my Jakey. He was a warrior."

Her Jakey?

"I wanted you two to find that and you did, so bravo." Lizzie gave me a little golf clap. "It made it so easy to listen in and plan my next steps."

She was spying on us the whole time, I thought to myself.

"Once I knew that you had it I knew I had to pay this Earth's Jakey a visit once the time was right. You'll make a suitable replacement once I get rid of that annoyance that you're so in love with."

Lizzie made another ice sculpture of Beth and stared at it for a moment.

"Pathetic." She said and shattered it.

"What are you talking about?" I demanded.

"Not to go all Bond-villain," Lizzie purred, "but this is just a dream after all,"

Lizzie raised her eyebrow, pushed me to the ground and sat on top of me, straddling my hips. I had flashbacks to Thanksgiving Eve as she continued talking.

"After I kill your little friend and take her power for my own, and once I open the rift above Skytop Tower, I will be able to mold the perfect Earth. The one I need, the one I desire, the one that brings me everything I want." I felt Lizzie grind her hips deeper into me.

I asked her, "What do you want?" *I* wanted her off of me but at the moment I squirmed and was trapped.

"The perfect life." She said with a smile. "I mean, my life is pretty great right now, but it's not perfect. Playing with my lesser, and *playing* with you has been fun, but I'm ready to end it now."

Lizzie bent down and had her face inches from mine.

"Why don't we have a date?" She said softly in my ear.

"What?" I heard her, I just couldn't believe her.

"Meet me here on New Years Eve and we can celebrate with a bang." She grinded her hips again. "You can even bring that imposter, it will make it easier for me to knock out everything at one time. A little murder, a little sex, a brand new world. Sounds like a party to me."

"You're nuts!" I tried to push Lizzie off of me but she didn't budge.

"Maybe," Lizzie said whimsically, "Maybe not. Either way, it's inevitable. Besides, it's just a dream anyway. This is all made up in your head."

Lizzie leaned down and brushed her lips against mine, looked in my eyes and smiled. I had never seen eyes so blue in my life, they looked unnatural.

"See you soon." She snapped her fingers and I woke up in a cold sweat. My brain was a scary place sometimes but holy shit did this take the cake. Lizzie looked insane. Those blue eyes seemed to pierce into me, drilling right into my soul. There was no way what she was saying was real right? That was just my head trying to make sense of all of this craziness.

That's when I heard Scott yell my name from the living room.

I jumped out of bed onto my freezing floor and threw open the door. When I opened it, it was snowing in my living room. I felt my mouth fall open and I looked over to Scott who was in his doorway.

"What the fuck dude?" Scott looked at the ceiling and we just watched the snow fall. I tried to remember a time where my life wasn't turned upside down with crazy multiverse shit.

"Lizzie was here I think," I said to him, "And I think I know her plan."

CHAPTER NINETEEN

"So let me get this straight," Scott said as we hopped in my truck and sped towards The Griffon, "Lizzie showed up in your head, but not in your head, and told you her whole plan?"

"It looks that way, yeah, considering the lock was frozen off of our front door." It freaked me out that she was in our place again. Everything I felt in the dream was apparently not just a dream.

"Holy shit man, this whole thing is fucked up."

"Yup." It was the only thing I could say.

I whipped into the parking lot of The Griffon and led Scott directly to the basement. It was early in the morning, and I was pretty sure I wasn't making my last day of classes before the break. Hopefully I could catch Professor Cline before he went to his. I walked up to the wall and placed my hand on the brick that started the bricks shifting into place for the gateway.

Scott's jaw fell open and he just stared at me. The wall shifted and contorted until a black and teal gateway appeared in front of us. I grabbed Scott by the wrist and instantly felt him lock his body down.

"What the hell are you doing?" Scott sounded genuinely terrified.

"Bringing you with me," I said as calmly as I could, "We have to go through here to get to the cave where Professor Cline and Beth are."

"The hell *we* do!" Scott tried to pull back from me. "There is no way in hell I am going through that thing!"

"Scott," I let go of his wrist and put my hands on his shoulders with my back facing the gateway, "Listen, I've kept a lot from you this year and I'm sorry. I need you to trust me, you'll be fine. I've done this a lot. Nothing to worry about."

Scott raised a skeptical eyebrow, looked at me, looked at the gateway over my shoulder and looked back at me.

"It's safe? Is it gonna make me feel weird? It's way too early for this shit." He had genuine concerns.

"Yeah, you'll be fine. No discomfort at all." I lied, it was the only way to get him to come.

I grabbed Scott's wrist again and we walked through the gateway. In an instant we were in the cave and Scott looked like he was going to throw up. He fell to his hands and knees on the ground and made heaving sounds.

I asked him, "You okay buddy?"

Scott looked up at me and shook his head "no". "I hate you," he said as he struggled to get his bearings.

"You'll be fine in a minute and then you can feel free to hate me more later when we go back." I chuckled, thinking that this is how I must have looked the first time through, "Anyway, this is the place."

I started to walk down the ramp, called out for Professor Cline and, with a bit of trepidation, Beth. After a moment Professor Cline appeared in the doorway looking like he was about to leave for class.

"Mister Howard!" He exclaimed and then looked behind me at the huddled mass of Scott on the floor near the gateway. "And you brought a guest? May I ask why?"

"We have a problem and Scott was kind of a witness to it." I started pacing a little, and tried to figure out what to say, when I heard another voice from the doorway.

"What the hell is he doing here?" Beth pointed to Scott and sounded pissed. She marched over to The Professor and I and luckily she wasn't on fire. Yet.

"I was just about to tell the Professor," I said to Beth while she stared at me, her eyes slowly getting flecks of orange, "Something just happened and Scott was there."

Scott made his way to his feet and stumbled over to us, holding onto my shoulder for support. I helped him into a chair behind me and turned back to explain what was going on to Beth and Professor Cline.

"So last night, after I left, I had a dream and…"

"A dream Jake, really?" Beth cut me off, sounding annoyed. "We don't have time for dreams, we have real problems, thanks to you."

"Lizzie showed up in my dream," I blurted out, "Except it apparently wasn't as much of a dream as I thought. She broke into our dorm last night and I think she told me her whole plan."

"What?" Professor Cline sounded concerned and Beth stopped talking. "How do you know she was there?"

"Because it was snowing in our living room," Scott said, slowly rising to his feet, "And our lock was frozen off." Scott walked over and stood slightly behind me. If Beth could shoot fire from her eyes, both of us would be dead with the looks she was shooting us.

I told them everything that I remembered: the way Lizzie looked, everything she said, and that I thought it was just my head making all of this up, and making me feel things. That was all plausible until I woke up and saw the snow. Scott backed up everything I said and I told them that Scott knew everything about what was going on here. Professor Cline didn't like that at all, but he understood and Beth was quiet the whole time taking turns scowling at Scott and me.

"This is very concerning." Professor Cline walked over to his computer and started tapping the keys. "What could be significant about New Years Eve?"

"New year, new me?" Scott said softly. I shot him a stern look and shook my head and I saw Beth roll her eyes. We locked eyes and she looked away and walked over to Professor Cline.

I was getting annoyed at this whole thing going on with Beth. I didn't ask for any of this to happen and for all I knew Beth and I were the ones hooking up, not Lizzie. Beth wasn't listening to my side of the story at all and whenever I tried to talk to her I got shut out. But right now we all had to figure out what Lizzie was up to, I'll try to sort everything out with Beth after all this is done. That's if there's a Beth, or even this Earth, left.

"I need to contact The Conclave," Professor Cline walked away from his computer and back toward the doorway he appeared in earlier, "I would recommend not staying in your dorm. You were heading to your parents today, yes?"

I nodded, "Yeah, I just have to grab my stuff."

"Excellent," Professor Cline turned back towards me, "Hopefully Lizzie won't find you there. We now have a time limit. I'm optimistic The Conclave will have answers and we can figure out how to stop her."

After The Professor left Scott, Beth and I remained standing in the cave. You could cut the tension in the air with a knife. None of us said anything, the awkward silence only being accompanied by the occasional ambient echoing from our cavernous surroundings. Beth walked back over to the computer and I just watched her silently. There was so much that I wanted to say to her but she just wouldn't listen. Anytime I would try to say anything I would get shut down after a couple of words. I guess she still needed time, but it looked like time on our Earth was running short.

"Nice place you have here." Scott was the first to break the silence.

Beth turned her head slightly towards us before turning back to the monitors.

"Don't you guys have to leave?" She sounded as monotone as when I first met her.

"Yeah," I said, "I guess so."

"Don't forget your jacket, Jake," Beth pointed over to the chair, her back still to us before sarcastically adding, "It's not like the cold bothers you anyway."

I don't know if it was her delivery, my feelings or everything I have been through this year but I felt an overwhelming sense of rage fill me. I had enough, I was tired of being shut down.

"You know, Beth, I didn't ask for any of this and I'm tired of you treating me like I wanted this to happen." I was trying to keep myself in check, not yelling or screaming, but talking as calmly as possible.

Beth stopped typing but kept her back to me.

"I've tried to say I'm sorry so many times, so many fucking times, but you cut me off every time. I'm sorry. I AM SORRY!" I could feel myself getting more angry the more I spoke. "Since I met you my entire world has been flipped and how the hell am I the one apologizing for it? Multiple Earths, having to worry about every goddamn decision I think about, possibly causing the end of the world and yet I'm here apologizing to a girl that doesn't want to hear it because I made a mistake! Because a girl showed up to my door that I thought was YOU! The girl that I've liked since the first day I met her but turned out to be an evil version of her from another Earth?! So sorry that I didn't see that one coming!"

I felt Scott put his hand on my shoulder and I brushed it away. Beth still had her back to me but I saw her hand grip the armrest of the chair a little tighter. I didn't know if she was getting upset or about to roast me where I stood but I didn't care. I was tired of being a passenger in this.

"So news flash," I continued my tirade, "I've been into you since day one. All this time I've been into you and I wasn't sure how you felt, especially over these last few weeks. Maybe you were, maybe you weren't. Maybe I was gun-shy just because of everything else that came bundled with you. I know some people have baggage, and yeah, I have my own, but nothing compares to what you brought to the table. But despite all of that, all of this danger and bullshit that you brought with you, I still found myself falling in fucking love with you."

I heard Scott smack his forehead behind me and mutter. "Seriously, dude?"

"There I said it, I love you. Since the first day we met. So when I thought you showed up at my door that night, and everything that the person *that I thought was you* said and did, I thought maybe things were finally working out for me. Turns out I was just fucking everything up." I felt my voice catch a bit but I continued. "So I'm sorry, I'll be sorry till the end of time. Oh and I guess that might be coming sooner rather than later so I guess soon it won't matter. The world could end tomorrow for all I care because all I want is to be with you and I fucked that up too."

Beth stayed silent, but I saw her grip release a little from the chair. I was trembling at this point, a mix of passion, rage and just exhaustion. Scott put his hand on my shoulder again and told me that we should go. I grabbed his wrist and walked him through the gateway, not looking behind me to see if Beth had anything to say or do.

I gave Scott a few minutes to recover and then we drove back to the dorm in silence. It wasn't snowing in our living room anymore, but I hurried up and gathered some clothes and my Playstation before I was about to go home for the holidays. Scott gave me a hug and told me that he will try to see if he could figure out something to help and I thanked him.

I had some time to think on the drive back home as snow started falling again. I was so damn sick of the snow at this point, it seemed like it was snowing like every other day. The snow made me think of all of the bullshit with Lizzie which made me think about Beth. I didn't want to yell, but I was so tired of not being heard about all of this. Should I have said I loved her? No, probably not. But I did, it's out there, I'm in love with Beth and I inadvertently screwed it up and may be causing the end of the world. I pulled over on the side of the road and had, what I think, was a mild panic attack for a few minutes before driving again.

My mind was still a muddled mess as I turned into the driveway. Part of me was thinking it would be better if I just didn't ever go back to the cave again. At this point I was probably doing more harm than good being there, a distraction that kept Professor

Cline and Beth from actually doing the work to save the world. But I made this mess, I needed to at least try to clean it up.

I walked in and was greeted to the smell of freshly baked cookies and a screaming brother and sister fighting over Super Mario Kart in one of their bedrooms. I avoided seeing them right away and instead made a beeline right to the kitchen where I gave my Mom a huge hug. She handed me a cookie and asked if everything was alright and said that I looked stressed.

I laughed internally, *She had no idea.*

I told her I was fine and that it has just been a stressful year so far. We talked a little and she asked about 'the girl I talked about on Thanksgiving'. I kind of avoided the question and just said we weren't really talking at the moment and I think Mom sensed there was something more but she just left it alone.

The next couple of weeks were kind of a blur. I went to the cave a couple of times but I never stayed long. Beth graduated from not talking to me to saying a couple of words here or there like 'could you hand me that' or 'thanks'. She was helping Professor Cline build whatever this thing was, which looked more and more like a glove of some type. In between building and the sparks that were flying from his tinkering he kept a watchful eye on me and Beth. I don't know if she told him what I said, hell at this point I don't even remember everything I said, but there was a tinge of sadness behind his eyes whenever he would look away and go back to his work.

I tried to spend a lot more time with my family but I still had a sense of impending doom. I tried to lift my spirits by taking my siblings to see the Hudson Valley's weirdest Christmas tradition, Eggbert, who is a giant animatronic, crowned, talking egg. The end of the world was coming and I was starting to feel like there was nothing I could do but just accept it.

Jen came by on Christmas Eve to visit the family. She spent almost as much time here as Scott did back in the day and my parents thought of her like another daughter. She showed up after dinner and the whole time she kept looking at me as if knowing that something was wrong. As Jen was leaving she asked me to walk her to her car and I did, knowing this was her way of trying to talk to me alone. My sister never left her alone and Jen never minded, but it was like having a growth attached to you. It was cute, but that left Jen and me with no chance to talk. The minute we were outside and out of earshot, the questions started.

"Why do you look like death?" Jen didn't bother to beat around the bush with me. "You barely said anything tonight."

I didn't want to tell her anything about what I may have caused, but I did want to tell her the truth as best I could.

"I think I screwed things up really bad with Beth," I said truthfully, "Like *really* bad. Kinda feel like it's the end of the world." Again, not a lie, but not the whole truth either.

"What happened?" Jen leaned back against her Corolla. She genuinely wanted to know.

I gave her an abridged version, leaving out Lizzie and multiverse stuff, that sounded believable based on my previous track record. I said that she came by after that night at The Griffon, we started hooking up, I told her I loved her and it freaked her out and we haven't really talked about it. I followed that up with that we had a huge fight about something a couple of days ago and that I think it's over with her.

Jen responded by punching me in the chest. I was wearing a thick coat but I still felt a little bit of a sting.

"Didn't I tell you not to lead with that?" Jen shook her head in disapproval.

"What can I say," I said as I rubbed my chest, "I'm an idiot."

"You are, but it probably isn't as bad as you think." Jen gave me a hug and a kiss on the cheek. "Just give her some time."

"Yeah, maybe." There was so much more that I couldn't tell Jen.

"Merry Christmas Jake," Jen said as she sat in the driver's seat and started the car.

"You, too," I replied as I carefully closed her door.

I stood in the driveway and waved to her as she drove away. I watched Jen make a left at the end of the driveway and then sat on the bench and just listened to the silence. Between the heavy coating of snow and the thick woods around my parents house, it was very peaceful. I heard some kind of rumble in the distance, probably a tractor trailer or something as I went inside to join the family for the tradition of getting Christmas pajamas from Santa's elves.

I woke up the next day to my siblings barging into my room at six in the morning and attacking me in my bed. I was still half asleep and I almost slapped the Rig to make a shield before I knew what was happening and came to my senses. They dragged me upstairs where Mom had already started making breakfast and Dad still looked half asleep, drinking his coffee and probably cursing the fact that he had kids that woke him up this early on Christmas.

We opened a couple of presents before breakfast, a tradition my parents started about six years ago to keep us quiet and content until after we ate and the living room turned into a warzone filled with bows and paper. After breakfast there was a knock at the door and Scott walked in. If my parents treated Jen like a daughter, Scott might as well have been my twin. Instantly my mom put a plate of food down in front of him and he ate it happily, all while giving me looks of urgency.

After we all opened our presents Scott and I descended the basement steps to my room so we could play my new games: Grand Theft Auto and Bushido Blade. After I closed my door Scott took a sheet of paper out of his pocket and unfolded it onto my bed. It looked like some type of weather map.

"Did you hear that rumble last night?" He asked in a serious tone.

"Yeah?" I said, "It sounded like a truck in the distance or something. You live further than I do, was it like near you or something?"

"No, further," Scott said and pointed at the map and I looked at where his finger was, "It came from near Skytop Tower."

I felt my heart drop into my stomach.

"Like from the mountain?" I asked.

"No, the air above it." Scott clarified his statement from earlier. "There is some really weird atmospheric stuff happening over there, like way off the charts. I've been wondering about the weather patterns and why this winter has been so brutal and my professor said in class right before the break that the weather patterns were very unusual."

I listened intently with a knot in my stomach.

"Because I'm a weather nerd," he continued, "I looked up weather map patterns at the library and compared them to the one I had in class when Professor Garland was giving his lecture. It looks like the pressure is building right above Mohonk Mountain."

"Do you think this is because of Lizzie?" I already knew the answer in my gut.

"Probably, yeah, but why?" He asked, but I didn't want to tell him why.

"Professor Cline might know," I started pacing nervously, "Lizzie did say something about Skytop Tower and New Years Eve. Maybe, like a pipe or something, the pressure is going to release and that has something to do with the merging of Earths?"

"I understand like half of what you said," Scott chuckled a little, "But it sounds that way, yeah."

"We should head over right now." I grabbed my keys from my nightstand and went for my door. Scott gathered his papers from my bed and followed me as we walked upstairs. I told my parents I'd be back and that we were going to visit Scott's parents for a bit and that we would be back for dinner.

My gut told me that Beth and Professor Cline were still in the cave. As we jumped in the truck, I really hoped that they were. I guessed that saving the world doesn't take holidays off.

CHAPTER TWENTY

Scott lay on the floor of the cave near the gateway after surviving his third trip through. I checked on him to make sure he was okay before calling out for Professor Cline. He must have heard the sound from the gateway because he appeared quickly after our arrival and seemed surprised that we were there. He was wearing a Santa hat and had a drink in his hand as we met by the computer.

"Mister Howard! Mister Connelly! Merry Christmas!" Professor Cline was in an unusually chipper mood considering we had a week until the end of the world. "What brings the two of you here? You should be spending time with your families!"

"Professor, are you okay?" I was concerned. The Professor was usually pretty straight laced but I'm pretty sure he was a little tipsy.

"Yes, my boy, I am fine." Professor Cline swayed as he walked over to his chair and had a seat. "Just coming to terms with my part in this mess that is happening." He leaned back in his chair and took a big breath.

"Professor?"

"Mister Howard," He addressed me but kept his eyes facing the roof of the cave, "I have been wracking my brain since classes let out about how to fix this. Elizabeth is still angry at me for being deceitful, over time I would hope that she understands that I did it for her protection. Lizzie's plan to unite The Multiverse into one that she has hand crafted seems impossible, but after doing some research, I have found something disturbing that may actually make her plan possible."

I was curious, "What did you find out?"

"I found out that Lizzie is entirely in control of an incredible amount of power." The Professor seemed very out of it; he was either talking to me or just speaking out loud. Either way, he was definitely drunk.

"We knew that but..." I started.

"She has killed nearly one hundred versions of herself to amass that power."

I stopped talking abruptly, and took that in. Holy shit. The Professor continued his ramblings.

"I sent Elizabeth home to visit with her father and stepmother. She thinks I am making some progress on," he pointed over to the glove-looking thing, "that. But I don't even know what it exactly is. The image of that glove just showed up in my head after all of this started and I began working on it. It's almost as if there is something missing, something I'm not quite seeing, that will finally let me realize how this will help."

I could tell The Professor was at the end of his rope and I felt really uneasy. I was certain if anyone would have a plan, it was Professor Cline, but he was almost as lost as we were. I felt a hand on my shoulder and Scott stood next to me looking a little less green than when we came in.

"Professor," I nearly forgot why we were here, "Scott may have found something."

"Mister Connelly," The Professor's gaze still hadn't moved from the ceiling of the cave, "Hopefully it is something I haven't considered. Right now, hope is all I have."

Scott handed Professor Cline the weather map research he found. Professor Cline fixed his eyes on it and I watched as they widened.

Scott explained, "There's something weird happening with the weather patterns and it's focused right above Skytop Tower. It's almost like..."

"Lizzie is building up atmospheric pressure in order to get enough force to power whatever device she will be using!" The

Professor shot up from his chair and nearly fell over. I grabbed his arm to steady him and he thanked me.

"Sure, I was going to say some of that, at least." Scott said.

"Yes! Of course! Of course that would be how she would amass the power required to do such a thing as combine The Multiverse! How could I have missed that?" Professor Cline was pacing in front of the computer rambling to himself, putting together the pieces of what he was missing. I silently watched him, not wanting to interrupt his train of thought as he continued.

"By building up the atmospheric pressure, combining it with the power she has amassed from other versions of herself and using a Rift Ripper she would, theoretically, be able to open a tear in the fabric of The Multiverse. She wouldn't be able to control it though, she thinks she can, but she would be destroyed along with everything else." Professor Cline typed on his computer and pulled up a weather map like what Scott showed us, but it looked like it was in real time. It looked like there was a slowly moving vortex swirling over Skytop Tower.

"Is she going to use Skytop Tower as a dimensional lightning rod or something?" I asked.

"Exactly!" Professor Cline and Scott said at the same time. They looked at each other and gave each other a little nod of approval.

"I know what the glove is for now!" Professor Cline exclaimed "It's to divert the energy!"

Scott and I watched the Professor with curiosity and he scrambled for some supplies and drew a diagram.

Professor Cline furiously drew arrows and shapes as he explained: "Lizzie needs to combine some of her energy with the Rift Ripper before the atmosphere explodes with the pressure that has been building. Once, or if, that happens, the tear opens and everything ends." Professor Cline drew an explosion before starting another diagram below it. His drawing reminded me of John Madden's excited marks on the screens of many NFL games. "The glove would have to be able to either divert that energy before it gets there, by being close enough to Lizzie to lure it out or by getting to the Rift Ripper and removing it from wherever it is. If the device isn't where it needs to be at midnight on New Years Eve, the explosion in the atmosphere will do nothing except sound like thunder and, presumably, pull Lizzie back to where she came from. The problem is that the device she is using needs to be grabbed as close to midnight as possible, just about when the pressure is about to burst."

This sounded like the most dangerous plan ever concocted. Professor Cline, sobered up, rushed over to the glove and started working on it again with Scott following close behind. There was one important thing that wasn't brought up through the Professor's ramblings.

"When is Beth coming back?" I asked.

"Elizabeth should be back tomorrow." Professor Cline responded from behind a shower of sparks. I saw that Scott wore a pair of welding goggles, was watching intently, and being more help than I ever could. "When I sent her home I had very little hope that I would have a plan of action. I feel confident that we are on our way now."

Hearing those words gave me some comfort, something I lacked on my way here. The Professor was reinvigorated and having Scott here seemed right, the only thing missing was Beth. Maybe after, dare I say if, we saved the world we could sort out something. Anything. For now it was probably better just to focus on a plan to stop Lizzie.

Scott and I didn't leave the cave till almost midnight. We drove back to my parents' house and he crashed in my room, just like high school. We did play a little bit of Bushido Blade, the most unfair fighting game I have ever played. It was fun, but dying in one hit was bullshit. We passed out at about two in the morning and I felt just a little bit of hope as I drifted off to sleep.

When I woke up, Scott was already upstairs eating and chatting with Mom. She handed me a plate of waffles and I sat down to eat. Scott had already told my mom that we were going to be out all day because of some 'weather experiment' that we were doing and she just told us to be careful and not to blow anything up. In high school Scott and I had a habit of making things explode, or melt, depending on how bored we were.

His fourth trip through the Gateway went more smoothly than the first three. Scott was able to stay on his feet and only needed to brace himself slightly to keep his balance. He took a deep breath and gave me a thumbs up before visiting Professor Cline, already hard at work on the glove. I didn't see Beth anywhere.

Professor Cline waved us over to show us the progress he made. I'm pretty sure he was up all night because this thing looked a lot different than it did yesterday. It reminded me of a mix of the old Nintendo Power Glove controller and the way artists draw Colossus in X-Men when he turns metal. It looked pretty cool, even though it wasn't completely finished yet, and looked like it was made with bronze and steel. If I were to put it on it looked like it would come about halfway up my forearm.

"I've made some modifications to the original design." Professor Cline was still wearing his Santa hat from last night and his eyes looked bloodshot. There was a giant Thermos next to him that I *assumed* was coffee.

"Have you slept?" I asked with genuine concern.

"A few minutes here and there," Professor Cline responded, "Every time I started to drift off a new idea would appear in my head and I would jump up and figure out how to implement it." He was talking really fast, like the only thing he was running on was caffeine. A lot of caffeine.

"Professor, why don't you take a break?" Scott said poking up from behind the workstation. "I know time is ticking, but you need to keep your mind sharp."

"There is no time for a break Mister Connelly," Professor Cline leaned back in his chair, "We have less than *six days* to stop Lizzie from destroying The Multiverse!"

"I get that," I said while I looked closely at the glove, "But you need to rest. Even if it's just for an hour or so." This thing really was cool looking.

"Hey Jake," Scott pointed towards Professor Cline and whispered, "He's asleep."

I looked at the Professor and saw that he was passed out in his chair. Scott and I tried to keep it down while we examined the glove.

"Do you have any idea how this is going to work?" I whispered to Scott.

"I'm not sure," Scott placed his hand under it and slightly lifted the glove off of its base and back again, "But it looks like it might be like a giant heat sink since he used copper and aluminum."

"So it would disperse the energy?" I asked Scott and he nodded his head.

I thought, *That's pretty cool, but who was going to wear it?*

About a half hour later, the sound of a gateway opening on the platform startled the two of us and Beth appeared in front of it. She turned her head toward us, took a deep breath, and walked down the stairs in our direction. She looked amazing, but that also could have been because I hadn't seen her in a few days. She was stone faced as she reached us and she then looked at the Professor.

"How long has he been out?" Beth's voice was low, a couple of notches above a whisper,

"About a half hour or so," I matched her tone, "He was up all night working on this."

Beth walked away from us and through the double doors on the far side of the cave. A moment later she returned holding a blanket, laid it over Professor Cline, placed her hand lightly on his shoulder and walked back over to Scott and me. We didn't say anything, Scott and I just watched.

"So, is there a plan?" Beth asked us flatly.

"More or less." I looked to Scott. "You want to explain what you figured out?"

Scott explained the weather patterns he noticed and all of the atmospheric pressure that was building over Skytop Tower. I chimed in with what Professor Cline told me about Lizzie killing almost a hundred versions of herself, to become more powerful, and that she isn't going to be able to control the tear she is trying to make. I tried to sound as business-like as possible. I tried to put my feelings aside so that we could focus on the task at hand. We only had six days, no time for a pity party.

Beth nodded, taking in all of the information we just told her, before looking up at Scott.

"I'm sorry I made you crack your head." Beth said. I couldn't tell if she was being sincere or not but I was pretty sure she was.

"Thanks," Scott said with a little shock in his voice, "I'm sorry I was being a dick and I'm sorry I called you..." he stopped talking and took a moment to finish, "That word you don't like."

Beth gave a slight smile and placed her hand on his elbow, then looked at me, still smiling. My heart skipped a beat.

"You don't need to say anything," Beth looked directly into my eyes, "I know how you feel. I..." Beth stopped talking for a second and looked up and to the right. "I may have overreacted. I'm sorry."

I didn't know what to say, but she continued.

"I'm still a little hurt," Beth added, "But we can figure that out later. Right now, we need to stop that bitch and we only have a few days to prepare."

I nodded in agreement and looked from Beth to Scott. It looked like we were all on the same page, united in the face of impending doom.

Professor Cline woke up a couple of hours later as Beth, Scott and I were trying to form some type of battle plan. We didn't come up with anything solid. The Professor walked over towards Beth and she stood up and gave him a hug. He gave her a kiss on the top of her head and that was that. All of the disagreements and bullshit over the last month or so was put aside so we could figure out how to stop Lizzie.

Over the next few days we all were doing what we could to prepare. I told my parents that Scott and I were going to New York City for a few days and staying there for New Years Eve while, in reality, we decided it would be best to stay in the Mohonk Mountain House so we wouldn't be far and could get more work done. Since I was a kid I've always been freaked out a little by the place just because the building looks like it could be haunted, but hell, it was nice in here and since they've worked with The Conclave for years it was warded and safe.

Scott and Professor Cline worked hard on the glove, while Beth and I did more combat training in between trying to come up with a better name for what they were building other than 'The Glove'. Nothing we came up with seemed to stick, so we just reluctantly settled on The Glove.

Beth and I were talking like when she first started warming up to me. Neither of us brought up what happened, and we both seemed to be able to keep our feelings at bay in order to concentrate on the task at hand. We agreed to not talk about anything we were feeling until after, or if, we came out of this alive. Anytime feelings might be creeping into our conversation we would just go back to the armory for some more combat training.

We wound up doing a lot of combat training over the next few days.

Before the four of us knew it, it was the morning of New Year's Eve. I woke up and looked out of my window and couldn't see outside at all. There was such a heavy snowfall outside, it was almost like a thick fog covering the area. I turned on the television and flipped over to the local news and they said that forecasts were calling for upwards of six feet of snow, possibly more. They were calling this the worst winter storm in recent memory, but they had no idea what was *really* going on.

I got dressed and walked over to Scott's room only to find that he was gone already. His bed didn't look like it was slept in at all so I figured that he and Professor Cline had probably pulled another all nighter. I walked down the hallway towards the double doors that led to the cave, swung them open and headed towards the argument that I heard as soon as I opened the door.

"Elizabeth, I can not have you do that!" I heard Professor Cline yell.

"Why not?" Beth responded vehemently, "I'd rather put my life at risk than risk anyone else's!"

"Either way, this plan is fucking nuts." Scott said.

The bickering continued as I approached. The Professor saw me and everyone started to settle down, raising my concerns. I had a really bad feeling about whatever they were talking about.

"What's going on?" I asked, not really sure that I wanted an answer.

No one spoke for a couple seconds before Scott broke the silence.

"Professor Cline and I made a slight miscalculation." Scott said with disappointment in his voice.

"How badly of a miscalculation?" I didn't like the sound of this.

"A pretty big one." Professor Cline added. "We may have made the dampening field too strong on the glove."

"How strong is too strong? Strong is good, right?"

"If I wear it, it nullifies my abilities." Beth said.

"So?" I said, "I was going to wear it anyway, wasn't I?"

"No, you weren't." Beth looked at me with eyes full of sorrow. "I wasn't going to let you wear it. I was going to wear it and face Lizzie alone."

"Are you nuts?" I was genuinely shocked. "That's a suicide mission! She is crazy and super powerful, why would you even try that?"

"Elizabeth still wants to wear it and face her alone." Professor Cline added.

"I wasn't going to put it on until I had her down or I was near the top of the tower, I wasn't going to wear it the whole time!" Beth persisted.

"No I..." I started to speak and Beth cut me off.

"I need to be the one to kill her! Alone!" She blurted out and I felt heat starting to come from her. "After all of the shit she has put us all through, killing my Mom, messing with our lives, our heads," Beth looked at me with tears of rage in her eyes, "After everything she has done, *I* need to be the one to end her!"

I walked over to Beth and reached for her hand. She looked down at her hand and looked back at me, her hazel eyes slowly losing the orange that was filling them. It was warm, not super hot, but warm enough that I felt pretty hot immediately.

"Beth, I get it," I said trying to calm her down, "After all that she has done, she deserves it. But there is no way you are doing this alone. That's reckless. We make a pretty good team, and I'm with you in this until the end."

Beth let go of my hand, crossed her arms and nodded her head in reluctant agreement. I heard Professor Cline and Scott both breathe sighs of relief as we came up with a new plan. Just as we were about to start, an alert flashed on the monitors and a countdown clock appeared and began ticking down. I did some quick math in my head and realized it was clicking down to 11:59pm. I looked at the Professor for an answer.

"The Conclave sent an emergency alert," He said in a dark tone, "They must have sent a probe out to check on the situation and started the Doomsday Clock."

"That doesn't sound good." Scott said.

"It puts a period on everything we're doing." Professor Cline replied. "We have a definite end point."

I was confused and pissed. "They can send a probe but they can't send help?" I questioned. It would seem logical to me that The Conclave would think this was a 'all hands on deck' kind of situation.

"They want us to clean up our own mess, according to my contacts." Professor Cline sounded a little frustrated with that statement.

"I'm wearing the glove." I said turning back to Beth. "End of story."

Beth reluctantly nodded.

"We have just under ten hours," Professor Cline said, "What are the two of you thinking?"

Beth and I looked at each other, neither of us having a good answer. We knew we had to get up there and I either had to get my gloved hand on either Lizzie or the Rift Ripper she was using at the top of the tower, or what we assumed would be a Rift Ripper.

"I need to fight her," Beth said darkly, "I need to kill her or, at the very least, distract her long enough for you to make your way up the tower and get to the top. And then," she paused, "kill her."

"You think that's easier than me just sneaking behind her to grab her." I asked.

"We don't know what kind of tricks she can pull." Professor Cline said. "Lizzie's base abilities are that of a Cryomancer, but we have no idea what the abilities of her other versions were. We also don't know how she is channeling them."

"Dude, she showed up in your head while she was in our place and she literally made it SNOW in our dorm!" Scott added, "Who knows what she can do and what the range is."

I walked closer to the monitors and watched the clock tick down. My mind raced at the task in front of us and the fact that the fate of entire worlds rested on our shoulders. As I was lost in thought I felt Beth's hand lace her fingers into mine and I looked down at her. She returned my look.

"We got this." She said as she looked back at the monitors. Beth gave me a little smile to try to reassure me. I missed that smile.

"I really hope so." I tried to smile through the nervousness I was feeling.

I gripped her hand a little tighter as we continued watching the clock count down. Behind me, I heard Scott and Professor Cline making some final adjustments to the glove and I hoped that all of our efforts were going to work out.

CHAPTER TWENTY-ONE

The clock read that we had just over two hours until midnight and it was time for Beth and me to head to the top of the mountain and, hopefully, save the world. I mean worlds. Since we found out Lizzie's plan, Professor Cline had been scanning the area around Skytop Tower to see if there was any trace of life up there. So far it looked like there was no sign of Lizzie, or anything else, just an intense amount of pressure in the atmosphere and a pulse from the top of the tower.

Scott and Professor Cline called me over to run through the finished version of the glove. Its main function was just like Scott said, a kind of heat sink to disperse the dimensional energy given off by either Lizzie or her device in the tower, but Professor Cline was able to tweak it a little bit, so that it could amplify whatever my Rig could produce to make it a little stronger. I slipped the glove on, flicked my wrist and a warhammer appeared that looked like it was made of iron and bronze. It was lighter than what I normally produced and Professor Cline, Scott and I took a trip to the armory to try it out. The Professor and Scott watched as I smashed some training dummies effortlessly, even shattering a couple. I flicked my wrist again and the weapon disappeared.

"I dig it." I said, nodding at both of them.

"Hopefully it gives you even the slightest of edges," Professor Cline walked to me and put his hand on my shoulder, "Be careful up there Mister Howard."

I nodded and started to head out of the armory. Scott was standing by the exit, looking incredibly nervous, barely looking at me as I approached. As I reached him, he looked me right in the eyes and I could tell he was barely holding it together.

"Promise me your're not going to fucking die up there."
Scott's voice cracked slightly as he spoke.

"I'll do my best," I said trying to keep the mood a little light, "I think you are still up on me in that Bushido Blade game. I can't die before I even the score."

Scott let out a nervous chuckle and gave me a hug. I could almost feel the fear coming off of him. He's been my best friend for as long as I could remember, I knew exactly what he was feeling. I felt the same way.

I left the armory and walked to the main room. I didn't see Beth anywhere as I glanced up to the countdown clock. Time was running out, we had to go. As I turned away from the clock I heard the doors on the other side of the cave open and Beth came through. She was dressed like the first day I met her, the day that changed my life, and she walked straight over to me. She looked determined, and a little scared, as she gave me a little look and that smirk that could make me melt. Before she got to me she grabbed my jacket that had been hanging on a chair since Thanksgiving and put it on. I smiled a little as she finally reached me.

"You're wearing my jacket." I tried my best to sound aloof.

"Do you not want me to?" Beth looked up at me with a little smile, but sure of herself.

"No," I said, "It's always looked better on you anyway."

I could tell this meant things between us were mending. Holy shit I wanted to kiss her, but this wasn't the time and we still had some things to talk about, as long as we stopped Lizzie. We walked towards the platform but didn't touch the wall for The Griffon gateway. Instead, Beth grabbed my hand and started to reach for her necklace.

My mind started racing. There was so much that I wanted to say to her, so much that I had been keeping in over the last month, and I didn't know if I was going to get another chance.

"Beth wait!" I said louder than I meant too. She looked surprised.

"What's wrong?"

"Before we go up there I just wanted to say something."

"Jake…" I cut Beth off before she could tell me not to say anything.

"It will just take a second." I took a deep breath. "Since I met you this year my entire world has been flipped upside down and I just wanted to let you know that I wouldn't change a damn thing about it, other than the last month or so." I looked her deep in her eyes, remembering what it was like when I first looked into them what seemed like an eternity ago. "I needed to get that out before we go up there and I just wanted to let you know that…"

"Jake," Beth smiled at me, "You don't have to say it. I know. I'm sorry too."

I left it at that, but I wasn't going to say that I was sorry. I was going to tell her that I love her. I wanted to tell her sincerely, not in the middle of my screaming tirade a couple of weeks ago. I decided it would be best to just leave it there. We had other concerns at the moment. Beth reached back up to her locket, held her hand to it and in a moment we were a short distance away from Skytop Tower.

The bitter cold hit me in the face as soon as we appeared, shocking my senses into an even more alert state than they already were. Heavy snow was falling in thick, big flakes. The only way I knew Beth was still with me was that I was holding her hand. The wind was howling so loud I couldn't hear Beth as she murmured some words and a little ball of flame appeared in front of us, guiding us toward our goal.

We followed the ball of flame closely, keeping a firm grip on our hands, for a few minutes until we got about halfway up the path to the tower. We took another step and we were out of the snowstorm, literally by one step. I looked behind me and saw that the snow was still falling just as hard, it was just like we were on the other side of a curtain, but there was only a dusting of snow where we were standing compared to what we just dredged through. I looked at Beth and saw her jaw tense up.

"She's close." Beth's eyes squinted closed slightly, "I can almost feel it."

Beth didn't let go of my hand as we headed up the path. My eyes were wide, scanning the area for anything that could be around. I had no idea what to expect, I was already in way over my head since the beginning. It was weird seeing the snow falling what seemed like one step behind us, almost like we were in a spotlight. There was a strange silence in the air as we continued.

As we approached the top of the path I saw Skytop Tower in front of us, a vortex of clouds swirling high above. There was some lightning crackling around it, it really looked like the opening splash screen of Castlevania, or the sky above Dana Barrett's apartment when Zuul arrived. The moment our feet crossed the boundary on top of the mountain the little ball of flame we were following turned to ice and shattered on the ground in front of us. Beth and I looked at each other, knowing that this was the place. I could feel the heat coming off of her, I assumed it was due to the rage of coming face to face with her mother's killer.

The view ahead of us was clear, there was no sign of anything or anybody anywhere. We didn't let go of each others hands as we carefully stepped forward towards the tower, which was still a few hundred feet in front of us. After a moment Beth and I felt a rumble in the ground and a patch of the fallen snow about thirty feet in front of us started to rise up from the ground into a shape. We watched this shape twist and turn into a form resembling a throne and out of the throne another shape began to emerge as if coming from the inside. This second shape formed much more quickly. It was Lizzie.

Lizzie now sat on the throne, legs crossed, playing with an icicle with a smile on her face. She looked exactly how she did when she showed up in my head, leather outfit, blond hair, electric blue eyes. This was her true form, a chilling mirror of Beth. Beth's grip on my hand tightened to the point of being a little painful as she stared ahead at this twisted version of herself.

"Jakey!" Lizzie sang my name gleefully as her voice rang like windchimes in the air. "I was afraid you were going to stand me up, it's not nice to keep a lady waiting like that. Naughty, naughty." Lizzie cast her eyes over and looked at Beth. "And you bought me a present, too! How thoughtful, I guess I can forgive you." Her smile widened, sending a chill down my spine.

Beth didn't say a word but my hand was getting really hot and I could feel her trembling with rage. I was honestly afraid to let go of her hand because I didn't want Beth to just frantically charge toward Lizzie and get herself killed. As I was thinking about what to say, Beth spoke.

"Murderer!" Beth screamed at Lizzie, years worth of angst escaping her lips. Beth tried to walk forward but I did my best to hold her back. I could feel that this wasn't the right time for her to attack, it felt like something was telling me to wait.

"Are you still mad about that?" Lizzie mockingly replied to Beth while draping her legs over the arms of her throne. "You need to get over it sweetie, she was just another bump in my road of conquests. Kinda like Jakey." Lizzie looked at me, licked her lips and blew me a kiss.

I had no choice but to let go of Beth's hand. She wasn't fully on fire yet, but my hand felt like I was holding on to a hot pan without an oven mitt. Beth didn't charge forward like I expected her to, she just stood there seething.

"This isn't going to work Lizzie." I said as I walked towards her, hoping Lizzie would focus on me and not Beth. "You've miscalculated. If whatever is on the tower goes off, *all* of the worlds will end."

"Oh Jakey, I know that." Lizzie shocked me with that answer. If she knew this wasn't going to work then why was she doing this? As if knowing what my next question was, she answered it. "Of course it will fail, unless I kill the little firestarter. She's the last bit of power I need. That's why I needed you to bring her here. Her death will give me everything I want."

"And what's that?" I heard Beth say. Her voice sounded like the day I stumbled into the cave, echoing and almost otherworldly. She was getting an orange glow in her eyes as she stared at her doppelganger.

"Oh I don't know," Lizzie sounded so whimsical it was alarming, She changed her seated position again and now she was sitting cross legged on her throne, a finger to her light blue lips as if she was deep in thought. "What do most simple people want? Power? I have that already but more is always good. Money? I have that too, a lot of it. Fame? Nope, good there." Lizzie looked at me and smiled an evil smile. "Love? I had it, it got taken from me, got some again," Lizzie shot me a wink, "And I want it back."

"This is about your Jake?" I said, trying to piece it together. "Your Jake died..."

"Jakey was killed!" Lizzie's tone changed immediately to dark and serious in a flash. "He was taken from me by some insignificant rebels foolish enough to challenge my power." Lizzie stood up on the seat of her throne and it began to sink into the ground. "He died in battle, after being stabbed in the back by one of the insurgents. I disposed of them all pretty quickly after that, kind of like I'm going to deal with this imposter." The smile returned to Lizzie's face as she turned her attention to Beth.

I could feel time was running out as I looked up towards Skytop Tower and saw the vortex swirling faster, lightning cracking within it looking like it was aching to get out.

"I'm not going to let that happen." Beth said, fire starting to pulse off her.

"You're not?" Lizzie sarcastically acted surprised, touching her hand to her chest. "I doubt that. Considering I'm remembering the right imposter correctly, your mother was pretty easy to kill. Almost as easy as *my* mother was now that I think about it." Lizzie started to walk closer to Beth, and away from me, as I saw Beth glance in my direction. Lizzie continued, "All I had to do was look like a weak, scared, pathetic little girl that followed her Mommy into the woods."

Lizzie kept walking toward Beth and I saw a new icicle form in her hand. She didn't try to hide it. I slowly started backing up, trying to sneak my way toward the tower. There was no way I would survive if I tried to get close to Lizzie.

"An icicle makes a perfect murder weapon," Lizzie continued, "It melts away, leaving no trace. Hold on a second." As I inched away, Lizzie waived her hand in my direction. Suddenly I felt myself back into a wall and ice locked my ankles and wrists against it. Struggling was useless, it made me feel like I was sinking further into the wall. Lizzie turned her head towards me and smiled.

"Keep being naughty like that and I'm going to have to punish you." She turned her attention back to Beth, but it was a moment too late as Beth used the momentary distraction to suckerpunch Lizzie in the face. Lizzie stumbled back a step and touched the back of her hand to her lips, a little trail of blood smeared on her face. Lizzie smiled at Beth.

Beth was practically on fire at this point, looking like a goddess. Her hair was blowing from some mystical breeze and her eyes were burning orange. Little torrents of flame were coming off of her fingertips. If I didn't know her, I would be terrified. Actually, I was a little, mostly because I couldn't get out of the ice bindings keeping me on this wall. I was about halfway between the tower and the coming battle between Beth and Lizzie and I could feel the heat from where I was. Beth charged at Lizzie and Lizzie cartwheeled to the side to avoid her.

"Physical violence?" Lizzie's mocking tone seemed to make the heat coming off of Beth hotter. "Come on, little lamb, you are better than that. Or are you just disguising yourself as a wolf?"

Lizzie took a swing with one of the icicles in her hand and Beth barely dodged out of the way. Beth was fast but Lizzie seemed faster, probably due to the other versions that she's killed. Beth screamed some unintelligible words and a box of pure flame surrounded Lizzie, momentarily trapping her. Beth used this time to dash over to me and melt my shackles. I fell to the ground, but quickly scrambled to my feet.

"Get to the top of the tower!" Battle Beth's voice echoed in my ears, "She's mine."

"Come with me," I pleaded with her, "She's too strong. You know this. We need to…"

"Go!" Beth cut me off and I moved back a couple of feet just from the force of her voice. "We don't have time for this. She's taken too much from me already. She needs to pay."

I nodded and looked over Beth's shoulder just in time to see the flaming box Lizzie was trapped in turn to ice and shatter. Lizzie stood there, staring at the both of us with a menacing grin.

"It's nice to see you have a little fight in you," Lizzie approached us slowly and methodically like Freddy Kreuger or Michael Myers, "I prefer that in my fights. It makes the kill more satisfying."

"Go! Now!" Beth pushed me towards the tower as her flaming sword appeared in her hand from The Rig. A huge wall of flame appeared in front of me blocking me from their view, separating us. I yelled Beth's name into the flaming wall but knew it was pointless. I knew my job, my only chance to end this, was to make it to the top of the tower.

I started running as fast as I could, probably faster than I have ever run in my entire life. I had no idea how much time we had left, but it couldn't be too long, maybe a half hour or so. As I reached the base of the tower I heard a chorus of chilling voices from seemingly everywhere.

"Where do you think you are going?" Lizzie's disembodied voice sounded almost musical.

I looked around and didn't see anything except Beth and Lizzie fighting in the distance, fire and ice erupting from where they were, and heard faint battle cries in the air.

"Lizzie!?" I asked the air, "I'm getting to the top of this tower, this needs to end."

"You're adorable," Lizzie's voice sounded so condescending, "Do you really think you're going to get past me?"

I looked again and still saw the battle between elements raging on.

"It looks to me like you're a little busy." I tried to sound like a badass, I'm sure it didn't come off that way. I was pretty fucking scared to be honest.

"Oh Jakey, you really do underestimate my power."

A shape formed in the doorway of the tower that looked like an ice sculpture of Lizzie and it started to walk towards me. I backed up a few steps and noticed two more Lizzie-sculptures forming on either side of me like the velociraptors in *Jurassic Park*. They walked in front of the tower and met with the first one I saw and the three of them stood shoulder to shoulder in formation at me and formed ice daggers in their hands.

"I don't want to kill you Jakey," they said in unison, "But I'm not going to let you stop me either."

They started to approach me and I flicked my wrist, forming the warhammer and shield that has worked for me so far.

"You're insane." I got into a defensive stance, trying to figure out what to do next. "There is no way we are going to let you do this.

The Lizzie-sculptures stopped and pointed in the direction of the fight. I carefully looked over trying to keep one eye on them. The fight was still raging, but I definitely saw more ice than fire being used.

"There is no way that imposter can beat me." the chorus of icy voices said. "She's weak, frail, too worried about helping others than realizing it's easier to just rule with an ice cold fist. She's too afraid of her own power to be any type of threat to me."

Time was running out, I said the only thing that I could think of to try to distract her.

"I don't know how any version of me could've loved a cold hearted ice witch like you."

The look on the Lizzie-sculptures faces immediately changed from happy to the enraged death stare that Beth would get whenever Scott would call her a witch. I knew I hit a nerve, I just hoped it was enough to make a move.

"How fucking DARE YOU!" they screamed and charged toward me in a blind rage. I charged forward as well, running as fast as I could with my shield raised, hoping this gamble was going to pay off. I closed my eyes and braced for impact.

I felt my shield connect with one of them and heard an ice-Lizzie shatter, my momentum propelling forward into the door at the base of the tower. I stopped myself before I slammed into the wall. I looked back and saw the remaining two turn and run towards me with rage etched on their icy faces as I slammed the wooden door of the tower shut and threw down the locking bar. I couldn't see Beth and Lizzie fighting, I couldn't see anything other than a faint light coming down the spiral stairs. Hopefully I bought myself enough time to run up the giant staircase and get to the top. I heard scratching and pounding coming from the barred door as I started my climb.

I didn't get too far ahead when I heard the door explode open below me. I kept running, my heart feeling like it was going to burst from the exertion and panic. I heard footsteps falling behind me and simultaneously I heard something clawing its way up the side of the tower. As I got just over halfway up I came across a window and stopped for a second to peek outside. I was able to see Beth and Lizzie, well sort of. There was a lot of ice and even less fire than before. Beth was losing. If I didn't succeed, Lizzie was going to kill her.

A Lizzie-sculpture popped up in the window from outside and nearly made me fall down the stairs. It crawled through the window like a spider, landing a few steps in front of me. I looked back and saw the other one a few steps below me and moving up fast.

I was trapped.

Both of them started taking stabs at me and I did my best to block and parry them, getting in a couple of swings here and there. They got in a couple of slices each on me, their ice cold daggers felt like they were burning my skin. The one behind me started to run swiftly toward me and my mind flashed for a moment to wrestling of all things. I put my shield up and ducked down slightly. As the sculpture made contact with the shield I tried to use its momentum to flip over me and into the other one. It worked and they both fell down on the stairs, each of them breaking in half.

I ran past them just as they began to speak. "Did you really think it was going to be that easy?"

I turned around quickly and saw a really horrifying sight. The four halves, two torsos and two pairs of legs, started to merge into almost a conjoined twin version of Lizzie. Four legs, four arms, two heads and a whole lot of anger coming at me. I ran like my ass was on fire while being chased up the rapidly narrowing staircase. As the staircase narrowed the monster reformed, adjusting itself to fit and get the best angle to reach me. It couldn't catch me fast enough and I was able to reach the top and slam the door behind me. I heard pounding as I took in the scene in front of me.

There was a Rift Ripper suspended in mid air, spinning rapidly in front of me. Sparks were starting to fly off of it in all directions, it almost looked like when the Professor was putting this glove together. I could feel the pressure building and I knew there just wasn't any time left to spare. I wanted to see what was going on below me and I peeked over the edge.

There was no more fire and ice being shot. Beth and Lizzie were both fighting hand to hand as far as I could tell. I could tell for sure that Lizzie had the upper hand, and my fears were confirmed for sure when I saw Lizzie drive an icicle into Beth's shoulder and kick her in the stomach. Beth fell to the ground and Lizzie jumped on top of her, ready to deliver the killing blow.

I panicked, I didn't know what to do. I screamed and grabbed the Rift Ripper just as lightning was about to hit the tower.

The last thing I remember was a searing pain through my body and an explosion.

CHAPTER ????

I opened my eyes and everything around me was dark teal and black, swirling around. There was no floor, no ceiling, no anything.

I was pretty sure I died.

I was pretty sure everything died.

I was pretty sure we failed.

I looked down at my body and hands and saw that I didn't have the glove or my Rig on. I was just wearing my normal clothes. I felt like I was swimming in jelly but at the same time floating in mid air, weightless.

I didn't see a light like when people say that 'they saw a light' that brought them back. No light anywhere, just almost total darkness.

I didn't feel like I was alone though. There was something here.

My senses seemed like they were heightened. I didn't know *what* was here, only that something was here. But I didn't feel scared, not at all. I felt eerily calm.

"Hello?" my voice seemed to echo endlessly. It reminded me of when I first entered the cave.

There was no answer at first, just the echo of my own voice.

I said hello into the void again.

"Hello." A soothing lady's voice said back. It seemed to come from all around me.

"Where am I?" I asked.

"You're here." the voice replied. "You're where you need to be right now."

What the hell did that even mean?

"Okay," I said, trying to get a more direct answer, "Where exactly is here?"

"Exactly where you are," the voice said, "You're between worlds."

"Between worlds? Like between life and death?"

"Yes, and no." The voice wasn't giving me any straight answers.

I floated in place. I wasn't sure I wanted to know what the answer to my next question was.

"Does this mean the worlds ended?" I closed my eyes as I waited for the response.

"Not at all," the voice replied happily, "You succeeded. The Multiverse is saved."

That gave me some relief, but I was still really confused. If we won, why was I here?

"You're here because you needed to be here right now," the voice said, seemingly reading my mind, "You needed rest, and now you don't."

"Does that mean I am going back soon?" I asked.

"Yes," the voice sounded happy and sad, "Everyone is waiting for you."

I wondered who everyone included.

"Is everyone okay?" I didn't know who this voice was and I didn't want to give it too much information.

"Yes, everyone is fine."

I breathed a little sigh of relief.

"Who are you?" I just wanted a name to the voice.

"No one important. Just someone who helps when I can," the voice said, "But I do need you to make me a promise before I send you back."

"Okay."

"I need you to keep taking care of her," the voice sounded like it was smiling, "she's strong, so strong, but you need to make sure she keeps her humanity. Keep love and care in her heart otherwise you have seen what she could possibly become. Promise me."

"I promise." I was just glad that Beth was still alive.

"Thank you, Jake," the voice said before adding "Beth was lucky to find you."

I felt what seemed like someone lightly touching my right hand and a soft kiss on my forehead. A bright, ghostly shape appeared in front of me. As the weird world I was in faded out around me I swear that the last thing I saw was a face that looked like Beth's Mom, Peg, smiling.

CHAPTER TWENTY-TWO

My eyes opened slowly as the room I was in slowly came into focus. I was in the Mohonk Mountain House, the room I had been staying in for the past week, and I saw that I was hooked up to some equipment. It looked like stuff that you would find in a hospital like monitors and IV's and things like that. I felt well rested, but my hand hurt. I looked down and saw that my Rig was still on me and my right hand was bandaged up. I was able to move my fingers, but there was a dull throbbing pain. I looked over at the clock on the nightstand next to me and it looked like it was just about to be noon. There was also a coffee next to the clock and from the aroma I could tell that it was my favorite.

I slowly sat up and heard an alarm go off from one of the pieces of equipment hooked to me. I leaned over to try and shut it off when the door to my room burst open and Scott appeared in the doorway. He screamed down the hallway for Professor Cline and ran over to me and threw his arms around me.

"You're alive!" Scott said before standing back up. He had a huge smile on his face and tears in his eyes.

"Yeah, it looks that way." I laughed as I sat up in the bed. I flexed my fingers a little and my hand hurt a bit but I reached over and hit the alarm, finally shutting it off.

"You scared the shit out of me man!" Scott slumped down in the chair next to the bed. "These last two weeks have felt like forever!"

"Two weeks?" I was stunned. "I've been out for two weeks?"

"Yeah man," Scott said, "You've been in a coma for just over two weeks, sixteen days to be exact."

"Holy shit," I said to myself quietly and then aloud to Scott, "What happened? Like with Beth and Lizzie. Is Beth okay? Is Lizzie dead?"

"No, but I don't think she will be showing up here anytime soon." Professor Cline appeared in the doorway, smiling at me. "It's good to have you back, Mister Howard."

Professor Cline entered the room, stood next to Scott and proceeded to tell me what happened after I blacked out. The story, according to what Beth told them, was that I grabbed the Rift Ripper just before the lightning hit it, but the lightning seemed to strike the glove directly. The glove prevented the lightning from hitting the Rift Ripper, but instead surged through my body, shot down towards Beth and Lizzie, and struck Lizzie in the face, and apparently scorched her pretty good. Beth had told them Lizzie's eyes had turned black along with her hand, which was glowing like it was lit by a blacklight. Seconds before Lizzie grabbed for Beth, Lizzie was struck in the face by that lightning bolt. She clutched her face, opened a gateway and jumped in, leaving Beth alive, but bleeding badly, on top of the mountain. Beth made her way up the stairs and found me. I was smoldering and smoke was coming from me. I faded in and out of existence. Like literally fading in and out, apparently, like Marty McFly. She was somehow able to grab me and ported us back to the cave.

Beth was exhausted, wounded, bleeding and crackling with leftover static electricity and she saved me. I've been laying in this bed ever since for the last two weeks. The Conclave also put new wards and protective measures up to try and prevent Lizzie from showing up here again.

"Is Beth okay?" I asked again. It was the first thing I thought of after processing everything that they had just told me.

"Elizabeth is fine, a little banged up, but fine." Professor Cline said. "We patched up her wounds but had to immobilize her left arm in a sling because she has some tears in her muscle due to Lizzie stabbing her very deeply in her shoulder along with some other cuts and bruises. She should be back to normal soon enough."

"Good." I lay back down in the bed. "I can't believe we did it."

"Yeah, man," Scott said. "This whole thing has been nuts."

"You were a tremendous help, Mister Connelly." The Professor placed his hand on Scott's shoulder, and then sat on the edge of my bed.

"Your hand suffered some burns but should be fine soon," Professor Cline took a breath before continuing, "But I would like to study you more. Being that close to dimensional energy can have some strange effects and getting hit with an insane amount of power, it's unfathomable. It's amazing that you are actually up and alert in such a small amount of time. It truly is fascinating." The Professor looked at me with a bit of curiosity in his eyes, "The fact that you were fading in and out is very concerning. You stabilized after a couple of days, but when you feel up to it I would like to see if we can figure out what is going on exactly."

"Of course, Professor," I nodded in agreement, "I'm just happy we won."

"Me too." Professor Cline warmly smiled at me as he stood up and started to leave the room. "I'm going to contact The Conclave and tell them that you are awake. I'm sure they are going to have some questions."

I watched Professor Cline walk out and close the door. I wanted to tell him what I saw when I was between worlds but decided not to, at least right now. Part of me was sure that Beth's Mom put the image of the glove in the Professor's head somehow, knowing it would help. I didn't want to bring it up until I had some more proof.

Scott moved his chair a little closer to me and gave me a light punch in the arm.

"I'm glad you didn't die," He said with a smile. "I don't know how I would have explained that to your parents."

"I told you I had to even up with you." I sat up again and took another sip of my coffee. "How did you know I was going to wake up today?"

"I didn't."

"Then why was my coffee here?" I asked.

"I've brought it every day since you've been out, every shift."

"Every shift?"

"Yeah," Scott took a deep breath, "Professor Cline, Beth and I have been taking turns everyday staying with you. Every time I came in, I would bring that abomination of a coffee, in hopes that you would smell it and wake up."

I could tell Scott was holding back some heavy emotions and he took a deep breath before he continued.

"Beth and I have talked a lot. I can see what you see in her," he said before adding, "Not my type at all, but I can see it. She's pretty cool." He laughed a little as he said it.

"I'm not one to say I told you so but…" I joked as I raised my eyebrow and gave him a look. He just nodded and said that he knew.

We sat there talking for another hour or so before I felt really hungry. I started to try to get out of bed and Scott jumped up to try and help me. Amazingly, I was able to stand on my own and felt fine. Better than fine, actually. In my head I knew there was no way I should be fine, I just got hit with the power of Zeus, how the hell am I even standing?

"Are you okay dude?" Scott sounded genuinely concerned with a bit of shock in his voice.

"Amazingly, yeah. I feel fine, other than my hand stinging a bit." I flexed my fingers a little as I looked at my bandaged hand. I wondered what the damage under the bandage looked like. Would my hand be all scarred up or would it look normal?

I tried to put the mental image of my possibly scarred up hand on hold and we decided to go to My Hero. Before we left we asked the Professor if he wanted anything. He didn't, so we left and headed over.

While we were talking on the drive over, Scott insisted on driving my truck since I just woke up and might be a little out of it which was good because all I could think about at the moment was Beth. I was actually a little scared to see her. We had a lot to talk about, she had to deal with a lot with finding out the truth about her Mother and everything that went along with that. I know I didn't want to tell her what I saw right away. Just like with Professor Cline, I wanted to see if I could get more information about it. I was keeping my little 'Journey to the Great Beyond' a little close to the chest for now.

Scott and I laughed our way through lunch and we tried not to bring up everything we had been through this year. It felt like old times, me and my best friend, just busting each other's balls and being ordinary morons. An hour or so later we decided to head back to the dorm and I figured I would go to the Mountain House later to get the few things I brought with me.

The walk from the parking lot was cold, but not bitter like it had been all winter. The sun was bright and the sky was clear. Scott said that right after New Years the heavy snow finally stopped and the local weather just attributed it to a nor'easter and called what happened a 'Thundersnow Storm'. That was a good enough explanation for everyone in the area but the truth seemed to be that when Lizzie hit our world she brought winter with her, and when she left, the storm took a hike.

As we approached DuBois Hall, I saw Beth sitting on the bench in front of it. She was wearing my jacket, mostly. Her right arm was in the sleeve but her left was in a sling under the jacket. She didn't see me at first, she was looking down at her hand and picking at a rip on her jeans. I stopped walking for a minute to just look at her.

I was glad Beth hadn't noticed me yet, I just wanted to look at her for a moment. My world since August had been turned upside down by a girl I bumped into when I wasn't looking for anyone. She was smart, funny, beautiful and the most powerful person I have ever met. Watching her sit there and play with a tear on her jeans brought a smile to my face. I just wanted to enjoy the moment.

Scott stopped along with me and after a couple of seconds snapped me out of my daydream.

"You alright, man?" Scott asked.

I felt like I was in a bit of a haze, "I am. Just give me a second."

As we got closer Beth stood up and approached us. Scott and Beth locked eyes, he gave her a little nod and told me he'd meet me upstairs.

We stood there for a while, neither of us saying anything. I was just happy standing here, alive, with her. I noticed a new patch on my jacket, near the shoulder where Beth got stabbed, and smiled. It was a cartoon pig holding a pineapple. I had no idea where she found that, but it was pretty funny.

"How's your arm?" I honestly couldn't think of what else to say. I wanted to tell her everything that I was thinking and nothing all at the same time.

"It still hurts a little, but it feels better." She said, looking down at my hand. "How's your hand?"

"It stings a little." I wiggled my bandaged fingers. "Getting hit with a lightning bolt will do that to you I guess."

Beth let out a little chuckle and it was the greatest sound I have ever heard.

"I'm sorry she got away."

Beth bit her lip absentmindedly and nodded slightly.

"I was losing that fight," Beth said in a haunted tone, "If you didn't somehow make that lightning come down and hit her, I wouldn't be standing here right now."

That statement hung in the air for a while, neither of us speaking.

"Hopefully we don't ever run into her again," I said, "I'm really hoping we scared her away."

"Me too," Beth sounded distant, "But if we do I need to be ready."

"We will be," I assured her.

Beth looked up at me, the sun glinting off of her eyes and she gave me a little smile.

"Thank you." She said and gave me a hug. I inhaled deeply, the smell of baked apples filling my senses. I didn't want to hug her too hard because I was scared of hurting her arm. I let go after a couple of moments and we just looked at each other, neither of us knowing what to do next.

I decided that this was it. This was my moment.

I placed my hands gently on her waist and kissed her.

After a moment, Beth put her hand on my chest and pulled back, giving me a surprised look. My head was screaming at me that I read the situation wrong, that this was the nail in the coffin. I was done.

In a moment that felt like an eternity, she raised her eyebrow and gave me that heart melting smirk.

"It took you long enough." Beth said with a coy smile.

I felt the smile grow on my face and I probably looked like The Joker.

"I've wanted to do this for so long Beth. I…" Beth put her finger to my lips.

"Jake, I know," She said sweetly, "I've always known. I love you too." Beth looked up at me and smiled. "Now don't make this weird and just kiss me again."

I leaned down and kissed her again, this time with a little more passion. I felt the heat rise in both of us and I swear I felt an actual electrical spark between us. As far as I was concerned this was all I wanted in life, something I didn't even know I needed.

Usually I question every decision I make, wondering what all of my other options would be. Given what I've learned about The Multiverse, every decision matters. It looks like this time, even with a couple of pretty major missteps, my life here on this Earth might actually be shaping up to be really great.

ACKNOWLEDGEMENTS

Congrats! You reached the end of my first novel! Well, I'm assuming you did. What kind of weirdo would just jump to the end to read the acknowledgements. Unless you're that kind of weirdo, then congrats on reaching the part of the book you came for!

It took me the better part of a year to write this and I have some people I need to thank starting with my wife, Gina. We've been married for twenty years and through all the ups and the many, many downs she's still hanging around. Thank you for sticking around through thick and thin and listening to me ramble about things I go on and on about. I love you.

Next up are my kiddos, Harlee and Tori. When I started writing and hadn't found my writing voice yet I bounced a lot of ideas off of them and had them read some of my conversations between characters to make sure they sounded natural. They are the first ones that knew the entire plot before I finished writing and were my enthusiastic cheerleaders (even though they aren't actually cheerleaders) the entire time.

Anastacia Carroll is my editing angel. After I finished my first draft I posted a screenshot and said that I was starting to edit. Within an hour, my friend of almost eighteen years Stacy sent that screenshot back to me with some preliminary edits and said that she would take a crack at editing my novel. Her input was tremendous, she helped flesh out some of the scenes I saw clearly in my head but didn't quite get all of the words I wanted to say out on the page. I know I was a straight up pain in the ass at times and, bless her heart, she never told me off. Thank you so much Stacy!

Christina Gallagher was one of the first people I reached out to when I started writing. We went to high school together and she used to live in the heart of Wallkill, around the corner from Rob's Pizza (yes, it's a real pizza place in Wallkill) and when I had some questions about the area I asked her. She read the first ten chapters of the first draft before anyone else and helped me cut some bits that didn't work and encouraged me to keep going with the story.

I have another pair of girls to thank, Erica Delbury and Olivia Margulis, two of my many nieces. Erica was my proto-editor before Stacy was around. Erica helped me focus the beginning of the book. I know it's a little detail heavy, but there was a lot more before, Erica helped me trim that down. Olivia did some tweaking of the cover that I designed with her photoshop skills. Both of them were a great help.

Christa Charter is the author of one of my favorite series of books, The Lexi Cooper Mysteries (Schooled, Pwned, Glitched and Griefed), but some of you may remember her as the Xbox 360 community manager Trixie360. I reached out to her a few times while I was writing and she always answered whatever questions I had. Thank you for being there for support when I needed it.

I would like to thank my beta readers for making the time to read my book and an extra thank you to Chris and Alayna who were the first ones to finish it. Your input was really valuable so thank you!

A general thank you to all of the jobs I've had in my life that made me wonder what other versions of my life might look like. The job I had when I started writing this (which I am not going to name and have moved on from) really sparked the idea for this book.

And, lastly, I would like to thank you. All of you that decided to read an unknown book from a first time author. Thank you for allowing me to share this story with all of you. This was one of the scariest things I have ever done, but something that I hope you all liked. I can not thank you enough for taking the time to read this. I love you all.

BEFORE YOU GO!

- Follow @halfazedninja on Twitter and Instagram!
- Go to https://spoti.fi/2lOAyCn for the (Un)Official playlist!
- Stay tuned for future adventures!

Made in the USA
Monee, IL
29 July 2020